BORN IN A RED CANOE

BORN *in a*
RED
CANOE

Katharine Johnson

SILVER FOX BOOKS

ISBN 979-8-9860388-0-3 (paperback); 979-8-9860388-1-0 (eBook)
Library of Congress Control Number: 2022905789

Cover and book design by Paul Nylander | Illustrada

Published by Silver Fox Books, Cloquet, Minnesota
https://katharinejohnsonbooks.com/

SILVER
FOX
BOOKS

For Dale with love and appreciation.
This book lives because of your encouragement.

CHAPTER I

I walked along the narrow strip of sand lining our shore and watched a black bear cub hurry to catch up to its mother. The soft waters lapped at my bare feet. I wrote in the sands.

I was born in a red canoe.
Mother died giving birth to me.

While I watched a bird feed its babies, waves erased my words. So, I wrote again, even though I knew the waters would wipe the sands clean once more.

Father named me Purslane—
An unwanted weed—.
I am Purslane, the weed.

All spring and summer, I wrote everything I knew about myself. Each night, waves erased what I wrote. In the morning, it was as though the words and I didn't exist.

I was born while the great comet glowed in the skies overhead.
Father hoped the comet bestowed me with magical gifts.

The damp and grainy sand stuck to my fingers.

My mother's name was Alcyone—not a weed, but a star of the Pleiades.
Father called himself Polaris after the bright and steady star of the North.

After I was born, Father moved us from his little hut to the nearest hamlet so I'd have a nursemaid. As soon as I was weaned, we moved back to his moss-covered log hovel deep in a forest near a placid lake and a meandering stream.

"The worst six months of my life," he said. "What could I do with a half-orphan on my hands? A girl at that. A girl who cried loudly. A girl who constantly wet the rags I wrapped around her bottom."

My earliest memories were of riding in a birch bark and skunk fur carrier that Father slung on his back. I snuggled close and smelled his sweaty neck as we tramped through the woods. Once I even watched a wood tick walk gingerly over the hairs on his neck and down his collar until it was out of sight. When I grew older and outgrew the skunk fur carrier, I was free to meander behind him as we foraged the wilds.

In the springtime we ate leaf buds from basswood and birch trees as well as the pungent new growth cedar and spruce tips. Father carved hollow tubes that he tapped into maple trees to collect sweet sap. After rains, he taught me to identify mushrooms that popped up in circles. "Fungi," he said, "Tasty, but you need to know which ones not to pick. My favorite are the morels of spring. Ugly to look at, but ambrosia fit for the gods."

I wrote in the sands.

I like little chanterelle mushrooms.
They're magical. Fairies must have planted them.

In summer Father and I picked berries of every color and dug cattail roots to eat. We burned dried cattails in our outdoor cooking fires. In the waning days of warmth, we waited for rose hips to form and hurried to pick wild apples and hazel nuts before the squirrels and birds got them all.

The lake we lived by was where I bathed and taught myself to swim as a child. I floated lazily as waves lulled me on sunny days. I imagined my mother arising from the lake and floating with me—holding my hand. I dove and felt pleasure in seeing the underwater wonderland through the light filtered from above. It was as though I floated and drifted in another world.

Father frowned whenever he saw me playing in the water. "Your mother died in that lake," he told me.

Despite his admonitions, I wasn't afraid. I wrote in the grainy sands.

I wish with all my might that my mother would tug me into the lapping waters to be with her.

Inside our hut, I slept on a loft above the stone fireplace. Father had knotted a thick rope and tied one end to a big round ring he pounded into the loft. To get to my bed, I gripped the rope and curled my feet around the lowest knot. Then I pulled myself up and braced my feet around the next knot, and so on, until I could lean my belly over the top and wriggle my way to my corn-shuck bed.

We had meager furnishings—a wobbly table, a bench Father slept on, two leaky buckets we turned over for stools, a wooden chest Father kept locked, a stone fireplace and a shelf where a few books gathered dust. One was a dictionary that my mother had written. Her beautiful script on the cover spelled ALCYONE'S DICTIONARY.

Alcyone. Alcyone. I loved saying my mother's name. I traced each letter with my finger. The name of a star unlike my name, Purslane—the name of a weed. When I learned to read, I found my name in Mother's dictionary.

Purslane: A weed. Gardeners curse it because it boldly sets root along rows of turnips, parsnip, and peppers. It is impossible to eradicate.

Did Father name me because—as he claims—it was what my mother called out at the moment her spirit soared from the red canoe to the heavenly Pleiades to look down upon us forever and ever? "Purslane! Purslane!" is what he said she'd cried in the instant I slipped from her womb onto the cedar-strip floor of the canoe.

Or did he, bereft of the love of his life, name me because he had hoped for a blessing and was instead delivered a curse? Whatever the reason, he'd named me Purslane, and I felt as unwanted as a weed.

Whenever Father was in a good mood and had sipped quite a lot of the apple cider he hardened each fall, he told the story of how he came to possess the skunk skin that lined the inside of the pack he'd carried me in before I could walk. After I outgrew it, he closed the leg holes so we could use it for gathering fiddle head ferns, wild plums, hazel nuts, and apples.

I had heard the story so many times; I memorized it with all his exaggerations.

"It was a dark—well not so dark—night because there was a bulging and gibbous moon. It was one of those spooky nights when the fairy beings that live in the sphagnum world light tiny torches called fireflies so they can pick worts in the gloom. Wort—remember that Purslane—is not to be confused with an ugly lumpy wart."

"But I digress. Along with the woodland sprites, I was out in the murk of night. I had ventured into the sylvan eeriness to relieve myself of a distressing bladder buildup from drinking too much wild grape tonic. Just as I was buttoning myself back up, I heard a roar and a snarl. Trees crashed, and I felt the earth trembling. 'Oh, Jove,' I yelled. Frightened out of my wits, I beseeched all the moons of Jupiter to which I have sworn eternal allegiance. I begged Europa, Io, and Callisto to help me slay the vicious creature that hurled itself toward me. I entreated Ganymede, 'Save me from the hungry beast that cometh looking for my flesh to satisfy his wants.'

"With the power of the moons strengthening my resolve, I tore a branch from the shivering aspen I had just nourished with my essence. I swung it at the beast hoping to stun it enough so I could run back to my bed and jump beneath the covers. To protect you, of course, my darling daughter."

I always broke out laughing at this part. My image of Father running and jumping to protect me from a beast of the night delighted me to no end.

"Crack! Crash! The branch fell to pieces in my very hands. Now, completely without weapon, I ran. In the density of the thickets, I stumbled over the very beast I was attempting to flee.

"We rolled and tumbled. He scratched. I scratched back. He hissed. I hissed. He growled. I growled. He clicked his teeth. I clicked my teeth. And then he did the unthinkable. He let loose a putrid, disgusting, awful, terrible, toxic spray that covered me like a fetid shroud. Now my dander was up. I reached out and grabbed the monster by the throat and squeezed. All the while I coughed, choked, gagged and tried to spew the foul stuff from my mouth, but finally the fiend lay still. I had conquered the great beast with my superior strength and intelligence!"

I held my sides as I laughed. Enjoyable as it was, I was sure it really hadn't happened the way he told it. He often filled our dark evenings with his stories. None were as amusing as the skunk story, but I'd listen just as intently. Sometimes he'd say, "Let me tell you a story about two foolish youngsters who thought they were in love, but didn't listen to their parents." Or "There once was a princess who lived in an enchanted palace and wore magical shoes that enabled her to fly among the stars." For better or worse, Father was an inveterate storyteller.

In my mother's dictionary she'd written: *Storyteller: Simply, someone who tells stories. Not so simply, one who embellishes the truth—or makes up elaborate stories.*

Except for his storytelling, I always knew my father as a sorrowful man. "It was only natural," he told me, "that my life, my heart, the air I breathed, and everything I touched would be filled with grief. It was destined to be so from the day I married your mother. The very Pleiades she came from is the constellation of sorrow and mourning. Some say each star is for a woman who died while giving birth."

I felt guilty for causing my mother's death and my father's sorrow. Once I told him, hoping to relieve his sorrows, that I didn't miss having a mother. My own had never held me in her arms or suckled me for even a short second before she fled this earth and rose on evening mists to join her constellation sisters. Father said he had furiously paddled the canoe to reach my mother's family who, according to him, were the Ice People living in a land where the wind sings to one's heart and can be found somewhere beyond ridges of howling wolves and valleys of trilliums.

Mother had insisted on going to the land of the Ice People to give birth and to be with her own nurturing kin. I never questioned Father on the discrepancy between his stories on how Alcyone came from the Pleiades to marry him and how she had a family here on earth. Given enough time, most of his stories had alternate versions, so I just listened politely and looked up as much as I could in my mother's dictionary. Sometimes I found another story there. Deciding which was true one didn't worry me much most of the time.

"Did you have a mother?" I asked wanting to know what it was like.

"Yes, everyone does," he replied. "Mine was most proud of me when I became a professor."

"What can I do to make you proud of me?"

"You were born under the comet. Every day I hope that your gift will be that of seeing into the future. You could become a famous fortune teller. We could travel the world together and become rich. Then I would be proud of you."

I didn't want to become a great fortune teller. I wanted to be wanted for myself, just as I was. At festivals, I watched Father pretend to be a fortune teller, and I didn't like it. I wished he was still a professor. Needing to know more about my mother, I took her dictionary off the shelf, paged through until I found the word *mother*.

> *Mother: Mine was a most joyous and beautiful woman. She died so young when the ice on a raging river took her from me.*
> *My grandmam became my mother after that. Her arms were soft yet strong as she enfolded me close to her.*

I was not so much sorrowful as a lonely child. I told myself I didn't miss having a mother. In truth I didn't know what it was like to have a mother. When I saw a doe gently nudging her little fawn, I wondered if that was what it was like to have a mother. Someone to watch over me? Was gentle? And nudged me in the direction she wanted me to go? I dreamed of a doe walking with me through the fallen leaves of the forest and feeling her warm breath on my shoulders.

At times when I watched a bird bringing food to its hatchlings in the nest, I did feel a sadness and a deep hollow in my stomach and chest. As I watched the sun gleam off each little ripple in the lake, I wondered what it was like to be a duckling following in its mother's wake, fluttering to her back, sleeping under her wing, hearing her heart beat.

Sometimes, I had a sensation that if I looked quickly, I would see someone sitting by me. At those times, I very much wanted someone—someone like myself sitting beside me, nudging me, putting a wing over me. Of course, when I looked, nobody would be there. Just some shadowy morning mist. Other times I would feel a hand on my back or shoulder. I'd look quickly, and as if in a dream, the hand would lift and disappear, but a soothing warmth lingered where the hand had been.

CHAPTER 2

Sometimes Father frightened me. When he drew long swallows from a bottle of what he called elixir, he'd shake a few last drops into his mouth and then stare at it for a long time. He'd be still and silent for a long time. When he did talk, it was about his plans to fly to the Pleiades to find my mother.

"When you show signs that the comet has gifted you with seeing into the future, we will travel to all the biggest festivals. People will come from far and wide to hear your prophecies and to hear their fortunes. We'll fill our pockets with silver and gold. Then, I'll be able to buy what I need to build a flying machine."

"What do you want a flying machine for?" My heart ached whenever he mentioned the comet and his plans to fly through the stars, if I became a fortune teller.

"Well, of course, it will fly me high in the sky, through the clouds, to the stars, and to the Pleiades where I'll find your mother and live happily ever after."

"What about me? Will you make it big enough for me, too?" I wasn't sure I wanted to leave this earth to fly through the stars and sky. I wanted to know my mother, to be with her, but she'd died. I couldn't imagine how she could be living on a star far away, or how Father could travel there.

"It's a journey for one. Just me," Father said. He shook the empty bottle and brought it to his lips in case a drop remained.

For days I'd been waiting for Father to open his trunk. The leaves on the trees had already been turning to golds and reds. Some had already dropped to the woodland floor. The moon had almost reached its fullness. He should be opening the trunk soon, but he'd been so forgetful that I feared it would be too late when he remembered.

Father's wooden trunk was the only beautiful thing in our little log hovel. Carvings of blooming flowers, trees, and a beaming sun decorated all the sides. A full moon, stars, and forest animals romped on the sculpted lid.

Finally, in the dim pre-dawn, a click woke me. I listened until I heard it again.

Father was on his knees unlocking the trunk. My excitement swelled. As quickly as possible, I crawled from beneath my ragged blanket, swung out of my corn shuck bed, and slid down the rope ladder to the floor below. My heart beat wildly as I sat on an over-turned bucket so I could watch Father dig through his trunk. The whole of my insides jiggled with anticipation as Father pulled out his old professor's robe. We were going to the Harvest Moon Festival!

I was fourteen years old. I knew because just before we set out for the festival, Father made another slash mark in one of the logs above our door. "Are you keeping track of Harvest Moon Festivals?" I asked.

"No," he said running his finger over all the slashes, "it's this many years since my beloved Alcyone died giving birth to you." His hand shook as he ran his finger over the slashes again.

Father didn't talk about my mother much, but every day, he sat in a corner for a long time with his shoulders slumped, drinking from a bottle. Once I'd asked him what he was doing, his voice faltered as he said, "I'm grieving for my loved one. For Alcyone."

I tried to grieve for my mother, too, but I didn't know how to grieve for someone I never knew. Once I tried doing what he did. Hunched over in a corner, I lowered my head into my hands, wiped my eyes and nose. I didn't have a bottle so I chewed my thumb nail instead.

At the festival, Father paid a few coppers to rent a wooden stand. He donned his professor's robe on which he had painted glittery stars along the sleeves, the front, and the back. I unrolled his sign.

FORTUNES TOLD BY
THE
*ALL-SEEING EYE
OF ETERNAL STARS*

"I hope you discover your gift from the comet soon and that it's clairvoyance," he told me as he tacked the sign in place, "then we'll change this to read: FORTUNES TOLD BY THE GREAT SOOTHSAYER GIFTED BY THE SACRED COMET."

I wrinkled my forehead. "What does that mean? Clairvoyant? Soothsayer?"

"Predictor of events. Teller of prophecies and fortunes."

"What about the sacred comet?"

"Oh, that. Well, Daughter, you were born at the time when the comet Halley flew overhead in the night sky. Great fortune and goodness come from the gifts bestowed on children born under the comet. You are such a child. I look forward to you developing your gifts so we can start reaping the fortune that comes with them."

I wasn't sure what Father meant by 'reaping the fortune' that comes with the comet, but I didn't ask because he tossed me two coppers and told me to go and not hang around chasing customers away. Then he started his spiel, "Step right up! Five thin copper coins is all you need offer the All-Seeing Eye of Eternal Stars to divulge secrets about your past and your future."

He needn't have shoo-ed me. I was eager to explore. A whole new world was before me. The festival with its sounds of squeeze box music, clomping horses, and bells jingling was pure magic. I drank in the colors and sights of prancing goats, dancing dogs, haystack jumping contests, caged birds, ring toss games, puppeteers, clowns, and pony rides until I was reeling in a state of ecstasy. The aroma of roasting chestnuts, turkey legs, and sizzling sausages provoked my salivary glands. Even the dust, kicked up by donkeys pulling creaky carts and making me sneeze, drew me far from Father's booth.

All winter, spring, and summer I had looked forward to the freedom to explore when Father was busy pretending to be the All-Seeing Eye and earning coins by making up destinies for unfortunate believers. Coins he used to buy a few supplies for the winter, but mostly for bottles filled with golden liquid.

Some girls, a little older than I was, walked right by as if they didn't even see me. Curious about my own species, I followed them, listening as they gossiped and giggled. They walked shoulder to shoulder and sometimes held hands. I wondered what it would be like to have someone my age to gossip and giggle with. What would I gossip about? They talked about school. About the preacher's son who always wanted to play hide and seek in haystacks. About teachers who wielded rulers against the heads of inattentive students. About a naughty book they passed among themselves. I didn't know anything about those things. I wasn't sure I would know how to giggle even if I had a friend to giggle with.

I bought a muffin when the girls bought a muffin. I stopped to watch a puppeteer pull strings to make wooden dolls dance when they stopped. I watched a pickpocket slide his hand into the handbag of the girl wearing a yellow ruffled dress with buttons down the back while she stood transfixed watching a juggler throw fiery batons into the air. I wanted to warn her, so I pushed the hair out of my face and cleared my throat. She turned and our eyes met. I froze. My cheeks burned as blood rushed to them as her eyes dropped to my dress and then my dusty shoes. She gave a little crooked smile. I thought she might say something, but before she could, one of her friends grabbed her hand, and they headed off together. My ears still burned as I looked down at my ragged dress and put my hand into my own pocket to hold my last copper coin.

Needing to relieve my bladder, I left the girls and wandered away from the dizzying colors of the fair. I headed for a stand of trees on the other side of a field at the outskirts of the town. There I would find shade and the privacy to do my body's bidding.

As I passed a crumbling outbuilding, I heard murmurings and goats bleating. I peered around a corner and saw two goats tugging at and vying to win a rare prize—a bonnet of sky-blue with an excess of trailing ribbons and delicate flowers adorned the brim. I eased forward to retrieve the bonnet before the goats completely ruined it.

That was when I saw them. The goat boy—young man, really—and a golden-haired lass who dressed in the same blue as the hat now being chewed by the goats. The two were entangled in each other's arms and legs, kissing up a storm. They rolled in the golden grasses of autumn. They crushed clover beneath themselves. They maybe even tumbled into some purslane. When the goat boy laid his hand on her leg, I was sure she would give him a big wallop, but no, she just murmured something into his ear and giggled. I would have liked to have watched them longer, but nature called urgently so I dashed away to the woods.

When I returned, the goats were gone. So were the two who'd been frolicking on the ground. So was most of the bonnet. I picked up three remnants of ribbon. They were soft and silky so I slid them into my pocket.

Back at the fair I watched a monkey dance and beg people to put coins in a cup while his master played melodies on a squeezebox. A withered crone clutched me by the arm and dangled a necklace made of chicken feet in front of my face. "Good for protecting ye from warts and flatulence. Just three little coppers."

I sneezed and pulled away. "Thank you. I don't need one."

Everyone—like Father—wanted money.

Tired and hungry, I spent my last coin on a corn pone dipped in honey, then I returned to Father's booth and sat in the shade beneath the planks. Through the spaces between the boards, I watched a beautiful young woman look both ways several times before sidling up to Father. She wore a dress the color of the ribbons in my pocket and no bonnet. She untied a lacy handkerchief and laid a silver coin on the wooden plank. I stretched my neck as long as I could and aimed my ear hoping no horses would clomp by so I could hear Father tell her fortune.

The finely dressed lovely said, "Woe is me! My father is the mayor of this squalid little village. He keeps a stifling tight rein on me. He turns away all and any of the young suitors who come knocking at our door. I'm afraid that he'll force me to marry one of the creaky old men he brings home. He brags about their wealth. He tells me what fine husbands they'd make and what good political alliances they'd be. But I don't want an old man. And I don't care about his alliances!"

"Tell me," she continued as she shooed a fly from her nose with her handkerchief. "Tell me, please, who do the stars say I will marry?"

Father of the All-Seeing Eye slid the silver coin into his pocket. His voice squeaked a bit as he said, "Well, you've come to the right place." He nodded his head up and down as he held her hand. With great dramatic effect he pressed it to his forehead and then to his heart. He looked skyward, his eyes searching beyond the crowded fair, beyond the clouds that slowly drifted across the deep blue and into the heavens where the eternal stars dwelled.

Under the booth, I trembled with delight and squeezed my arms around myself to keep from laughing.

After a long intense moment, Father the pretend All-Seeing Eye reached to hold her other hand, too, and droned in a deep-throated voice, "I see a multitude of suitors who seek you for your beauty. The young ones are but pesky gnats you must quickly flick away. The old ones see you and become like frolicking goats in spring grasses hoping to recapture their youth. Unfortunately, when beauty fades, so will the attentive ardor of all such men. Your father, the honorable mayor, hopes for wealth to come his way through your marriage. Remember, even after beauty fades; wealth remains."

I held my hand to my mouth and bit a finger trying to hold back a laugh that threatened to expose my hiding place. A fly buzzed near my nose. I swatted it away thinking *pesky gnat!* Father gave me a warning kick and went on with his message.

"You hope for romance and excitement. The true husband is the one who sees your soul shine as brightly as any star in the heavens and will be as steady as Polaris the northern star. Bide your time for that rarest of moments when a gallant one will hold you to his chest where his heart beats true, and he says, 'Fair one, I love you, and I will love you even when the roses blooming on your cheeks fade.'"

When Father said those last three words, he lowered his eyes and looked into hers. I bit on my finger again. Ridiculous, I thought. *As steady as Polaris? His name was Polaris, and he wasn't as steady as anything!*

"But, but," the mayor's daughter stammered, "How will I know the man who sees my soul shine as brightly as a star so that I don't flick him away like a gnat before he has time to fall in love with me?" As she spoke, I noticed bits of straw stuck to the skirt of her dress.

"Come again next year," Father said. "And I will tell you all about your heart's secret powers that will allow you to discern a man whose own heart beats true."

"No! I need to know now. I don't want to wait a year." With that, she untied her lacy handkerchief and placed two more silver coins on the board.

Father's eyes popped. He paused. He shifted from foot to foot. He scratched his palms and held his forehead. He had just slid the silver coins into his pocket when a dozen or so pigs from the greased pig catching contest broke out of their pen and ran into the midst of people eating their lunches of hot cakes, sausages, soured cabbage, and whatever else. Pandemonium broke out. One frisky young boar butted the fortune-seeking lass right in the behind knocking her off her feet. I took the opportunity to tug on Father's robe. He scowled at me and signaled for me to scram. I beckoned him to stoop down so I could tell him something.

He did. I furiously whispered that I had seen the lovely lass and goat boy tumbling in the grasses.

When the chaos and mayhem were over, my father tipped a nail keg over and bid the young lady to sit and recover from her fright. She did and spent the next few minutes exclaiming, "Oh! Such disgusting animals! Pigs! Gracious me! Alas! Poor me!"

She frowned and wrinkled her forehead a lot, waved her handkerchief to cool her flushed face, and brushed dirt from her frock. My insides shook with glee as I watched her through the spaces between the boards of the booth. With her grand display of delicacy, one would never guess that she'd just been rolling around on the ground with the goat boy. If I wore a dress as beautiful as hers, I wouldn't roll in the dirt.

When she calmed, Father stood in front of her and solemnly placed his hands on her head. He plucked a straw from her hair and with a flourish tossed it to the wind. It floated. It wafted. He watched it. She watched. I watched. It landed on a pile of pig dung.

That was when Father brightened and began telling her fortune. "A straw floating on the wind," he said, "without any direction, but going this way and that. Up, then down. What was its fate? Dung! The All-Seeing Eye of the Eternal Stars is showing how easy it is for a lovely person like yourself to waft with the wind, looking for pleasures, wherever they may be, with no thought of the future. Let the straw landing into dung be a warning to you."

Needless to say, the fine young lady stood, kicked the nail keg, and stomped away. I crawled out from behind the booth. Pretending to be a well-dressed young lady, I frowned and wrinkled my nose as I stepped over the heap of dung with the straw. Then I kicked the nail keg and stomped away.

CHAPTER 3

Later that day, I watched a puppeteer jerk the strings on his wooden dummies to make their feet click and clack. He tried to make it sound like the dummies talked by changing his voice and not moving his lips. It didn't work. I wiped sweat from my palms. The frozen smiles on the dancing dummies frightened me. I turned away as fast as I could, but still heard the click and clack. Click clack! I feared they were following me, so I turned back twice as my heart pounded in my chest.

When I thought I was safely away and could no longer hear the click and clack of the puppets, I heard a voice call, "Little girl! Little girl! Come here. I need your help."

I flinched thinking it was the puppeteer. My heart thumped as I looked around. I was the only little girl in the swarming throng at that moment so I asked, "Me?"

A man with a shiny black cane, a black mustache that curled impossibly at the ends, and wearing a dusty black suit, crooked a finger at me and said, "Yes, you." He stood upon a wagon and reached for my hand.

Noticing a black box next to his feet, I did not take his hand. "What do you need?" I asked.

"An assistant," he replied. "You're perfect," he said. "I have a dress just your size. We just need to run a comb through your hair. And scrub that smudge off your face."

I reached up to pat my hair. It indeed had not been combed for many days.

"What would I have to do?" I asked not eager to put on a dress, unsnarl my hair, and scrub my face.

"Hop on up with me and I'll show you."

15

I looked around. Lots of people walked by eating roasted corn on the cob or buttery scones. A father lifted his son to his shoulders. A mother bought a muffin for each of her children. I could always jump off the wagon if I didn't like being an *assistant* so I climbed up.

"*Voila!* Look at this." He opened the black box that reached higher than my knees and was about as wide. I looked in. Nothing.

"This is my magic disappearing box," he explained. "I put things in and make them disappear. Then I pass a hat and the chumps—I mean wonderful people— fill it with coppers and sometimes even a silver coin so that I'll make the things reappear again right before their very eyes. Magic!"

Magic? I was tempted to touch the box, but didn't. "And you want to make me disappear?"

"Presto, my dear."

"I don't want to disappear," I said turning to get off the wagon.

"Come back. It's safe! As safe as can be!"

"Where would I disappear to?" I stood near the edge of the wagon, ready to hop off. My skin itched. I looked around for the girl with the yellow ruffled dress. Maybe she'd like to disappear in the black box.

"Into the ether, into the glorious firmament, into the azure expanse with the moon and stars. Into thin air!"

I wasn't sure what he was saying, but he sounded like Father when he put on his robe and magically became the great All-Seeing Eye. I wanted to laugh. "How would you make me reappear, or would I be lost forever in the azure expanse whatever that is?"

"How? Well, that's the secret of magic, but I'll tell you this much, it has to do with this cane." He held it close so I could see a carving of a snake and other strange markings winding round and round the whole thing. "I don't even understand the inner magical workings of this cane. I think it has something to do with the mystical symbols circling it. All I know is that when I tap it three times, whatever or whoever is in the box disappears. When I tap three more times, they then reappear. *Voila!*"

"What if you forget to tap three times for them to come back?" I asked.

"Well, now that would be a problem. That's exactly what happened to my last assistant. She disappeared just fine. When it was time for her to reappear, I tapped twice and was ready to tap the third time, when a big bear appeared from nowhere, jumped on the wagon, knocked me over, grabbed my bag of apples, and ran off.

By the time I recovered and tapped the third time, it was too late. My assistant did not return. I tried time and time again. No luck. Gone! She was a lovely. I do miss her so."

He wiped his eyes, but he need not have done that. I hadn't seen a single tear. He might as well have put on a professor's robe. He told stories just like Father. I jumped off the wagon not wanting a thing to do with him and his disappearing box.

"No. Don't go. Come back. I never carry bags of apples on the wagon anymore so nothing like that will happen again."

I kept walking. He jumped off the wagon and pleaded, "You're perfect. I will make you reappear. And . . . and I'll pay you a copper if you'll do it."

I stopped. I never had earned a coin. A man and woman walked by with their two children. Butter dripped down their chins as they bit into corn on the cob. My mouth watered. I looked back at the black box. I didn't like it, but for a copper? Finally, the lure of some money was so great I straightened my back and said, "For five coppers. I'll do it once, but you have to promise to bring me back from wherever you send me."

"Three coppers."

I thought about buttered corn. "Five or I'll be on my way right now."

"All right. Five it is. Come back now."

The magic man with the cane and box handed me a gauzy black dress. I headed for the shed behind which I'd seen the goat boy and the mayor's daughter. I put on the dress, spit into my hands and rubbed my face clean. I almost tore all my hair out trying to straighten the tangles with my fingers. When I had it smooth enough, I twisted it into a single braid and tied it off with a bit of flowering vine that wound its way up the wall of the shed.

When I returned, the magic man showed me how to step just so into one corner of the box and bend my knees to my chest as I hunkered down. "You have to be in this exact position," he said.

"But there's more space," I said as I felt sweat drip from my underarms. "If I put my feet over there, I'd be more comfortable."

"No," he said. "It has to be this way because I'm going to move this piece like so." He did—pushing me even further into the corner.

"Don't do that," I complained. "Now I'm really cramped." I jumped up and started to climb out.

"I have to," he said as he winked at me. "Sometimes I need room for other things. Hunker down again." He patted me on the head. "That's good. I'm going to close the lid so you'll know what it's going to be like. I'll keep it closed until I pass the hat and then tap three times. Even if you're feeling crushed and can't breathe, don't wiggle, don't say anything, and remember that two coppers are yours when we're done."

"Five coppers," I insisted.

"Yes, of course. Remember, after I tap three more times, I'll open the lid and give you a hand out. That's when you stand and smile at the onlookers."

We practiced one more time. I still felt cramped and a little scared in the box. He didn't tap his cane at all so I didn't disappear. I kind of looked forward to that happening. What would it feel like to be floating in the sky looking down on the festival? It would be so much fun to tell Father about my great adventure of disappearing and reappearing; and if I saw the girl with the yellow ruffled dress, I would have something to tell her, too.

The magic man took the flowering vine out of my hair because he said it might get loose on my disappearing journey. Then he started his spiel, and a crowd started to gather. "Come one. Come all. Come see this beautiful young lass disappear before your very eyes."

When the crowd was big enough, he opened the lid, held his hand out to me, and helped me step into the box. I snuggled in. I hunched and crouched. He reached in and wrapped the skirt of the dress around my knees. When he closed the box, I heard him rap three times. Then he opened, not the top of the box, but the front side so the crowd could see. They oohed and aahed. "It's empty!" someone shouted.

If they couldn't see me, I must have disappeared into the ethereal firmament. I was confused. I didn't feel *disappeared* at all. I still felt suffocatingly cramped. The wooden box still felt rough against my back. It smelled of musty old wood. I could hear the jingle of coins being dropped into the hat as the man encouraged the crowd to be more generous so the magic would work, and he could make me reappear again.

Finally, I heard three more taps, and the magic man opened the top. He reached to help me stand. "*Voila!*" He gestured with a sweep of his arm and twirled his cane. Then he whispered to me through clenched teeth, "Smile."

My knees shook a bit as I looked at the awed crowd, but thinking of the frozen smiles of the puppets, I did not smile. I was glad to be back from the glorious firmament that had been cramped and musty smelling.

After I changed out of the magic man's dress, I ran to Father's booth to tell him about disappearing from the black box. He mumbled, "Sham. Bogus! That greedy, good for nothing used you to bilk money from fools."

I showed him the five copper coins.

"Good thing you're not a fool," he said as he plucked them from my hand and started to walk away.

I hurried after him. "I'm hungry," I said holding my chin high. "Maybe we could buy something to eat, like corn on the cob, or buy a new dress for me. It doesn't have to be new. Any old one without any rips and isn't so tight on me." I showed him the dress I wore. "Look at all the holes."

Father didn't look. I clenched my fists and stared at his back as he kept walking. "I earned those five coppers. I should get to keep at least one." I chased after him, but a gaggle of geese waddled in front of me. I was trying to step around their droppings, when a good woman beckoned me to where she had a flat griddle propped upon rocks that surrounded burning embers.

"Sit and rest," she invited. She wore a scarf wrapped around her hair, and a faded apron covered her dress. She squinted her eyes as she invited me a second time. "Sit for a spell."

Father hadn't even looked back to see if I was still following, so I unclenched my fists. The woman pointed to a stump by her fire. I sat. A brown and white nanny goat was tethered to a small red and blue cart nearby. The goat chewed leaves it pulled from the ground. *Purslane. The goat likes purslane.* Purslane—my name. I hated it even more as I watched the goat lift its tail and splatter its droppings on a patch of purslane.

"What's your goat's name?" I asked.

"Gloria," she said.

"That's a beautiful name," I said. "I'd like a name like Gloria."

The woman kept scraping skins off potatoes as she said, "What is your name?"

"Purslane. It's the name of a weed. An unwanted weed."

She shredded the potatoes on a wire mesh into a bowl. "Yes, Purslane is a weed. Gardeners curse as they pull it out, but it's also good and delicious. Poor people don't have to pay a penny for all the purslane they can eat."

I thought about what she'd said. Maybe purslane was good for something, but I had my doubts as I saw flies land on the goat's fresh dung. I watched the woman add a handful of flour, a great glob of butter and two dashes of milk, then stirred it all together with a wooden spoon. The mixture swirled in the bowl. It turned from white to gray and ugly. *Ugh!*

"Hand me the salt box from the cart," she said.

I stood and searched through various things piled there until I found the salt. I felt a tug on the hem of my dress. The goat nuzzled my leg and chewed on my hem. I patted her on the head and pulled my dress away.

The woman mixed a few pinches of salt into the potato mash, then she scooped a dollop of butter onto the hot griddle. It sizzled and spit. She ladled a blob of potato mash onto the sputtering butter and flattened it into a perfect circle with the bowl of her spoon. After a minute or two, she flipped the potato mash over. Like magic, the ugly gray had turned into a beautiful golden crispiness. A most heavenly aroma tickled my nose so my mouth started watering.

What the good woman said next delighted me and my hungry stomach. "The first cake will be yours."

At those words, I forgot about how angry I was with Father. I forgot about the chewed hem of my dress. I felt transported into a realm of happiness. *The first cake would be mine!* My stomach growled and begged.

I was shaken back to reality when the woman said, "There's a basin with water under the cart. Wash your hands and face. Then you can eat."

I did as she told me as fast as I could so I could hurry back to my stump. The aroma of the frying potato cakes was even more tantalizing.

"There's a honey pot somewhere in my cluttered cart. See if you can find it."

I hopped up so fast that my stump tumbled over. I searched through the scramble on the cart. Corset, hammer, dented pots, gunny sack of goat feed, water jugs, rags, books of every faded color, shoes, hanks of yarn, a blanket, ball of string, bag of corn husks, a jug of dried beans, potatoes in a rucksack, an old wooden trunk, a dried-out frog carcass, and finally, the honey pot.

Ignoring the goat when it butted my leg, I walked slowly holding the honey pot with both hands. The woman had already flipped my potato cake onto a tin plate and was frying another. "Go ahead, scoop some honey for yourself."

I looked for a spoon. "Fingers were made before forks and spoons," the good woman laughed.

Digging in with my finger, I wiped the golden honey onto my cake, folded it in half and took my first bite. If there were heavenly angels, they sang. If all the strawberries of summers gathered, they could not be more delicious. My shoulders relaxed as I took bite after bite.

The woman watched me. "Never tasted a lowly potato flat cake before?" she asked. My eyes were probably spinning in my head. My mouth was full, savoring the buttery honeyed goodness, so I shook my head *no*.

"I don't suppose you'll be wanting another." Her eyes shone with her smile. The goat maaa-aaa-ed.

"Yes, please," I said, glad my father had taught me to say *please* and *thank you*.

I ate three flat cakes while sitting on a stump, mesmerized by the sputtering butter and awed at the miracle of a grey blob turning into a golden crispy deliciousness. And best yet, I was in the company of a kind woman who fed me potato cakes and a goat that wanted to eat my dress.

When I had my fill, the woman set out a sign she said would bring hungry fairgoers to her humble stand which wasn't a stand at all, just a cart and a skillet set on stones above a fire on the ground.

"I'll be needing your stump for paying customers," she told me, "but if you're of a mind to help me, see that chestnut tree over yonder? It's dropping its nuts. Take this basket and see if you can fill it, but be careful. Don't pick up the burrs. They're sharp and nasty."

"I can do that." I eagerly took the basket, waved my hand, and scampered to the tree. There I spent the rest of the day bending and picking in the shade. When I returned, my stump was occupied and a line of hungry people exchanged coins for potato cakes. It occurred to me that they were getting something good for their money—not like those who paid Father to have their fortune told or those who paid to watch me disappear from the magic box. The woman was busy at her skillet and tending the fire, so I put the basket by her feet. As I turned to go, I heard her whisper, "I knew your mother."

When I looked back to her, she was already flipping a hot cake so I wasn't sure if I'd heard what I thought I heard. It was hard to know with the calliope music starting up, the goat maa-aaa-ing, the butter sizzling, the monkey man playing his squeeze box, and all else going on.

I wondered if I'd really heard the words *I knew your mother*. I'd never known my mother, but I hoped she would have been just like the potato-cake woman.

No one was at Father's booth paying to have their fortune told, so I showed him the rips in my dress that I had outgrown. I begged him to use the coins I'd earned from the magic man to buy me a dress. I hoped for one that was like other girls wore. One with buttons. Or a bow. Father dug in his pocket, looked at the few coppers he had left, and went directly to the rag man's booth and picked out a burlap dress made from a gunny sack. "You'll have room to grow," he said as he handed it to me.

I shook my head and didn't look at him. I hated the roughness of the burlap against my skin and the drab color, but I had nothing else to wear because Father had traded my old dress and one copper coin for the dress made from a sack.

CHAPTER 4

The second day of the festival was warm and welcoming. In the early morning I could already hear the music, smell sausages roasting, and see colorful banners waving in the breezes.

No one lined up at Father's booth. His sign flapped crazily in the breeze. It reminded me of his long underwear hanging and flapping on a tree branch where he hung it to air after a long winter. As Father adjusted his robe, a most pompous man with a big belly arrived and pounded on the booth.

"What's the noise all about?" Father asked.

"My daughter!" the mayor screamed. "That's what this is all about. You told her some mumble jumble about finding the man who could give her pleasure and see her soul shine and hold her to his chest to hear his heart beat and a bunch of other drivel. The result of your so-called good advice is that she ran away with the goat boy last night.

"But, but, but," Father stammered, "I told her that if she drifted without direction like a straw in the wind, she'd end up in a pile of dung, just like the straw I had plucked from her hair."

"Pile of dung, eh?" The mayor turned redder, his jowls shook, he pointed a fat finger at Father and said, "Are you saying my daughter belongs in a pile of dung? That's what will happen if she marries that goat boy. Never! If I catch her, I'll lock her in the garret until she's old and withered." With those words the mayor ripped down Father's All-Seeing Eyes sign and trampled it before stomping away.

Father gathered the muddied sign and tried tacking it back up. "Better find a way to earn some coins," he said to me. "Maybe the phony with the magic disappearing box is still here."

I didn't want to listen to Father tell his made-up fortunes or disappear in the black box, so I headed off to see if the potato-cake woman was at her griddle. I hurried, zigzagging past smiling families and past children holding their mother's hand. I made a wide arc around the puppeteer and his clickety clack puppets.

A trio of girls all wore high-waisted, high-collared dresses the color of roses in bloom. Even though the girl in the yellow ruffled dress wasn't with them, I chafed against the burlap of my own shapeless dress and yearned for one like theirs. The girls laughed shrilly as one told of the mayor's daughter running away with the goat boy the night before, and nobody knew where they went. "I heard that she climbed out of the attic window, and he caught her in his arms when she jumped. Isn't that romantic?"

"It would be if he wasn't just a goat boy." They all laughed again.

"Oh, the embarrassment the mayor has suffered."

Another said, "He and his wife deserve this embarrassment for spoiling her so."

I worried about Father. If everyone heard about the mayor and his daughter, nobody would want their fortunes told. I looked back at Father's booth. The wind had torn his sign even more, and no one stood waiting for their fortune. *How were we going to get coins to buy the few things we need for winter? And for Father's elixirs?*

I circled back to his booth. He sat on a stump looking at his shoes that had worn through at the toes. He wasn't even trying to entice people to come for advice from the All Seeing-Eye of the Eternal Stars.

"Hey ho," I said trying to be cheerful.

He didn't look up. "Is that phony wizard here who put you in a box and made you disappear?"

"I haven't seen him. I was hoping to earn a few coins by disappearing, but he's not here."

"He was a fraud," Father grumbled. "You never disappeared when he tapped the box. He just kept you hidden behind a false wall. Maybe he got run out of here for bilking people out of their hard-earned money."

"Maybe I can help the woman who sells potato flat cakes. Maybe if I help enough, she'll give you one, too."

He didn't answer so I scampered away feeling a bit guilty that I had somewhere to go, and someone kind to be with.

The potato-cake woman was setting her blackened iron griddle on rocks that surrounded glowing embers. "Here you are. I'm glad to see you. Come sit a while. Help me a bit and have two or three of my test cakes," she invited.

"I'll help," I said, happy to see her. "What do you want me to do? Get the honey? The salt? Feed your goat?"

"All of those things, and pick chestnuts again. Your mother used to sit under those chestnut trees. It was a long time ago—before you were born."

I sat straighter. I remembered that she'd whispered she knew my mother. "My mother had been here? Where I pick nuts? Please, tell me about her."

"That very place. She came to the festivals with your father. She was newly married to your father. While he played at being the All-Seeing Eye, she played her strings and sang. Her voice was so beautiful that birds even fluttered to the branches above her to listen. That was your mother. People tossed coins into a straw basket at her feet. She always smiled her thanks and kept singing. Many of her songs were gloomy. She said her father and mother, and grandparents had all died. That made her very sad."

My mother's parents had died. I thought about how full of sorrow she must have felt before saying, "She died when I was born. I never heard her sing."

"Oh, how terrible. I wondered what happened to her. When she was carrying you in her womb, she sang to you. She hoped you were listening inside her belly." The woman stirred some flour into the potato mash as she said this.

"Father never sings. He just tells stories."

The woman shook her head and tsk-ed. "Yes, so I've heard. Your mother earned most of the coins they took to market. I think they would have starved without her. Salt," she said nodding to her cart.

I got up and after finding the salt box, I tugged my dress from the goat's mouth, patted her on the head three times as if to make her disappear and sat back down, eager to hear more.

"Do you remember any of her songs? Maybe you could teach me."

She ladled a spoonful of the potato mash onto her sputtering griddle. As she spread the mash into a perfect circle she sang.

On the shores of Kawishami
I await the birth of my child
Child of my flesh and bone.
Child, you grow within my waters.

You will bloom like a flower.
You will be who you will be.
Child born when the comet is o'er.
Who will you be, child of mine?

I sat mesmerized. The woman sitting before me had known my mother and heard her sing. I looked down so she wouldn't see my tears. I felt a pang in my chest. My throat thickened. "Tell me more," I said.

"I only knew her such a short while. She was very pretty. You look like her. She made people happy with her lovely songs. Even though her parents and grand-parents had died, she wanted to go home—to the hills and valleys she'd known— perhaps to find her people from another village." The woman flipped a potato cake in the blackened pan.

Maybe I could go to those hills and valleys and find her people. "Why did she have to die?" I asked.

The woman looked at me, her eyes misted, and then slid the cake onto a tin plate and handed it to me.

She scooped her ladle full again and spread mash on the griddle. "That I don't know. Unfortunately, sometimes it is the good who die and the bad seem to live forever. The world is full of mysteries. Some glades quiver with magic," she said. "Some lakes have misty mystiques. Some unnatural beings live past death. Some loamy hills swell with mystery and charms. Some veined stones hold enchant-ment. Some people sing to conjure dreams and exquisite powers. Some are born under the comet."

I swallowed my mouthful of potato flat cake. *Glades, lakes, loamy hills, veined stones, and the comet. The comet in my mother's song. Father told me I was born with it, too, and that meant I would have a gift from the comet. I wished I understood it all.*

Just then, a long line of hungry festival goers formed, waiting for the good woman's potato cakes. She looked at me whispered, "Portals and phases. Portals and phases." She turned away and spread more mash on her griddle. It sizzled and spit in the hot butter. I stood from my stump seat unhappy that our conver-sation was over. I had no idea what she meant—if anything—by glades with mag-ical mystiques, misty lakes, and portals and phases. As I was about to leave, the woman nodded to her cart and said, "In the little wooden chest you'll find your mother's dress."

Confused and shaken, I sat on the edge of the cart and pulled a pale green silken dress from the chest. It was as lush as the first delicate leaves of spring violets nodding their colors above the duff in the forest. I smoothed the dress with my hand feeling the silk glide under my fingers. I drew the dress to my nose and breathed in deeply. Musk, lavender, chamomile, and mint swirled, filling my senses. I pictured a woman with wavy dark hair hanging past her shoulders. I took another breath. The image expanded and I looked into her soft brown eyes that sparkled with golden stars. Another breath and I envisioned her wearing the soft green dress I now hugged to myself. In my vision she sat under the chestnut tree singing and playing sweet melodies on a stringed instrument. I breathed her scent again wanting to take her in and hold her image close. I slid my hands over the softness over and over. My heart filled with happiness and sadness.

"Time to quit lolla-gaggling!" Father broke into my reverie. He scowled at the dress I held. "Leave it," he said.

I stroked its smoothness again, folded it, and reluctantly tucked it back into the chest. I nodded to the woman as Father led me away. She looked at me and whispered, "Some misty lakes give back what they take away. Take the dress. It is yours."

Father tugged me by the arm. "I'll get it later," I whispered back to the woman.

"We need to earn money," Father said. "I'm going to the fields to see if any farmers still have potatoes or rutabagas that need pulling. You stay here and find a way to earn a coin or two. Maybe even find some lying in the dust. If nothing else, sell that dress she said you could have. It should bring at least a silver coin Maybe more."

With that he left me alone.

CHAPTER 5

I did not want to sell my mother's dress, yet I needed to earn some coins so I walked around the festival grounds at least ten times. I offered to help at just about all the booths, but nobody needed me. I didn't know any songs to sing while sitting under the chestnut tree as my mother had. Tired, I went to Father's booth. I picked his robe from the ground and folded it over the plank. The ruined sign still flopped in the wind so I took it down. Our life together was in ruins, too. Maybe I could convince Father to find my mother's people with me. We could find family there. I stroked his robe and imagined him being a professor again. Maybe even an astronomer. It would be our chance to mend our lives, to begin again.

Squeals brought me out of my reverie. I thought back to the time the pigs had gotten loose, running free through the festival lanes and butting the mayor's daughter in the behind. I got up and followed the sounds of oinks and squeals until I found the fencing where pigs ran and youthful boys and some not so youthful men tried their hand at catching a greased pig to win a pouch of coins. A contest was in full swing so I straddled the fence to watch. Mud and slop flew in all directions as contestants chased the pigs unsuccessfully.

A bell sounded to end the contest. No one had caught the pig. A new round was announced. Strapping boys and young men dropped silver coins into a pouch. While I watched that mess, I began to see what the contestants did wrong. I made a plan. All I needed was a silver coin and then I could be there in the sludge and dung catching a pig and winning a bag of coins. When the bell rang again, the contestants, humiliated and dripping with muck, shook their heads and climbed out of the fencing. I hopped off the fence and ran to potato-cake woman.

"Please," I said, "I can win a pouch of coins if I catch a pig, but I need a silver coin to do so."

She frowned, but she gave it nevertheless. I quickly untied my shoes and left them next to her stool with the promise that if I didn't come back a winner and repay her coin, the shoes, worn as they were, would be hers.

Full of hope I hurried barefooted. When I dropped my coin into the pouch, everyone watching guffawed loudly. "Save your coin, Missy. You'll not be catching a pig today."

Nine of us paid to test our pig catching skills for that round. The pigman loudly announced the rules:

No cursing

No spitting

No biting

The bell rang as he opened the gate of the pen where the pigs had been greased. They ran out helter-skelter spattering filthy sludge behind them. The other eight contestants chased after them, but the hogs escaped every attempt to be caught. I stood stock still just to the center of the ring. I hoped the pigs would think of me as a wooden post and run close to me to avoid the whooping and hollering chasers. Time ticked by. I began to worry that the bell would sound before I had my chance. Then I spied a pink and black spotted porker running toward me. I stood as still as could be with my knees shaking in anticipation. And then, right as he was about to pass by, I stuck out my leg.

He tripped and squealed. I fell upon him. He squirmed. I grabbed a front leg. He kicked. I held on for dear life. He twisted. I twisted with him. Sludge, grime, dung, and filth spattered my face and open mouth. I spit even though it was against the rules and held on. He oinked. He squawked and struggled to be free. He tried to roll. I held on even after I heard the bell ring. The onlookers roared and hooted! They clapped their hands and cheered! I still held on. Finally, the pigman came and lifted me off his biggest and strongest hog. He handed me the pouch of coins. "Here. Now scat and don't ever come back."

I grinned, happy as could be, and held the pouch to my chest. A long line of new friends followed me out of the pig ring. They congratulated me and patted me on the back. Some begged for a coin. A ruffian even said, "One is always happier when sharing a meal with a friend. How about if I be that friend and we enjoy some roasted corn and a sizzling sausage or two?"

"No, thank you. I'm not hungry," I answered even though my stomach ached in its emptiness.

Another roguish looking fellow said, "Pretty girl, you need to clean that pig muck off yourself. I'll hold that pouch for you while you washed at the well."

"No!" I held onto the pouch tighter. I turned to the lot of them following me and said, "I don't need any help. Now or later. Thank you for asking. Go now and quit following me!"

I wanted nothing to do with the whole lot of them. Soon enough the line following me had thinned to three. Muck and sludge still dripped off me as I headed to repay the potato-cake woman and retrieve my shoes.

"Hold onto that pouch. Don't let go of it," she warned, "Better yet, stay by my side 'til your father comes. "There are aplenty of quick fingered pick-pockets keeping an eye on you and just waiting for their chance at that pouch."

I sat on the stump next to her griddle that was momentarily vacant. I looked around and sure enough, I counted three slouchy-looking characters loitering, waiting for their chance at my or someone else's coins.

"Better yet, you might want to sit up there on my cart," she said. "No one will want to come near me with how you look and smell." She wrinkled her nose.

Even the goat took one sniff of me and backed away as I climbed onto the cart. My dress hem, soaked as it was in the pig muck was safe from her chewings that day. Swinging my bare feet, I watched the festival goings on, counted the hungry folks who bought potato cakes and chased flies off myself.

The sun was lowering in the sky when Father returned from the fields. I saw him come from a long distance. He dragged his feet and rubbed his shoulders.

Hoping to cheer him, I handed him the pouch and said, "I wrestled a greased hog to the muck when no one else could."

Father jingled the coins in the pouch as he looked at my dirty feet and muddied dress. Without an *atta girl* or a *good going*, he tied the pouch to his own waist and said, "Well, you sure got dirty. It's time to buy our winter supplies and head for home before we have to stumble in the dark."

"And I need shoes what won't fall apart in the snow. And a better dress that doesn't scratch and itch." Filth and dung dried on the one I wore. "I won the pouch of coins, now I should at least have some say in how we spend it."

Father started walking away. Over his shoulder he said, "Time to go."

I looked at the chest that held my mother's dress, jumped off the cart, gave the goat a quick pat, and waved to the woman as she fried another potato cake. She didn't look up, but I'm sure I heard a whisper that sounded something like *Dress*.

Did she really say *dress*? If so, was she reminding me to take my mother's dress, or that my dress smelled bad and needed to be washed after rolling in the muck?

I protested to my father the whole way back to our hovel. He'd spent all my winnings, but not on shoes or a dress that wasn't a burlap bag. He carried a huge sack stuffed full of elixir and tonic bottles. They jingled, jangled and clanked all the way through the woods and fields as we trudged our way home. On my back, I lugged a sack only half-full of food supplies we needed for the long winter.

I grumbled, "We'll need more flour and corn meal than this!"

He replied with a grim *hurrumph*.

I griped, "You could have gotten more oats and molasses. They'd taste good. This measly bit of food won't last us the whole winter!"

"*Hurrumph*."

CHAPTER 6

Back at our hovel, life returned to our monotonous routine of humdrum. We scoured the woods for rose hips, berries, nuts, and whatever squirrels and birds had left behind.

One chilly day I sat on a log that had drifted to our shore. I thought back to the good times at the festival, the potato-cake woman, and the girl in the yellow dress who'd smiled at me. I took it upon myself to try giggling in case I ever had friends to giggle with. I was doing my best to mimic their unending laughter when Father ran to me and pounded me on the back.

"What were you choking on?" he asked.

I never tried giggling again.

Every winter when I was younger, Father brought out the McGuffy Readers he'd bought once at the festival. He sat patiently with me as I learned the sounds that went with the squiggles on each page.

The first reader taught me to be good, kind, honest, and truthful as I learned to read. We skipped around in the second reader. Father mostly focused on the parts about astronomy. He told me that I could read about biology, zoology, and botany on my own, but I was better off just going outside and learning from nature.

We never did get to the other four McGuffy's. Father preferred to teach me himself. He'd been a professor before he married my mother, so he still enjoyed delivering long impromptu lectures on whatever topic came to his mind. Alone in the woods with only the two of us and Father's memories, I was a willing listener.

On the shelf beside the dictionary my mother had written, was a worn, red leather-bound tome entitled *1001 Poems to Memorize*. From time to time I memorized one of the poems.

I often took my mother's dictionary down from the shelf and held it close to myself. With my finger I traced her beautiful script on the cover that spelled ALCYONE'S DICTIONARY.

> *Harvest Moon Festival:*
> *A joyous time*
> *And most of all, a friend who makes potato cakes.*

I thrilled reading those little lines. My mother had had a friend, too—the potato-cake woman. I felt closer to my mother even though I'd never known her. We shared a friend. I'd smelled her scent on the dress. I wish I had taken it so I could hold it again.

One evening, Father and I sat outside around our cooking fire and looking up at the stars. He pointed to the constellations. He called the big and little dippers Ursa Major and Ursa Minor. Big Bear and Little Bear.

"You know a lot about the stars." I said.

He stood and walked to the lake shore so he could see a greater expanse. "That's what I should have been," he said. "An astronomer! I could have stood proudly at a telescope with the best of them—Ptolemy, Copernicus, Kepler, and Gallileo. Even those from China, India, and Egypt. Instead of crawling on my knees and getting my hands dirty looking at plants like a boar digging for roots, I should have been an astronomer of the stars in the sky!"

"If you'd been an astronomer, you could have named me after a star instead of a weed." It excited me to think of what name I'd have. Ariel, Sirius, or maybe Cassiopeia.

"No." Father sat back at the fire and opened a bottle that he'd bought at the festival. "Purslane is what you mother cried out at the moment of your birth. So, astronomer or not, Purslane would have been your name."

"You still could be a professor like you were," I insisted. My cheeks burned to think that he'd still have named me after an unwanted weed.

He lifted the bottle to his lips. A fire simmered hotter in me. I'd disappeared in a magic box and rolled in the mud to earn coppers and a pouch of silvers. All I'd gotten for that was a scratchy burlap dress, and he'd bought himself more bottles of the golden liquid with the rest of the coins.

The sight of his bottles and the feel of burlap against my skin annoyed me, so I scowled and asked, "What's in those bottles you always buy?"

"Elixirs and tonics. Elixirs to prevent the vapors. Tonics to ease my lumbago. This one is an elixir." He took another sip.

"I'm thirsty, too. I would like some elixir to prevent the vapors," I told him without having the slightest ideas what they were.

"Oh, no. These are for the prevention of *adult* vapors and easing of *adult* lumbago. Never put so much as the tip of your tongue to these golden fluids, as tempting as they may look."

I didn't like the bottles of elixirs. Father became short tempered after drinking them. When he slept, he'd snore so loudly I'm sure he scared all the bears in the woods.

Another night, as we sat around our cooking fire, I asked Father to tell me about my mother and my birth. "Again?" He frowned and took another swallow of elixir. "I've told you all there is to tell. Your mother wanted to be with her people when you were born. The moon was full and that portentous comet streaked across the night sky. We were half-way across the lake, when a thick fog dropped, and the wind blustered. The canoe spun wildly. I couldn't see anything in the fog. Alcyone—my dearest love—cried out 'Purlane. Purslane,' and you were born in the red canoe. When the storm settled and the fog lifted, I lay on the sandy shore holding you in my arms. The canoe was nowhere to be seen." Father choked out the last words, "Alcyone was gone. Gone to the Pleiades. It is there that I must go to find her again."

He'd talked about going to the Pleiades to find my mother many times. I couldn't believe he really thought he could fly through the skies to her. Even though I felt a twinge of anxiety, I told myself that it was the elixirs that made him think so. And his sorrow. I felt his pain. We'd both lost her in that storm. "Alcyone." I whispered to comfort myself. Her name was so beautiful; the potato cake woman said she had been beautiful, too.

Father held his bottle to the skies. His eyes distant as he said, "Alcyone, my wife, a star of the Pleiades, came to Earth in a fiery ball to be with me. We were both stars—meant for each other. My name is Polaris like the bright star of the North. We were meant to be together."

He didn't have to say it. I knew. He and Mother were stars. I was a weed, rooted in dirt, and I felt as unwanted as a weed.

———————⸨⸩———————

One day, even though Father was sullen, morose and lost in a stupor, I gathered up my nerve and said, "You know what would be a good idea? You could be a professor again. Just think, we could move where there's a grand university. You could teach, and I could go to school. And have friends. We'd both have friends."

Father didn't move for a long time. Had he even heard me? It seemed like an eternity before he looked at me and said, "That's all foolishness. No more of that professor stuff for me. No more All-Seeing Eye. No more anything here. The only place I'm going is to the Pleiades to be with Alcyone."

Father fell asleep murmuring *Alcyone. I'm coming. Alcyone.* I didn't sleep at all that night.

The next night, Father and I sat by our outdoor fire. Grease dripped into the flames and sizzled as we cooked the grouse Father had snared earlier in the day. He looked up at the dark sky speckled with pinpoints of light. The moon had waned to a sliver. A few sips of elixir, the fire, and the anticipation of eating the roasted grouse to eat, warmed Father to a story telling mood.

"This is a night exactly like the night I saw a star fall from the Seven Sisters. I was still a professor. A highly respected professor of plant physiognomy and the spiritual relationship of plants to the universe.

"On a week-long break between school sessions, I camped out in a vast forest where I'd been researching and looking for enigmatic and rare plant species to add to my collection. A star streaked from the Pleiades and zoomed toward mother earth. Within an instant it plummeted smack-dab into the middle of my campfire."

I crossed my arms and looked to the sky wishing, hoping that something would plummet into the middle of our campfire. Father brushed a hand across his forehead and stared into the fire.

"At the moment of impact, the star exploded. When the blinding light faded, a beautiful woman rose from the embers of my fire. I was stunned speechless to see a glowing being before me. I stopped. Stopped breathing. I think my heart even stopped. The brilliant presence swayed with the breeze. She looked as human as any earthling who has ever sat around a fire roasting a plucked grouse. As human as you and I listening to the fats drip and spit upon hot rocks, and sucking our fingers after tearing flesh from bones."

Father's eyes gleamed in the glow of the fire. He waved his arms to take in the whole of our fire with the grouse dripping and spitting over the flames. I fidgeted, waiting for the story to be over, and the bird to be cooked.

"Flames swirled about her body and crackled at her feet. Her hair swirled like wispy smoke around her head. Her face was as radiant as these embers below our cooking grouse. Her feet looked like flames themselves."

As I tried to imagine the scene Father set of the woman rising from flames. I wondered if she had cried from the burning pain. I said, "But. . . ."

He shushed me and continued. "The beautiful star woman of the Pleiades raised one hand. The wind stopped blowing. The leaves on the trees did not rustle. The forest creatures stood still. Thoughts tumbled through my head. Should I bow in reverence? Offer a gourd of cool spring waters? Unsure, I sat mute not knowing what to say or do.

"The silence swelled as I stared at her. The river stopped rippling. The night owl did not *whoo*. The fox did not chase the hare. The bear dared not scratch a tickle on his nose.

"In the great hush, the moon glided from one side of the sky to the other. When it paled as morning light crept above the horizon, the being flickered once, twice, three times. Then she stepped out of fire and held her arms out to me."

"What happened then?" I asked eager to know where the woman went and just as eager to start eating the roasted grouse.

"She became my wife. I want to be with her. I need to be with her, not living here in some forgotten woods. You don't know how much I miss her. Soon, I'll leave to be with her." He stretched both arms like he was encircling the skies. "I will travel the heavens to find her."

Father took the grouse off the fire while I pondered what he'd said. Then he shrank into himself and his own thoughts and stared into the fire. I pulled a leg from the grouse. It tasted of bitter ashes, and my stomach revolted.

CHAPTER 7

The snow became too deep for Father to snare anything. The lake ice too thick to chop with Father's dull axe so we couldn't even drop a line through a hole to fish.

The slab of bacon and other supplies we'd bought with my pig catching money soon dwindled to almost nothing. By my figuring, we had yet to survive two full changes of the moon before the snow and ice dripped from our roof, and buds on the trees fattened and leafed out. I often wondered about what Father had said. *Was it possible for someone to travel the heavens looking for someone who'd died?*

We still had a handful or two of flour, another of ground corn, six scabby potatoes, a tin of raisins, as well as a bowl of fat we'd saved from frying bacon. Also, there was a small clay jar of mushrooms, another of dried cranberries, and a few sprigs of mint hanging from the rope I climbed to my bed.

So little food and yet the winter raged not showing any signs of letting up early. My stomach clawed with hunger constantly as I portioned each bit of food hoping it would last through the winter. I thought of all the coins that I'd won struggling in muck to win and that Father had spent more on elixirs than on food. One way or another, I would make sure that we would never spend another winter starving.

In my hunger, I couldn't help but think of the sizzling cakes made by the potato-cake woman. I remembered the silken feel of my mother's dress and pondered the words *portals and phases.* What had the potato-cake woman meant?

Father drank elixirs more and more frequently. He didn't seem to mind or care that we had so little food. Even with all that medication, or maybe because of it, he became as tempestuous and stormy as the weather.

At other times he was so silent and lifeless that I worried about him, so I'd say, "Tell me about the haunted house you once visited." Or "I want to hear about the trip you took down a mighty river when a muddy monster tore apart the whole great boat so you and others had to hold onto splintered boards and kick your way to shore before he tore you apart." Or "Tell me more about the time you had to run from hungry natives in the Amazon and nearly got squeezed to death by a boa constrictor."

But Father was seldom in his story telling mood. "Bah!" he answered one blustery day. "Don't bother me. I need to think. To plan. To invent."

"Plan what? Invent what?" I asked.

He waved a dismissive hand at me like I was a pesky mosquito, but I persisted, so he answered, "A catapult, if you must know."

"What's a catapult?"

"A sling, a hurler, a propeller, a flinger, a launcher, a tossing machine. Any device that will shoot me halfway to the Pleiades."

"Why do you want to go to the Pleiades, and why only halfway?"

He looked at the half-empty bottle he held. His eyes were veined with red. He wiped his nose and said, "I can swim through the ethereal mists the rest of the way to find your mother."

As ridiculous as it sounded, I asked, "When will we go?"

"There's no we. Just me. It would be too dangerous for you. This is a journey for one."

"How long are you going to be gone?"

"For an eternity. There is no coming back from a journey such as this."

"An eternity? But what'll I do when the fire goes out? Or the snow gets deep past my knees and my shoes fall apart? Or the snares are empty and there's nothing to eat? How will I find my way to the Harvest Moon Festival?" These were all problems I could already solve, but I wanted him to think I needed him so he wouldn't go.

Father took a long drink of golden elixir. He didn't look at me when he said, "You can take care of yourself. You were born under the comet. You should've been showing some sign by now. Something that makes you special. For years I watched for . . . I hoped for . . . But . . ." He slurred his words something terrible. "But nothing. No sign. You're old enough. It should be showing . . . some glorious sign is what I've been waiting for." He tore at his hair. "Something to bring riches. Something—anything—to get us out of miserable life. But . . . Nothing. Nothing. All for nothing."

A spasm squeezed my chest. Father hoped I'd bring riches. He was leaving because I couldn't bring riches. That I was just plain me—Purslane, a weed. Unwanted. What a great disappointment I was to him. What did he expect from me? I was only fourteen.

Father's words cut me deeply. Tears ran freely from my eyes. Blood pounded in my head. My voice rasped like gravel as I yelled, "What do you mean? I'm old enough? What do you mean by *nothing*? What do you mean by *bringing riches*? I'm your daughter! Doesn't that mean anything? And you want to leave me? To go chasing around among the stars? Leaving me? Alone!"

At that instant, I wanted him to be like the fathers at the festival buying their children buttered corn. Or to be like the potato-cake woman, to look at me, talk kindly to me and feed me something warm and good.

My stomach ached with emptiness. He lifted his bottle to his mouth.

Fury boiled within me. I swatted the bottle as he took a drink. The golden liquid splattered. It soaked his shirt and pants. He yowled as if in pain. His eyes narrowed to a pinpoint of darkness. Before he could roar or say a single word, I grabbed the sack of elixir bottles, stomped outside and swung the sack against a tree. Again. And again.

CHAPTER 8

My fury spent, I flung the battered sack aside and ran far into the woods. I ran from Father, from hunger, from the hovel. The boiling rage I'd felt drained away little by little, but a fear replaced it. No matter how far I ran, the awful sound of the bottles cracking against the tree haunted me. How could I go back? Father would be furious. The heat of my explosion was soon replaced by shivers as the blustery wind blew through my skimpy dress. The shivers turned to iciness. I fell into a mound of deep snow. I could either lie there and freeze to death or return to face Father's wrath.

When I stumbled into the hut, I was so cold and miserable that I could barely stagger to the fireplace to thaw in its warmth. Father said not a word, but poured warm water into a mug. Then he crushed a few mint leaves and handed the mug to me saying, "You have seen my misery. It hangs on me like moss from an old tree. I can't stay here. I must go."

His misery? What about mine? I didn't say those words. I didn't want to stir his anger. Besides, he didn't care about me, just himself.

Father rationed the two bottles of elixir that hadn't broken during my tempestuous outburst. I wished for him to be different, but he wasn't and never would be. Our hovel was no longer a home to me. It provided shelter from the blustering winds and swirling snows, but that was all. Home was supposed to be like a nest high in a tress where a mother bird fed her hatchings and protected them from the winds. Home was even a patch of grasses laid flat by a mother doe and her fawn lying side by side for the night. I had even felt more at home sitting on the stump by the potato-cake woman's griddle, listening to her kind voice and eating golden fried cakes. I daydreamed a home faraway with my mother's people. A home surrounded by violets and trilliums. A home with plenty of food, warmth, and happy people.

I fried potato skins in a little bacon fat for our next meal. Then I melted snow to boiling before adding a leaf of mint for a weak tea. Sadness and fear added to my loneliness as the days passed. Father barely ate, not even the day when I set a whole boiled potato slathered with bacon fat in front of him. The silence between us grew steadily as the wind rattled our one window. He sat for hours chasing the vapors away or curing bouts of lumbago with the help of the elixir from the last bottle that hadn't broken. Often, he didn't even go to his bench to sleep. In the morning I'd find him slumped at the plank table snoring. As golden liquid in the bottle measured less and less, Father became even more glum, silent, and morose.

I didn't understand his long silences. Perhaps they were to punish me for having smashed most of his bottles. I wondered if he missed the colors and sounds of the festival as much as I did, or was it only my mother he missed? I asked him, "Father, do you miss the festival and all the people? Do you miss being the All-Seeing Eye and telling fortunes?"

Father groaned, "Never! I hated going there. I don't miss it one bit. There is nothing left there or here for me. I can't stay malingering forever. You know how to fend for yourself. I've taught you that much." He emptied his last bottle in a big swallow then flung it against a wall. It crashed with a splintering noise. The shattering of the glass frightened me. So much was broken. Especially the man sitting before me.

Without any elixirs, Father seemed better for a day or two. The snow had started melting so he set snares. We escaped starvation with a newly caught hare, squirrel, or grouse to roast over our fire.

One night I dreamed about the canoe whirling me to the land of my mother's people. So, the next evening as we gnawed the flesh from the bones of a roasted squirrel, I asked, "Where did you get the red canoe I was born in and where is it now?"

Father thought for a moment, then said, "Your mother wanted to go to her people even though her own mother had died long ago, and her father and others had died in a great fire. She said she wanted to give birth while feeling what she called the song of the wind in her heart.

"It would have been a walk of many days. She was close to giving birth so that was not possible. One morning, after a gusty night, a canoe blew onto our shore. We didn't know where it came from, but your mother said that the comet must have heard her pleas and sent the canoe to us. We quickly packed to go. I paddled as hard as I could. When we were only half-way across the lake, a heavy fog enveloped us. Then a blustery wind whirled and twirled the canoe. I thought we'd be swamped by the waves. Your mother cried out in pain that a baby was coming.

"I couldn't even see the shore through the fog. When the wind picked up the canoe and swirled it round and round, I thought we were done for, but then the winds subsided and the fog cleared to a light mist. Unbelievably, I lay right here on the shore. Right by our hut. You were in my arms. The canoe was upside down in the middle of the lake."

"What happened to my mother?" My heart squeezed, knowing the answer.

"For days, weeks, really, I walked the shores, searching for your mother, but found nothing. Not even a scrap of her clothing. It was the worst day of my life—the day you were born should have been the best. A daughter born of the comet. If only your mother had lived."

Father's hands trembled as he spoke. He looked off into space, his eyes searching for and seeing something I couldn't see.

I put my hands on his trembling ones. "We could go to her people. Just like she wanted. We could feel the song of the winds in our hearts, too." I said hopefully.

Father shook his head. "Bah. Wind song. Wind song. She made it sound wonderful. I've never been there. She's not there now. I'll never go."

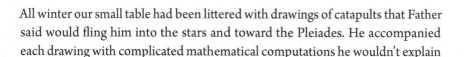

All winter our small table had been littered with drawings of catapults that Father said would fling him into the stars and toward the Pleiades. He accompanied each drawing with complicated mathematical computations he wouldn't explain to me. He never was pleased enough with the drawings or the reckonings he so carefully noted.

When winter gave up its grip, I welcomed the melting of the ice, the violets bravely peeping through the duff in weak sunlight, and the coming of robins, geese, doves, sparrows, warblers, and all my other woodland friends. We hadn't starved to death, but the burlap dress hung even more loosely on me.

Father muttered constantly about flying off to the Pleiades. In search of his true love. I felt abandoned already as I heated our only dented pan. When it was ready, I dropped in a bit of bacon grease and two dried mushrooms—one for each of us— and stirred in a little blob of flour. All the while, I made my plan. Before Father had a chance to leave, I'd convince him to go with me to find my mother's people. There the people would welcome us, and we'd find a home—the home I dreamed of.

Even with the coming of spring, Father's gloom increased. He no longer set snares and traps so we had no roasted grouse over evening fires. When he stood, he stumbled and trembled. His moods switched from grumpy to grumpier. Night time was torture for him. He couldn't sleep. When he drowsed a bit, dreams he called *fantasmagoric* haunted him. He kept me awake with his moaning and groaning. He began seeing things. He often waved his hands wildly about and shouted, "Go away! Go! Leave me alone!"

Because of his unpredictable moods, I spent my days in the woods. Thinking, planning, dreaming of being with my mother's people, and longing for what Mother had called Wind Song.

I watched fox kits play in the dappled sunlight. Ducklings swam after their mother in the lake. Sometimes I followed fawns that began roving further and further from their mother's side to explore a sunny glade or to drink at the lake or to nuzzle a toad in their path.

Like the fawns, I roved further from our log and birch bark hut. I felt guilty I was abandoning Father when he might need me, but when he was in his dark moods and paid no attention to me whatsoever, I needed to find sunshine, and something else I yearned for and didn't have a name for. What was it I wanted so badly that I felt an ache, a hollowness in my deepest being? Did I want the mother that I had never had? Would I be wandering further and further from *her* side as the fawns did as they grew? Did I yearn to be like the girls I followed at the festivals? The girls who walked arm in arm giggling and gossiping? I missed the company of a kind woman who made potato cakes. I even missed things I couldn't put a name to. I was empty. With his silences, Father had already abandoned me. I wanted something or someone to fill my emptiness, so I became even more determined to seek my mother's people.

When I wasn't looking for berries and leaf buds to eat, I memorized poems and read my mother's dictionary.

Loneliness. From the word alone.
One need not be alone. To feel loneliness.
Not even if one is married.

At night, I thought about what I had read. My mother had been lonely, too. I wondered what Father had been like back then. I dreamed about a red canoe. In one dream I was birthed, not from my mother, but from the canoe itself as it spun through cresting waves, tilting this way and that. I awoke with the strangeness of the dreams still haunting me. The canoe carried me to a land—a land of hills and valleys filled with trilliums and violets all year round. A land with kind, smiling people.

The next morning, I wrote in the sands.

I wish I had a red canoe.

That evening when the moon was but a sliver, and all the stars shone as bright specks in the sky, I asked Father, "Tell me how to get to my mother's people."

"Why do you want to know?"

"So, we can go there."

"Too dangerous. Too dangerous."

"Not if you go with me. We would be together. We would both be safe." I hoped Father would understand the logic of my argument, but he didn't.

"The only place I'm going is to the Pleiades." He rubbed his hands against his face and then stirred the handful of spring mushrooms sizzling in a pan on glowing embers. I had mixed a potato flat cake batter as best I could with our last potato and mashed cattail root. As it sputtered in bacon grease along with the mushrooms, I hoped it would be half as good as what the good woman made.

Father scratched his arms and chest. "I was a professor once. A very respected professor," he said and then stopped to stir the mushrooms again.

"Eighteen! A mere lad of eighteen! That's how old I was when I already knew more scientific names for plants than men twice my age. I knew the physiognomy of them all, too. I'd been studying since I was eight."

Father looked off into space. "I should have studied more astronomy. Plants are the stuff of dirt. People walk upon them. But the stars? The moon? The wisdom of the planets? Now, that would be something."

"You can do that now!" I was excited that he was talking about being a professor again. "We can go to a big village or town. You can be a professor of the stars and planets! We can live like regular people and have friends and lots of food, and. . . ."

Father interrupted as though he hadn't heard a single word I'd said, "When I get to the Pleiades, that's what I'll do. I'll become a professor of the stars—of the universe!" Father stood tall and proud as he spoke. When he finished, he stumbled along the shore staring into the sky.

How could I ever pull Father back to this world to travel with me when he was already dreaming of his next life among the stars?

CHAPTER 9

Father's trembling and confusion became worse. He often took longer walks and didn't return until the next day. I'd find him curled beneath a tree, or lying flat in a bed of bracken ferns. In the hovel he was preoccupied, so deep in his own thoughts that I had to remind him of simple chores. "Bring in some wood." "Scoop a pail of water from the lake for us to wash with." I was so worried, I asked, "Father, what's bothering you?"

He looked at me as if he didn't know me, and then at the sky as he answered, "I'm leaving soon."

He'd said that before but now his lethargy and forgetfulness had become so bad, he'd forget to eat if I didn't remind him. I hoped he'd forget about leaving, but I was distressed to think I'd be on my own. Even if he didn't go, but stayed with me, he was in such an awful condition, I'd still be on my own. I had to do something. "Father, let's go to my mother's people. We'd have a home there with plenty to eat."

"I'm leaving, but not to go there." He stumbled to the table.

"First, let's go there together. Then you'd be free to leave, if you still want to."

"No use. I don't know how to get there. Quit such foolish thoughts."

Foolish thoughts? Who was it with the foolish thoughts? Me, who just wanted to find my mother's people here on earth. Or him, who wanted to fly around in the star sky looking for my mother? Either way, I didn't know which direction to go. Neither did he.

49

On a warm sunny day, I headed deep into the woods. Fiddle ferns popped up everywhere. Wintergreen leaves showed glossy green in the midst of brown duff. Birds sang with my every step. In a small pond, tadpoles were beginning to turn into. Frogs. A green snake slithered past my boots. I kicked leaves from under a. tree. Worms wriggled to get out of the strong sunlight. Everywhere I looked, life was wiggling, waggling, swimming, and singing.

On my way home I plucked cedar buds and wintergreen leaves for tea. As I knelt to gather some fiddle heads and tiny mushrooms for soup, I wondered about what the potato-cake woman had whispered—portals and phases.

I hurried home so fast to look through Mother's dictionary that I almost stepped on a woolly bear caterpillar and knocked my head on a wasp nest on a low branch. Father was out on one of his many searches looking for catapult components as I pulled the book from its shelf. With great anticipation I ran my fingers over my mother's name lettered on the cover A-l-c-y-o-n-e. My fingers shivered as they turned pages until I came to the bold lettering that spelled PHASES.

Cycles that repeat.
For example, Polaris has phases of goodwill followed by drunken bitterness
directed toward those who dismissed him from his job at the university.
Or, on a more pleasant note,
the cycles of the moon as it changes shape
from new moon to full during the waxing phases,
and then returns to a sliver during the waning phases.
Time and again.

My throat caught as I thought of Father being dismissed from the university. He'd never told me that. No wonder he wouldn't even consider moving and getting a professor's job.

Carefully I opened the dictionary again. I turned the pages past placate, platitude, Pleiades, plight, poetry, poison, and Polaris to get to portals.

Portal: Entrance

That's all. Just one word. I turned the pages to the *Es*. I found Enigma and Enlighten and finally—Entrance.

Entrance: Appearance or arrival through doorways when accenting
the beginning (EN-trance).
Fill with wonder or fascinate when accenting the end (en-TRANCE).

I understood. Father always said that was the way to get people to pay for their fortunes was to fascinate or entrance them with the mysteries of the future, but what did the potato-cake woman mean when she said *portals*? Doorways? Entryways? And how did the phases of the moon fit in? I didn't think I knew, but maybe I was getting an inkling. Was it possible to enter portals to another world with some moon phase? Or just one special one? If I could figure that out, maybe I could find the portal to my mother. If . . . If she still was in the world between the living and the dead.

——————⌒——————

Father came home long after dark. I had already climbed the rope to my bed and was falling into the dream world when he blustered into our hovel. I pretended to be asleep. I heard the ripping of page after page of his catapult drawings. I shuttered to think of the rage he might be in, but hoped he was giving up on his plan to fly through the ethereal sky to find my mother.

That night I dreamed I fell into a rushing river. I called for Father to rescue me but he didn't come. My voice echoed off the deep walls of a rocky canyon. I kicked and thrashed, trying to swim against the current. The puppeteer I'd seen at festivals stood on the shore. He laughed cruelly and threw his puppets into the river with me. They frightened me as they skipped, clicking and clacking, while dancing on the waters and laughing at my plight.

I awoke. Sweat dampened my hair, my clothes and the corn shuck bedding beneath me. Father snored on his bench below. I climbed down my rope ladder and tiptoed out the door. The full moon was high in the night sky. It gleamed, casting its light on the placid lake surface. The smooth waters of Kawishami looked like a huge moon. I wished the waters would tell me their secrets.

I walked to the shore and wrote in the wet sands.

I wish I had a red canoe.
I wish I could enter portals of the dead to see my mother.

CHAPTER 10

I begged and begged to go to the Harvest Moon Festival that fall even though Father didn't want to go. Finally, he gave in. My winning argument was we could earn money to buy needed winter supplies and elixirs.

"Bah!" He said. "We'll go, but just for one day. It's just a bunch of frauds, scammers, schemers, swindlers, thieves, and imposters. They'll try to get every last coin for a bottle of snake oil or a smoke and mirror trick. No one earns an honest living anymore."

I wanted to argue that the potato-cake woman was honest. And she'd given me all the sample cakes I could eat in exchange for a few easy chores, and the pig man had given me the pouch of coins as promised. But Father had just said we'd go. I didn't want him to change his mind. I needed to get my mother's dress, and I hoped to untangle the mystery of portals and phases.

Following Father's footsteps through the fen, stepping on the same tufts of sedge as he did to keep from sinking into the morass, I had a deep feeling that this would be the last time we'd go to the festival together. I wanted our long walk to be a jolly one so I asked him if he knew a song we could sing. He brushed a spider web from his face. He looked at me. His eyes were glazed. He looked as though he were not in the midst of the wetland, but far, far, away. A strange tingling filled my body. It was like he'd forgotten I was right there following his every step. Maybe, I thought, his body was there, but his very soul had already catapulted to the Pleaides.

Long ago when I was but a wee child, I had pestered Father to tell me story after story. After he had run out of stories about magic rings, lost princesses, talking bears and the like, he told a horrible story about a man who died. His soul flew to the high heavens to join his one true love, but his hollow body had been doomed to walk the earth forever. I hated the story and suspected he had made it up so I would quit begging for more.

That was what he looked like to me now—a hollow man who was looking for his one true love and didn't care a smidgen for his daughter following him. He turned away from me and with his next step he slid off the path and sank to his knees in swampy black waters. At first, he just let himself sink. I feared he'd blame me and curse all the moons of Jupiter and slippery paths, but no, instead he reached a hand to me. I couldn't remember when we'd touched hands, much less held them. I took a hold on his in both of mine. His was cold. I felt him thaw at that touch. He looked at me. The man inside him, for good and for bad, had come back.

Holding my hand, Father did not try to pull himself free of the rank mud, but began to sing.

To the fair we must go.
To the fair. Hi ho! Hi ho!
See the peddler sell his wares.
See some dancing-prancing bears.
Eat some muffins dripped with honey
As the monkey takes your money.
Pay a penny for crispy cakes
That the good woman daily makes.
No more fortunes will be told
Even though they're worth some gold.
We will sing a merry tune.
Underneath the harvest moon.
To the fair we must go.
To the fair. Hi ho! Hi ho!

I laughed as Father sang. We held hands. A man I had never known before was there knee deep in marshy waters. Instead of drowning his sorrows in elixirs, he was singing! A butterfly landed on the spider web that still clung to his beard. A fly buzzed above his head. He kept right on singing. My chest swelled with a happiness I had never felt with him before. I wanted the song and merriment to last forever.

After a while Father climbed out and even though he was wet and muddy with a spider web in his beard, he seemed not to care. The rest of our trek was not as cheerful as when Father had been making up songs and singing, but he was definitely in a better mood than I'd seen him for a long time. As we walked, he told me about the plants along the path. "A pitcher plant—flesh eating. Don't put your finger near. Look. A whole family of jack-in-the-pulpits. Don't eat the roots. Better, yet, don't eat any of it." He picked a handful of sphagnum moss and showed me the little insects living in it. I kept track of all the mushrooms we found. He told me which were edible and which were not. We munched on a delicious nutty-flavored mushroom.

"Chanterelles," he said. "Fit for kings."

"And queens," I added. "They have a lovely name. I would like a name like Chanterelle." I popped the last bit into my mouth. I thought of my own name. Purslane the weed.

"Chanterelle," I whispered to myself pretending it was my name.

The closer to the festival grounds, the quieter Father got. I wished we were back in the swamp with him singing and sinking up to his knees in murky water. A cacophony of sounds greeted us as we got near. I heard squeeze box and calliope music, horses neighing, pigs oinking, drums beating, and barkers pitching their wares. A new fortune teller had taken over Father's booth. A woman dressed in filmy layers of scarves and skirts, brightly colored orange, red, purple, and green twirled as we walked by. Gold and silver sequins caught the sun's rays and glinted so brightly I had to squeeze my eyes almost shut. Her sign read: LADY MAGDA'S PALMISTY. YOUR HANDS TELL YOUR FUTURE. Young and old gathered waiting for her to stop twirling so they could have their fortunes read.

Awestruck, I watched her scarves float in the breeze. Father grabbed my hand and started to pull me away. In that instant Lady Magda quit twirling and looked straight at me. Her eyes piercing. She whispered a word. I didn't quite catch it—something like *careen, serene, selene,* or maybe *dorine.* Whatever it was, the word meant nothing to me, but I was intrigued by the colorful woman even though I didn't like that she had Father's booth.

Father pulled me away from the whirling and twirling. He muttered something about finding a way to get a few coins and left me by myself. I headed to find the potato-cake woman, but the whole area where she'd been during other festivals was now a tent show. Placards advertised oddities like The Alligator Girl. The Boy Ape from Borneo. The Woman with Chicken Claw Feet. The Feathered Man. I was fascinated but had not even a single copper coin to pay entrance to any of the tents so I continued wandering. Two wooden puppets jerked on strings as the puppeteer told a story. One ran from the other who meant him harm. Their frozen faces, one smiled, the other sneered giving me a chill up my back so I hurried away.

Finally, on the very fringes of the festival, I found the potato-cake woman, her goat and cart. "Sit down," she invited. "It's good to see you. I was afraid you weren't coming."

"Thank you," I said, feeling more than a little bit sad that she and her griddle were far from the center of all the festival busyness and that there wasn't a bustling crowd around to be lured in by the aroma of her wonderful cakes. Here at the outer edge were wagons and carts stacked with rags, dented kettles, bent nails, broken glass, bruised apples, and herbs that looked like dried grass. The sellers themselves looked as ragged, dented, bent, broken, and bruised as their wares. The whole of it lacked the color, sounds and mad activity that I had so loved at the festivals of old.

The woman didn't say anything, but a sadness seeped from her every pore. She looked at me a long while before picking up another potato to peel. I had the feeling she was looking at my burlap dress and how skinny I had become since the last festival. I wanted things to be like they had been so I asked, "Do you need some help? I'm a good peeler."

She handed me a chip-bladed knife and said, "Don't peel too many. Doesn't look like there'll be much of a crowd coming way out here."

"What happened?" I asked.

"Gossip is that a greedy rich man owns the whole tent spectacle. It's whispered that he bribes the mayor of villages for the privilege of bringing his whole hullabaloo to festivals. They take over. What used to be a *harvest* fest is now an up-roar full of oddities. Worse yet, soon they'll pack up their tents, painted ladies, lots of money, and we'll be left here with empty pockets."

I hadn't heard a word like *hullabaloo* before, but I could guess by the way she spit the word out that it wasn't good. Empty pockets I knew about.

"I liked the old festival better," I said.

"That rich man even brought his own food wagons. They're painted bright yellow, orange, green, and red. They sell spiced sausages, roasted turkey legs, sweet breads, pies, and exotic fruits. No one will want fried potato cakes."

I wanted to tell her that I would like one, but I was all choked up and a tear fell onto the potato in my hands. I hadn't even started to peel it. Even Father pretending to be the All-Seeing Eye and the magic man who made me disappear in his black box were better than this. I doubted if there was even room for the greased pig catching contests.

Before too many more tears could fall, I put knife to potato and started to peel. Sour bile rose in my throat when I looked up at the colorful tents that took up most of the festival space.

"This will be the last year I come if it's to be like this," the potato-cake woman said.

The knife bit into my finger. My red blood seeped into the flesh of the potato and looked like a blooming flower of pink.

"There. There," The woman said patting me on the head. She got up and dug around in her cart. She tore a strip of a rag, uncapped a clay jar, scooped out some honey, spread it on my wound and wrapped it tightly. She kept holding my hand, and stroking the cut finger. It was the second time that day someone had held my hands. It felt good.

As we sat together, I thought of singing with Father in the swamp. "Let's sing," I said.

She still held my hand and began to make up a silly song. She lifted her face and smiled as she sang.

A grumpy old bear
Lost his hair.
Ha-rumph. Ha-rumph.

A lazy old cat
Fell asleep in my hat.
Meow! Meow!

"Your turn to make something up," she said.
I looked at her goat and sang.

A hungry old goat
Ate my coat.
Blaa blaa. Blaa! Blaa!

We took turns making up verses, laughing, and singing.

A big old cow
Sat on a plow.
Moo moo. Moo moo.

A sly old fox
Stole some socks.
Ha ha! Ha ha! Ha ha!

She and I held hands the whole time and laughed at the end of each verse. A heady joy filled me until I tingled from head to toe and wished to feel that way forever.

CHAPTER 11

When Father returned, our singing and exuberant cheer fled in an instant. He looked awful. Horrible. Terrible. Dreadful. Desperate. And he smelled like he'd swallowed half a bottle of elixir. He was but a hollow, shrunken shadow of the man who that morning had sung and held my hand while knee-deep in sludge.

"What's wrong?" I asked. The potato-cake woman let go of my hand, got up, took a dented bucket from her cart, turned it upside down and pointed for Father to sit.

He did. Resting his elbows on his knees and holding his own face in both hands, his voice broke as he said, "I can't take care of you forever. I'm leaving soon so I asked at the mayor's house if they'd take you for a serving girl. He slammed the door in my face. He didn't even say a kind word. It was as if I was a rag seller or worse."

A shiver ran up my back. What did a serving girl do? And Father can't take care of me? He hadn't for a long time. I cooked. I patched. I reminded him of his chores, but he must have taken care of me years ago when he strapped me to his back in the skunk fur carrier. He was so miserable I was sure I could convince him that we could either find a village with my mother's people, or better yet, a portal to my mother, so we all could be together.

Father continued, "Then I made my way to farm country. You'd think farmers or their wives would need a good helper. I trudged through fields, stepped stones to cross creeks, made my way past barking dogs, and even got chased by a nasty flock of geese and had to out-run a charging bull. Unfortunately, the big farms all had passels of growing kids to do the work.

"Finally, I got lucky. At a small farm I was able to convince the bachelor that a dairy maid would ease his work burden."

The potato-cake woman stood up. She shook a finger at Father and glared. "You can't just go around giving your daughter to some stranger!"

"But, but, but," Father stammered. "She'd have plenty of milk to drink. The bachelor said she could sleep in the haymow. That's plenty warm even in the cold winter. There's even a barn cat to chase the mice."

"Hay mow! Barn cat! Mice! She knows nothing of those things. Much less how to milk a cow!" In her anger the woman kicked the bucket Father sat on and almost knocked him over.

They argued about me while I was right there looking from one to the other. The potato-cake woman was the one concerned about me, not Father. I wanted to kick the bucket, too.

Father looked at his boots. The stitches were breaking, and the boots were only one more long walk from falling apart completely. Looking at me, he said, "You can learn to milk. It's easy. And cows are plenty good company. And a cat, too."

"Learn to milk! Bah! And you call yourself an educated man? Can't you tell just by looking at your daughter that she is destined for better things? She was born the year of the comet!"

Destined for better things? And that comet stuff again? Father was disappointed I didn't have a gift that would make us rich. What better things could I be destined for? Bewildered, I looked back and forth from the potato-cake woman to Father as they argued. My chin trembled. I crossed my arms and held onto my elbows as though holding myself together. How could Father even think of sending me to some farmer he and I didn't know?

"And butter. Fresh butter. The bachelor showed me his churn. Churning is as easy as milking. It is a good churn, it is. It cranks easily. You could have all the butter and milk you want. And there were hens of all colors clucking all over the yard. You'd have eggs, every day, too. And a chicken for the pot once in a while."

The potato-cake woman kicked again. Father tumbled from the bucket and sprawled onto the ground. She stood over him shaking her fist. "You fool! You don't have an honest copper coin to your name. Or did you sell your daughter to that farmer so you could buy more of that fire water you're so fond of?"

My insides quivered, and I felt faint.

"She needs to do something. It's not good for her to just wander around in the woods doing nothing. Besides, he said if she was a good worker, he'd marry her. Maybe even take her into his house."

The full force of the potato-cake woman's kick caught Father smack in the ribs. He cringed into a ball. I reached out a hand to help him up. He ignored my hand, but between moans, grunts and groans he managed to wheeze out, "Enough! Don't kick me again. It wouldn't be such a bad life with plenty of milk, eggs, and butter."

"You better not have sold her. I'll have you put in the stocks, and I'll even throw the first stones if I ever find out you did."

Father stood, held his side, stumbled, and righted himself the best he could. He held his hand out to me. "Come on. Let's go home."

The potato-cake woman slapped his hand away from mine, took it in hers and led me to the cart. She opened the chest and handed me my mother's beautiful green dress. I pulled it to my face to feel the soft silk again. I breathed deeply of her lingering scent as I escaped the reality of my situation for a moment. Aromas of flowers mixed with mint, parsley, and basil filled my nose.

Unbidden images danced in front of my eyes as a lovely woman sang under a chestnut tree. Her voice floated through the leaves. They trembled in the beauty of the song—not just a silly jingle, but a real song. Birds of all kinds even winged their way to listen to her melodies. I wanted to hold the dress to myself forever.

"Where'd you get that dress?" Father's voice but a hoarse whisper that shook me back to reality.

"I bought it from you at this very festival the first time you brought this girl when she was but a-crawling baby. You were grief stricken and already needing coins for potions and elixirs to soothe your sorrow. I saved it all these years, hoping someday to return it to Alcyone's daughter."

Father flinched at the mention of my mother's name. Humiliated, he shrank and withered like a mushroom left to dry in the sun.

The woman noticed and said again, "Alcyone! Alcyone! Alcyone would have wanted better for her daughter."

Father moaned and held his chest as though painfully struck. "We need to go now."

I whispered my mother's name to myself and smiled as I remembered the words *Alcyone's daughter.* To the potato-cake woman, I wasn't Purslane the unwanted weed; I was Alcyone's daughter. I savored the beauty and softness of the dress as I folded and tucked it under my arm. *Alcyone. Alcyone.* Then I tugged my hem from the goat's mouth for what I hoped wasn't the last time. Wiping away tears that threatened to fall, I stood before the potato-cake woman.

"Thank you for potato cakes when I was hungry. For trusting me with a silver coin so I could enter the pig-catching contest. For the song my mother sang, and now for her dress." I had filled my emptiness sitting on the stump at her side. I had staunched my hunger with cakes from her griddle. The tears would not be stopped. My throat caught more than once but I still managed to add, "I hope we will see each other again. Maybe I'll be able to re-pay you for your kindness." My voice snagged as though caught in brambles and no more words could come.

"You are always welcome wherever I am. I have little I can give you other than your mother's dress and her song, but take these potatoes, too. Plant them. Think of me when you eat their harvest." She handed me two potatoes. Her eyes glinted and a tear formed at the corners. "Your time will come. Good things await you. Remember portals and phases." She looked at my sack dress and tattered shoes, then turned away.

Father, who'd stood silent during all this, took my hand, and we turned to go. I looked back at the woman twice. She was packing her griddle and potatoes and putting them on her cart. She was leaving, too. The goat maa-ed.

To reach the path through woodlands and wetland we needed to cross on our way home, we first had to walk the whole festival grounds. We passed tents proclaiming oddities and never-before-seen-curiosities and fast-talking shills. We skirted around dancing dogs dressed in pinks, purples, and yellows looking sad and nervous. I made sure we avoided the puppeteer and his frozen-faced puppets who only moved if their strings were jerked.

When we came to the row of food wagons, the colors and aromas slowed Father. "I have a couple of coins," he said. "Let's get a bite to eat before our long walk."

My stomach had been painfully hungry all day, as I had not eaten more than a handful of mushrooms and a few berries I'd plucked on our walk to the festival. I thought about the potato-cake woman and how she had always given me the first cakes off her griddle. I felt a deep aching void knowing I might never see her again.

We walked by each wagon judging which food would be the best bargain for a coin or two. Finally, we agreed on sausages that cost two coppers apiece. Father turned his back to me as he pulled a pouch from under his shirt. I heard coins clinking together. Not just a coin or two, but many. He handed the coins to the woman then tucked the pouch back under his shirt. The sound of coins clinking together made me think he had more than he said, but I was famished and the spicy sausage smelled so good that I forgot about coins as I took my first bite. I finished the hot and fatty sausage in the blink of an eye. Father must have been as famished as I was because he, too, was soon sucking the last bits from his fingers.

I was licking every last morsel from my fingers when a young woman in the next wagon called out. "Selene. Is that you?"

I looked around. There was no one nearby but Father and me. The young woman was mashing rutabagas in a tin bowl. The yellow and orange sign advertised BEST BAGA CAKES. She wore her hair braided and wrapped high on her head. She was beautiful even though a jagged scar ran down her left cheek. She looked straight at me and asked again, "Selene. Is that you?"

I said, "No. My name is Purslane."

She wiped her hands on her apron, looked me up and down, then said, "And so you are. Well, a pretty girl named Selene bought a beggie cake and soured cabbage from me . . . oh, three or four villages," she pointed in a vague direction and continued, "that a-way just this summer. She was with a man and woman. You'd look just like her if you combed your hair. And wore a decent dress."

I flushed red-hot and hugged the bundle of my mother's dress close.

Father was a few steps ahead of me so I hurried to catch up and tried to pat my hair smooth. I would rather have stayed and talked to the rutabaga-cake seller. There was something about a girl named Selene who had combed hair, wore a real dress, and ate beggie cakes with soured cabbage that fascinated me. I wanted to know more. And what had Lady Magda, the whirling, twirling woman, whispered to me? Could it have been *selene* or *serene?*

Trudging unhappily through stubble-filled fields and a scraggly stunted woodland, Father and I each fell deep into our own thoughts. We hadn't gotten far into the muddy swampy area that sucks people into knee-deep sludge when Father broke our silence by grumbling about the sausage he'd eaten. "All potato, grease, and leeks! Not a speck of pork or any four-legged animal!"

I felt rumblings and tumblings in my own gut letting me know that the sausage hadn't agreed with my stomach, not even a hungry one. I ran into the woods to relieve my distress. I wondered if Selene, whoever she was, had had a turbulent stomach after eating her beggie cakes and cabbage. I reached into my pocket to hold the two potatoes the woman had given me. I felt reassured just knowing they were there.

Father was silent for a long time after he joined me on the trail. When he did begin to speak, he said, "No matter what you or that woman who kicked me say, you will be better off at the farm with chickens, eggs, cream and butter to eat. I promised to bring you to the farmer today. If I don't, he'll come after you."

My head rumbled and tumbled more than my stomach had at hearing Father's words. Then I remembered the smell of elixir on Father and the clinking of many coins in his pouch.

I turned to him head on and screamed. "You sold me! You sold me to the farmer!"

CHAPTER 12

In my loft that night I dreamed I was lost at the festival. I wandered, looking for the potato-cake woman. The rows of painted wagons were a never-ending swirling maze of reds, yellows, oranges, greens, and purples. As I looked for a way out, masked people tried to grab me with their bony hands and arms. An alligator with people legs snapped his jaw at me and licked its lips. A headless woman dressed in a filmy red gown carried her own sobbing and wailing head by the hair. A laughing puppet chased me. His wooden legs clacked and clattered as he ran.

I awoke with my heart beating fiercely. Shaken and jarred by the dreadful images and plaintive voices, I shook off my raggedy blanket and brought myself to a reality worse than the dream. *Father sold me to a farmer! He was leaving me!*

I calmed myself by imagining the two of us paddling a red canoe, crossing Lake Kawishami in the fullness of the moon. I would not let Father leave me, whether by catapult or otherwise. I had to make him realize that my plan for the two of us to find my mother's people was best. No farmer. No flying through the skies. Maybe, even for a little while, we could be happy together. We'd be part of a big family.

Even if he wouldn't go with me, I was determined to find my mother's people. I would run, swim, trudge through deep mire—even claw my way up high mountains—but I would not marry the farmer no matter how many chickens and eggs I'd have to eat, or how much butter I could churn.

I must have slept again, because when I awoke our hut was silent. So silent I thought I could hear leaves falling from the trees outside. Father wasn't snoring or tossing and turning. Enjoying the quiet and steeling myself for the day, I lay as long as I could before climbing down the rope to build up the fire and set water to heat for tea.

What a mess! Father's professor's robe and shawl had been flung across the room. Buckets, cooking pots, books, papers, specimen jars with plants—all tossed and tumbled every which way. *How had I slept through all that?* The door was wide open and leaves blew in. No wonder I thought I could hear leaves falling in the silence. I looked out. I called for Father. I ran up and down the shore shouting, "Father! Father!" My voice echoed back at me and faded into the morning mists.

Pelicans, geese, and ducks flew up from the lake. A doe and her fawn leaped from the shore and ran into the woods. Father wasn't anywhere to be seen. He had gone! Left me. Abandoned me! My chin quivered as I screamed one last time, "Father!"

Sobbing with the reality that I was truly alone, I gathered up Father's robe from the floor and held it to my chest. Shivering, I slipped it on and pulled it tightly around myself imagining him as a professor. I picked up a book that lay sprawled on the floor, too. The title was utterly incomprehensible to me. *The Complete Physiognomy of Plants and Their Spiritual and Mystical Relationships with Humans and Other Mammals.* The author's name was proclaimed in bold letters: Professor Stere North—Father's real name.

I pulled *Alcyone's Dictionary* from its shelf to see what my mother had written about it. Wiping my tears away, I found her entry with all the other Ss like skunk, sublime, and symbiosis.

Stere: Dear Husband is Scottish.
To my misfortune—and maybe his own—his parents Mr. and Mrs. North
named their son Stere—meaning Star.
So, he decided that he is Star of the North: Polaris—the star the whole north-
ern sky revolves around while holding its own position. The guiding star.
Dear Husband thinks all revolves around him and that he guides all.

Mother had understood Father. I nodded as I looked up what else she'd written.

Polaris.
The name Stere prefers to call himself.
Even though I already had the name of a star,
he renamed me Alcyone as he pointed to Polaris.

'There I am,' he said, 'a star of the Little Bear, sometimes called the
Little Dipper.
And there you are, Alcyone, part of Pleiades, a constellation that looks like a
much smaller dipper. Both have seven bright stars.
Seven is the most magical of all numbers. We are pure magic.
Together we can do anything.'
Sometimes I don't know what to think of Dear Husband and his ideas.

I agreed with my mother. Sometimes I hadn't known what to think of him, either. Also on the table was a diagram of the Milky Way and the course Father planned to take to reach the Pleiades. His path zigzagged past the moon and Mars, then veered off and away from the sun. From there an arrow pointed to Orion and the constellation of Taurus and then to the Pleiades. Alongside the celestial map, he'd drawn a catapult and a series of strange galactic traveling devices. Cones, discs, triangles, balls, darts, and wheeled carts with domes. *Could he really reach the Pleiades in such contraptions?*

The last thing on the table was a map with a note attached. Father must have written it just before he hurried out the door. His handwriting was terrible, but I could make out the words.

Purslane, when you awaken, I will already be on my way to my Alcyone.
Forget about looking for your mother's people.
Follow the map to the farmer.
Just think of all the eggs, milk, and butter you'll have.
Go now or he'll come after you. Father.

CHAPTER 13

My stomach knotted. Sour bile rose in my throat. I froze to the very spot I stood. My mind raced. *Why? Why? Why? Was I really just a weed to be trampled upon? Or pulled out by its roots? Was I something that could just be discarded, left alone, without so much as a "Fare thee well?" Was I a rag that could be tossed aside? Worthy only of being sold as a milkmaid on a broken-down farm?*

My legs shook so violently that I crumpled to the floor and sobbed myself into a fitful state. I pounded the floor moaning and weeping. When I could cry no more, I curled into a ball and slept. I awoke to a rustling and a scratching, I sat up, wiped my eyes and blew my nose on the hem of my dress. The sun was already high. I had cried a long time.

A whir caught my attention as a snowy white owl flew in through the doorway and landed on my bed loft. A raven perched on the table. A skunk wandered through the open door, too. A dragonfly swooped in, followed by another. I watched a wooly bear caterpillar crawl in and out of the crannies between the stones of our fireplace. Perhaps he searched for a place to sleep during the long winter. Woodland creatures had taken over the hut as I had bawled a puddle of tears. The hut could be their home. It was no longer mine.

The raven hopped onto the farmer's map. He pecked at it until it was no longer readable. I managed a half-smile and said, "Thank you, I didn't want that anyway." As I said those words, a chill ran up my spine. The farmer would come after me if I didn't go to him. How much time did I have before he came? I began to imagine him as an ugly squat evil troll with slimy hair and snaggleteeth. I needed to plan. I needed to leave to find my mother's people.

A moment of uncertainty seized me. How ridiculous was I to think I could paddle a canoe I didn't even have across the huge lake? Or walk for days upon end not knowing which way to go? All the while hiding from the farmer who might or might not come looking for me? Was I as daft as Father? It was too much to even think about so I decided to hide from the farmer in the woods. A moment later I decided to run along the lake shore, hoping to find a way to my mother's people. Go? Stay? Hide? I didn't know.

Still dithering, I sat at the table and watched the owl preen its feathers. A fox peeked into the doorway. Its fur shone golden in the sunlight. I didn't even blink, trying not to scare it away. All of a sudden, its ears perked, and it scampered away. I looked to see what had scared it. Way down the shore was a man carrying a stick headed toward the hut. The farmer? I jolted into action stuffing my mother's dress into the skunk fur carrier with the two potatoes the woman had given me at the festival. Then I threw in *Alcyone's Dictionary* and Father's book. I tossed Father's robe to the floor and looked around. There was nothing else I wanted.

I bid the forest critters farewell saying, "Birdies and beasties, welcome. Shelter yourselves here from storms and tempests."

With the skunk fur carrier strapped to my back, I ran to the woods leaving the door open.

Turning often to look for the farmer, I dodged between trees and scrambled around bushes. I ran until my sides ached, and I could hardly catch my breath. Needing to rest, I hid behind a huge boulder. I didn't hear or see the farmer. The day turned chilly so I shivered as sweat dried from my back and underarms, but I stayed hidden for what seemed like half the day.

A hollow prickling filled my whole being as reality settled in. Not only had Father abandoned me, but he'd sold me to farmer who was coming to get me. My stomach ached with hunger. I thought of eggs and butter and a roasted chicken. Maybe it wouldn't be so bad with the farmer. I'd only had eggs once and that was when Father had come upon a duck's nest on the shore. We'd cracked the eggs into a pan and stirred them with wild leeks. It had been just a taste, but my mouth watered to think of how delicious they'd been.

The sky clouded over, and the wind picked up threatening rain. My legs cramped from crouching behind the rock, so I decided to creep back to the hut to see if the farmer was there waiting. If he was, I'd stay hidden. I had just turned to retrace my steps when the earth shook beneath my feet; the trees trembled, and the wind swirled sweeping away my clarity of vision. I clung to a small tree to keep from falling. As light fog descended, the trembling quieted, and I heard a "Hey ho!"

I immediately froze thinking the farmer had caught up to me. Standing just off the trail was a man with a beard so long I could believe he never cut it. A foxtail circled his head for a hat. His clothes were patches upon patches. Plaid squares on his elbows. Flowery patches on his pockets. Stripes on his knees. He looked dotted, dappled, spotted, or stippled like there were tiny spaces here and there and everywhere. I shrugged this off attributing it to my hunger and the trembling I'd had just experienced.

"Hey ho!" he said again.

"Hey ho!" I answered not sure what it meant but I liked the cheerful sound of it, and he didn't look like any farmer I'd seen at festivals. I stopped across from him and looked him up and down the same as he was doing for me. I was aware of my dingy sack dress that wasn't keeping the chill of the day from giving me goosebumps.

"Yuse fum arount hereabouts?" he asked.

"Down by the lake," I said looking at his face that without too much exaggeration of physiognomy, could be described as a mushroom for his nose, another for his chin, dried wrinkled apples for his cheeks, thin lines for a mouth, and two blueberries for eyes.

"Kawishami?" he asked.

"That one," I said looking at his boots. Unlike the rest of him, they were sturdy, unpatched, almost new with just a few scuffs on the toes. And shiny.

"Peoples drownt dere. Lake full up oft magick," he said.

"Oh." I didn't know what else to say, but I remembered the potato-cake woman saying something about the magic of misty lakes.

"Yuran stomacht got hungers?" he asked.

I was hungry. And tired. I had wandered too far. "No," I fibbed because I wanted to sneak back to the hut to see if the farmer had left.

"Wifet makin' soop en such. Cooks goot."

I was curious now because I hadn't known that anyone much less this odd man lived in the same forest as we did. And I was hungry. "Are you from around here?" I asked.

"Jist up dat hill. River ont da downt side." He pointed to a tree-covered rise

I hadn't noticed before. I saw a thin line of smoke rising through the trees, but couldn't make out a house.

More curiosity filled me. Something else grew within me. Another person. An invitation to eat. A woman cooking. Smoke rising from a chimney. Warmth. "Maybe I am a little bit hungry," I said.

"Goot. Wifet be happy. Youse be goot medisin for Lily. She sad. Not smilen onez tiny bitty."

"Why is she so sad?" I asked as we neared their small house that looked as dotted and grainy as the man.

"Bedder she tellen youse," he said as he wiped a tear away. Her namet Lily. Mine's Willem." He turned and beckoned me to follow.

I did. "Mine is Purslane."

"Purslane's delickous," he said. His eyes twinkled.

Nervously, I laughed. I hoped he meant the plant.

Willem carefully wiped his boots on a reed mat by a door that was made of matched birch trunks sliced in half. It had a deer's seven-pronged antler for the pull.

"Lookee 'ere!" Willem said as we entered. A tall slender woman with coppery hair neatly braided and piled on top of her head turned from the fireplace.

Her eyes opened wide when she saw me. "Company! Oh, my, this is unexpected, but such a delight!" She patted her hair and wiped her hands on a towel. Then she encircled me in a big hug. She smelled like basil and sweet grass and cedar all dancing together. I melted into her embrace and my world stood still until she broke away. Holding my hands, she said, "I welcome you."

Nodding at the man she said, "Willem, you surely have brought me the best of all gifts."

"Yer welcometh. Weez got the hungries in da tummies," he said.

"Well, Lordy, Lordy. Hold on a minute. We haven't even been properly introduced."

"Pahdon me manner," Willem said. "Lady Lily, dis herz Purslane. Purslane, dis herz Lady Lily."

"Please forget the Lady part. No need to stand on ceremony here. Willem does pretend so at times. Just call me Lily. Purslane? What a lovely name. You and I are named after plants. You are just what I need to chase the black clouds away. In the meantime, you and Willem have come just in time. The soup is hot and savory. The fry bread is sizzling. And cranberry mint tarts are cooling on the shelf."

My mouth watered. My heart warmed. We sat on wooden chairs that had been carved from logs. A colored stone inset formed a beautiful lily in the middle of the plank table. The aroma of the soup wafted of rosemary, basil, and wintergreen floating in a broth in which wild rice, mushrooms and bits of hazelnuts swirled to the bottom of my wooden bowl. I soon felt warm and joyously happy as I listened to the kindhearted banter between Willem and Lily.

When my bowl was almost empty, Lily asked, "Who are your people and where do you live?"

I had to stop and think. At the moment, I felt so far removed from the hovel and Father that it was as though I had to look through a telescope from the wrong end. Finally, I was able to say, "I'm Polaris' daughter. And Alcyone's, too, but she died when I was born."

"Ah," Willem said, "Star people names, but wit a dotter namet fer a plant." Then he added, "She liveth ont da shores ov Kawishami."

"Oh," Lily put her hands to her face. "That's where the awful drownings took place." She patted tears from her eyes.

"Dat very lake," Willem said with a catch in his throat. He stroked his beard. I thought he might shed a tear, too.

"Well, you are truly a great distance from home," said Lily pulling herself together. "What brings you so far?"

What did bring me so far? Should I tell them about Father abandoning me and that I was running from the farmer? "I was out walking. I had just turned to go home when Willem called out to me. I was hungry and maybe a little bit lost, but now I'm not." I rattled on, telling everything, not knowing how to stop. It was good to talk to someone other than Father. I did stop when Lily put a cranberry mint tart in front of me.

"A spot of tea?" she asked. "We have blueberry, wintergreen, plum, and wild leek."

"Blueberry, please."

As we ate tarts and drank our tea, I looked closely at Lily. Just like Willem, she looked dotted, dappled, spotted, and stippled like there were tiny spaces here and there and everywhere. Other than that, I found her to be the opposite of Willem in every way. She was tall and slender; he was short and rotund. She spoke perfectly well while he spoke in a way I'd never heard—not even at the festivals.

Her face was as smooth as the pebbles I found on the shore of our lake that Father said had been worn smooth by centuries of waves. Her cheeks were the color of wild summer roses. Wisps of her coppery hair curled on her forehead.

Like Willem, her clothes were worn but perfectly patched. She wore a lovely pair of carved leather shoes that looked as new as if they'd been made that day. I couldn't quit looking at them when she stood to get the teapot.

"You're wondering how two raggedy and patched people who live so far in the woods have such splendid shoes," she said with a smile.

I admitted that I had.

"Willem and I have a wonderful story to tell of how we came together," she said.

"But, be yee warned," Willem said. "It does-it gets scar-r-ry, scar-r-ry in pahts."

The woods were darkening around the little house. I needed to get back to the hovel for the night, but I also wanted to hear their story so I sat back and sipped my tea.

"I wast a shoozmaker," Willem said. "I maked da bestest shooz und bootz ov enyone aroundt fer meny miles."

"My father was a rich merchant. He sent me to the best schools to become a lady. Even though I liked book learning, I wanted to be a dressmaker. A seamstress. I loved sewing more than anything and could embroider tiny blue flowers on corsets or tat dainty laces to decorate a collar. I don't brag as easily as Willem does, but I do think that I could sew the straightest seams with the tiniest stitches."

Willem cleared his throat. "Oncet I wuz deliverink bootz to da fancee houz ov a ritch man who claimt he wuz frend ov all kings, duckz, und barens in all of U-rope. As soon as a shervant let me int da door, I heard skreems. Big skreems."

"They were my screams. I was there to deliver dresses to the lady of house for an upcoming Mayflower festival. After the lady tried them on, and I made some adjustments to the length and waists, they fit perfectly. The lady was delighted. She sent me to the reading room where she said her husband would pay me for the dresses."

"Ooof!" said Willem. "Dis iz bad memmoreez."

"The man of the house tried bargaining with me for a lower price, but I stayed adamant that my asking price was fair for the fine fabrics, the imported ribbons, the silk lace, and the work I had done. He got very angry. First, he struck me and then he began attacking me. I kicked and screamed and kicked and screamed some more."

"Und I runned to safe her. I hitted da man hart wit an inkpot. Den I grabbed Lily by her handt und ve run."

"Servants ran after us yelling 'You kilt him. You kilt him.' They chased us all through the town. We scared horses pulling carriages. We tumbled over a tinker's cart. We crushed flowers in garden after garden. We ran!"

"Ve runned fer dayz."

I shivered fearing what came next. Lily took a thick golden wool shawl from the back of her chair and wrapped it around me. "This will keep you cozy," she said with a smile.

The shawl hugged my shoulders and did warm me to the very core. I thanked Lily as she said. "It is yours now. I won't be needing it." Her voice broke as she continued their story, "We ran for what seemed an eternity until we came to Lake Kawishami."

Willem wiped tears from his eyes. After a moment, Lily said, "Now we live in these quiet woods. We've been here many changes of the moon. We have a goat and a couple of chickens. Willem makes our shoes. I patch our clothes. And now you have come. Just think, Willem, our guest is the daughter of star people."

Their story was curious and frightening. I pulled the shawl close around me and said, "I'm glad you got away." I believed their story as much as I didn't believe any of Father's. I felt at home here. Taken care of. I wondered what it would be like to live with a father *and* a mother. To have new shoes. To eat delicious soups and tarts every day.

With the flames of the fireplace behind her, Lily looked even more spotted and stippled than she had when I first saw her. I tried to shrug off the unbidden angst I felt for these two wonderful people.

"Tell Purslane whyz we'z so sad," Willem said.

"It's this way," Lily started. "Willem and I have been here ever since we fell through the ice, drowned, and the lake gave us back. We have been so happy that we forgot our time here was predetermined. Now *they* tell us this chapter of our being is up. Period. Done. Our re-assignment is soon.

"We begged to stay here so we could be together, but they said our old selves were due to expire, and there were births pending, so we must shed our old selves to become re-embodied." At this point Lily and Willem both sobbed uncontrollably. Lily barely stammered, "We might be separated and not even remember each other in our new lives. We could pass at the market and not know it."

Lily's story frightened me. She said they'd drowned. I remembered that the potato-cake woman had once said that some magic lakes gave back what they took away. *Could Kawishami be such a lake? Had I entered a portal? Were Willem and Lily the living dead that the lake had given back? And . . . was it possible that the lake had also given back my mother on that foggy, blustery day when I was born?*

Willem wiped his eyes and blew his nose while Lily softly cried.

"Who is this *they* who are doing this to you?" I asked.

"It's the Infinitely Wise Council of Andromeda that makes these decisions. Have you heard of it?"

I hadn't, but wanted to know more. While they talked, Willem left the table and began looking through a trunk. He pulled out pieces of leather and pairs of boots.

"Well, I remember this much from my book learning. There are three councils. One in each galaxy. All earthly beings originated in one or another galaxy countless generations ago."

"Originated?" I asked. "My mother gave birth to me."

Willem stepped in here. "Yaass. True enough. But fromt wherez did her mudder and all the mudders before her come fromt?"

I had not thought about that before. My head began to ache just a little bit from trying to consider it. I took a sip of tea and ate the last of my tart.

Lily dabbed her eyes again. "The ancestors of all the people and animals here on earth originated far, far, away. Willem and I are from stars in the Andromeda Cloud. Others are from the Magellan Cloud. And yet other people are from stars right here in the Milky Way."

That sounded right to me so I said, "Father told me that each cloud cluster is made up of stars and planets and that my mother came from the Pleiades."

Lily smiled and continued, "Yes, and each cluster has its own Council, and its own set of laws, but there is a Council even greater than the Andromeda, Magellan, and Milky Way all put together. The final laws come from that—the Eternal Infinite Omni-Council. Some call it the Great Wisdom."

"Andt now, da Andromeda Council, in its ownt wistom, sez ve haft to livet all over agin int bodies oft babies, or maybe efen tigers or monkeys."

Willem knelt as he measured three pairs of boots to my feet.

"And if we refuse, we will be sent to separate penal colonies on barren and remote rocks spinning somewhere in Andromeda. Forever. Without anyone to love."

As Lily and Willem told of their plight, the spaces between their dots and stipples grew larger and further apart. I wanted to hug them, to press them back into themselves, but I realized it would be of no use. They would have to leave to begin again. They were such good people, they deserved a good new life, and not have to spend eternity on a bleak rock spinning in space.

"Won't you be together?'

"Maybe never again. Not even if we refuse; we wouldn't be sent to the same penal colony."

Willem pulled off my ragged shoes. After he gently fitted a boot on each of my feet, he looked at me with eyes filled with an inner glow. I clasped my hands to my chest and said, "Thank you. Thank you." My face exploded into a smile. I'd never had such beautiful boots that fit so perfectly. I ran my hands over the smooth leather and said again, "Thank you."

As I stood to embrace Willem and Lily, a leaf fell on my head. I looked up. The roof of the house was turning to dust allowing leaves to blow in with the breeze. The stones of the fireplace rolled into a heap. The bowl from which I'd just eaten disappeared in a puff of dust. In a brief moment, the walls crumbled. Willem and Lily now looked like shimmering mists that rose from the lake on a chilly morning. I wanted to cry out to them, to make them stay. I didn't want them to leave. They reached out to each other at the last moment. And then they were gone.

I stood alone in the middle of the rise. The woods around me were silent. No owl hooted. No hare scooted. No fox darted through the trees. Leaves swirled in the breeze. I caught one as it floated by. Another landed on my head. How could there be nothing—no Willem, no Lily, no reed doormat, no iron soup ladle, not even the colorful stones from the table? Nothing but wafting leaves?

Hollow, miserable, and lonely, I walked the length of the whole hill, looking for one sign, just one, that Willem and Lily had been as real as I was. As real as the shawl I wore. As real as the boots that hugged my feet. I stood still and listened to the silence. A silence that filled with turbulence as the air around me settled into a new reality. A silence that was as solid as a wall.

As I turned to leave, a warmth surrounded me—profoundly deep warmth. A soft touch brushed my cheek. The warmth comforted me, but I already missed Willem and Lily and wished with all my might that they would reappear.

Faraway a night owl hooted eerily. I awoke as if from a dream, groggy and woozy. The full moon was waning to a new phase. Reluctantly, I stepped into the trees, leaving the light and warmth behind me.

CHAPTER 14

Fearing the farmer would be waiting for me, I didn't return to the hut, but slept on under the sheltering branches of a cedar tree. Even with Lily's shawl pulled tightly around myself, I still shivered through the night and hardly slept, so I arose early. In the dimness before the sun peeked over the tree tops, I flinched and hid behind a tree when I heard branches snapping. As I hid, I wished for the warmth and safety of Willem and Lily's little house. I wished they were there so I could ask what I should do. I wanted to escape the farmer and find my mother's people. I couldn't hide every time I heard a noise. I would never get there hiding behind a tree. Even if I had to face the farmer, I would have to take the first step on my journey into a life without Father.

Willem and Lily had been loving and caring. I wished for family. I would not settle for the farmer with all his eggs and butter. I would find my mother's people and be family with them. I straightened my shoulders and stepped from behind the tree. There was no farmer, just two squirrels chasing up and down a tall tree.

Relieved, I spent that first day following the shore, but staying in the woods. I had made my decision by turning my back, not even looking at the hut as I'd skirted around it to set out on my own.

That night I curled into the deep hollow of an ancient oak that grew on a hill overlooking the shore. Not a single ripple disturbed the lake in the evening stillness. A night bird sang a lonely melody. The moon had started to wane from its fullness during the festival. Potato-cake woman had whispered *portals and phases.* Had I entered a portal when I followed Willem along that stony path? How would

I know if portals opened during the waxing or growing phases? How would I recognize one? I had entered a portal to Willem and Lily only because Willem had called "Hey Ho!" to me. Tired from always being on the alert and walking too much, I fell asleep in the midst of all my wonderings.

The next morning, a chill in the air and a clawing hunger provoked me to leave the sheltering hollow of the tree. Geese flew overhead noisily honking. They headed to a warmer climate for the winter. I would be heading to the opposite direction—to a colder climate. I shivered and pulled Lily's shawl tighter around me.

I found some crawfish at the mouth of a rivulet that fed the lake. I gathered dried leaves and strips of birch bark. Looking around, trying to find stones or anything to spark a fire, a speck caught my eye way down the shore. A dark speck. A person? Walking my way? A man? The farmer?

My heart thudded. Sweat broke out on my forehead. My throat tightened. I dashed into the woods, scrambled through bushes up the hill, and crawled back into the hollow of the oak. With a jolt, I realized I had left footprints in the sandy shore. The farmer would know I'd run into the woods. I unfolded myself from the hollow and tore armloads of branches from hazel nut bushes. Back in the hollow, I stuck the branches into the ground front of me and hoped I was well hidden.

Soon enough I heard twigs snapping and felt the heavy thud of someone treading his way toward my hiding place. I held my breath and tried to calm myself. Through the tangle of hazel nut branches, I saw the slouched figure of a shabby man. Step by step he came closer. My heart stood still. I didn't even blink.

The farmer coughed. It started with a bark and continued grating in a most harsh way. When he coughed again, it became raspy and he bent over as if in pain. At the very end of his seizure, he spat a gob of slimy yellow-green ooze. I clamped a hand over my mouth as my stomach threatened to heave.

When he stood, he bellowed, "Come out. Come out from wherever ye are. I own ye now. I paid yer father plenty of coins. He signed a paper. Ye're mine now."

I froze. Not only from his voice so close, but a tiny movement by my feet caught my eye. I watched an ugly furry orange and brown beetle crawl out of an old acorn shell. It spread its wings and with a short flight, landed on my arm. *Noooo!* It tickled. I dared not move to shake it off.

"Show yerself. I know yer here somewhere."

I shivered in the mighty tree's hollow. Fear rippled my skin and set my nerves on fire as I stiffened to stay as still as possible despite the beetle.

"And if ye help me find yer cheating father, ye'll not be hurt. I've got gallows waiting for him. The ones I use for cows too old to give milk. If ye don't show yerself now, maybe I use the gallows for both of ye fer causing me so much nuisance."

The beetle probed my arm with its long snout. It itched. I held still. I felt a sneeze coming. I counted to ten. I counted to twenty. I prayed to Jove just as I'd heard Father curse the mayor when he ruined his All-seeing Eye act. *Jove, send your mighty thunderbolts to strike down the farmer. Save me!* It hadn't worked for Father, but I tried anyway.

"Show yerself now, and it'll only be ten lashings. If I have to find ye, it'll be twenty!" He coughed wretchedly and spat again. The beetle crawled further up my arm.

I cringed into myself. *Jove! Now would be a good time for that thunderbolt. Please!* The beetle flew to my forehead. I wanted to scream. I tried to frown, to raise my eyebrows, to wiggle my forehead as much as possible, but the beetle stayed.

After another coughing and spitting spell, the farmer stomped on up the hill, further from my hideout, but still coughing and yelling. One moment he shouted threats, the next he cajoled and begged me to show myself. I stayed curled and cramped in the hollow the rest of that day. Even as night fell and the farmer was far enough away that I could no longer see or hear him, I remained hidden. My legs lost all feeling. Hunger clawed my stomach. The beetle stayed with me exploring my arms, my legs, my shoulder and even my nose.

When the sun rose the next morning, I didn't hear the farmer calling or hear him crashing through brush. I hoped he had given up and was far away. Little by little, I dared stretch my legs and push the branches away. Gallows or no gallows. Ten lashings or twenty. I needed to crawl out. I picked the beetle from my arm and gently placed it on the acorn shell.

CHAPTER 15

Even though the sun rose with the morning, it did nothing to ease my fears. In my world, not a beam of warmth shone through my distress and anxiety. Father had abandoned me. Worse yet, he'd sold me to a farmer. For hours while the sun traveled to its highest in the sky, I stayed in the woods, ready to dash into the oak hollow to hide again, but there was no sign of the farmer. I lost all sense of time and even reality, but finally crept back to the lake shore and looked in all directions. No farmer. I looked at the sands. I saw no new footsteps so I warily began my journey once again.

After some days of walking, I began wishing that I would magically find my mother's people around the next cove. I was tired of being alone, not knowing where I was going. Always hungry. Always fearing the farmer would jump from behind a tree and overcome me.

One evening as I searched for a place to shelter for the night, I felt queasy. It was a queasy different from the gnawing hunger that was always with me, so I sat on the sandy shore and kicked off my boots to free my toes for a bit. The ground beneath me shivered, then quaked. The lake waters rippled and slapped the shore. My vision turned hazy. Feeling disoriented, I stood and looked around. A path leading from the shore up a hill became visible. I quickly put my boots back on and headed to the path hoping to find something to eat. As I followed the path, my vision still wavered. It was as though a sheet of paper with a picture on it had been wadded up tightly and now opened little by little as my vision cleared. It was then I spied a woman bending over some dented tin buckets.

Behind the woman was a little house made of trash. Clay and straw chinking held a confusion of cart wheels, crinkled tin sheets, broken glass, and jugs stacked one on the other. Tangled vines thickly covered one wall that I could barely see through the jumble. Pumpkin, squash, potato, and colorful gourd vines scrambled out of tin buckets, twisted and crept along the ground. Other buckets sprouted tomatoes of yellow, orange, and red. Blue and purple flowers snaked along the path right up to the doorway of the house. Birds flitted everywhere. Three puppies chased each other and their own tails. Two more slept in the sun. Four curled up and slept among some flowers.

I looked from house to dimming sky. The moon was but a skinny crescent. Then I remembered feeling queasy as the earth trembled once before. It was the same as when I found Willem and Lily. I had entered a new portal! Would I find my mother? I hoped so.

"Hey ho!" I called to the woman as I approached.

She stood and squinted at me. "A friend you be, come sup with me. Be you foe, turn around and go." Her voice was a melody, a lilting tune.

"A friend, I am. A hungry friend," I said. "I have two potatoes we can share for supper."

"No need for that," she sang. "I have squash and potatoes a-plenty."

Up close in the shadowy evening, she looked more bird than woman. Feathers wove in and out of braids in her hair. A feather shawl draped around her shoulders. Her face was just bone covered by taut skin. Her movements were fluttery and quick even though she shuffled her feet as she walked.

Just as I had followed Willem, I followed the bird woman—I instantly had thought such of her—to her house high on a hill overlooking the lake on one side and a red willow wetland on the other. At the door, she wiped her feet on a reed mat. I did the same, thinking of Willem and Lily again. Inside, she twittered while lighting four small candle lamps. "Never get any company this way. Of course, I don't need much with the puppies and birds."

As if on cue, a passel of chubby puppies tumbled through a small door that swung back and forth in the corner of a back wall. They greeted me with snufflings and licks. I gathered one up in my arms and felt its soft tongue lick my chin.

"Perch on whatever you find comfortable. And play with the dogs while I stir up a squash slurry for us." I looked around and saw a bench under the lone window. One room was the whole of bird woman's house. A stone fireplace in the far corner. The table in the center was made of tree trunks for legs and branches laid across making a most un-flat surface. There was one large mossy bed for the dogs. I wondered where she slept until I saw a circle of branches filled with cat-tail fluff in another corner. Of course, she'd made herself a nest.

I pet the puppies as the woman sprinkled seeds into the mashed squash. "Help me set bowls on the table," she chirped. "And there's a bottle setting on that shelf. Bring it for our drink."

She tucked the pot she'd been stirring under her arm and shuffled her way to the table. I brought the bowls and bottle. Together we sat—shoulder to shoulder—on a narrow plank and ate. "Usually, I just make a slurry of squash alone," she sang proudly, "but I've added sunflower seeds and beet greens to make it special for you."

I could have done without the 'special' part. Especially the beet greens. The slurry looked unappetizing with brownish green color and un-mashed lumps, but I was hungry, and I had eaten worse many times.

When we finished eating, the slurry pot was empty, and I must admit that I had two bowls of it. Bird woman uncorked the bottle I'd brought to the table. She handed it to me. I must have looked confused because she warbled, "Dearie, if you be wanting a glass or mug, you'll be waiting a long time. I have no such nice-ties here. Just heft it to your lips and drink."

I did. The amber liquid was as thick as honey, and almost as sweet, but it stung my tongue a bit, heated my throat, and tasted like a mingling of wild berries, herbs, and roots.

"Delicious, isn't it? I make it myself when the berries are ripe," the bird woman sang as she took the bottle from me and lifted it to her own lips. She passed it back to me. After the second sip I decided it was as tasty as she had proclaimed. After my third sip, it no longer stung my tongue, but smoothly slid into my throat that welcomed the warmth. We passed the bottle back and forth many times so I feared it would soon be empty.

"Tell me how you came to be here. I've never had company other than the puppies before."

I didn't know where to start. Father selling me? Father leaving me? Escaping the farmer? Finally, words tumbled out. "I was on my way to find my mother's portal, but then a man—a dreadful man that Father sold me to—followed me. I've been hiding from him."

The bird woman lifted her hands and said, "Well, praises be to Gyronia, god-dess of lost souls! You are safe here with me and the puppies."

"Have you seen such a man walking the shores?"

"Oh, my stars, no! Worry yourself not. I won't let that horrid man near you. Tell me more about yourself and start from the beginning. Let's do it this way, you tell a story about yourself, and then I'll tell you one," she tweeted as she passed the bottle yet another time.

I began. "I was born in a red canoe."

She stroked her feather shawl and said, "I was born in a high four-poster bed."

"My mother died the instant I was born."

"My mother was a famous *prima donna* opera singer."

"My father was a professor."

"My father sailed ships on the boundless seas and sent caravans of camels traversing barren deserts looking for the finest porcelain and silk for his markets."

"My name is Purslane."

"What a terrible name! That's a weed. One that's delicious, but a weed no less. My name is Elizabetta Anastasia Maria Francesca. No edibles in my name."

As the night went on, I told her about Father pretending to be the All-Seeing Eye, the potato-cake woman at the festivals, Willem and Lily, Father's elixirs, and his desire to go to the Pleiades. I ended by saying, "I was on my way to find my mother's people when the farmer began chasing me."

"I lived in a glorious cobblestone paved city far away," she said as her eyes turned dreamy. "I was fickle, spoiled, choosy, and fussy about everything. My favorite thing was to attend festive balls always wearing new silk-embroidered dresses with frills at the neckline and hem."

She told how she had been a big disappointment to her parents who complained that she was more interested in rouging her cheeks, piling her hair high in fashionable coifs and dabbing exotic perfumes behind her ears than studying French literature, Egyptian history, Philosophy of the Holy Greatness, Goddesses of the Universe, and all the other courses at the Kyrghizia Academy for Young Ladies.

"Then," she said, "one day while promenading along the shores of an azure lake with a suitor who was more interested in his own reflection than in admiring me, I became bored silly. I began looking for some excitement or some way to escape that stroll when I saw a band of rogues throw a sack into the lake.

"Before the sack hit the water, I heard puppies yipping and yelping within it. At last, I thought I could escape the tedium! I ran into the water fully dressed. With no consideration of the fact that I couldn't swim, I dove to pull the bag to shore."

I couldn't imagine bird woman doing anything of the sort. Myself, I could roll in mud trying to catch a pig, but I couldn't envision anyone jumping into a lake with her hair coifed high, wearing a fancy dress and necklaces of sparkling gems.

She continued, "I sank. I gasped. I swallowed water, but I finally grasped the bag and struggled to the surface. Without a moment even to take a breath, the weight of the bag and my many layered skirts pulled me under again. Time after time I thrashed to the surface, just to sink again."

Bird woman stopped to chuckle at this point. "Can you imagine that? All the time I was sinking and gasping for air, my conceited suitor continued on his way without even noticing I was no longer walking by his side. He didn't even miss me!" She sipped from the bottle again and passed it to me and chuckled some more before continuing her story.

"In desperation, I prayed to the Great Bird God to pluck me from the waters. He must have heard me because an eagle flew down, clutched me in his talons and flew me and the sack of puppies high above the lake. I convulsed trying to expel the water from my lungs. One convulsion was so great that my dress tore from the eagle's talons, and I dropped to the earth. The last thing I remembered before darkness overcame me was the awful cracking of what sounded like every bone in my body."

Her story was as wild and as fanciful as any of Father's, but I believed every word of it. I flinched at the thought of all her broken bones. "It's all right, dearie," she said. "I feel no pain. That same eagle and at least a dozen white birds flew me here to await my time. They petitioned flocks of birds to care for me. That's why you see so many flying in and out."

She pointed up. Earlier I had noticed a tangle of branches hanging from her ceiling. Several birds had flown in and were roosting for the night with their heads tucked under their wings. I was getting drowsy myself, almost falling asleep right there at the table. Needing to be on my way to find a hollow tree to curl into for the night, I thanked her for the food and drink and said, "I must be off now before the night is too late."

She fluffed the feathers of her shawl and said, "I won't have you out wandering at night among the mischievous sprites, *nisses, tomtes, mazokus,* elves, and gnomes who delight in the light of the moon to ply their shenanigans. And worse yet, farmers who'd threaten you with lashings and the gallows. You'll spend the night here. The puppies will be delighted to share their bed with you."

I had never slept in a nest of moss with a wiggling litter of puppies, but after I'd been licked and snuffled countless times, they settled down, and we all fell asleep. My night was filled with dreams. Dreams of puppies that were drowning, but my legs were mired in muck so I couldn't reach them. I dreamed of a red canoe floating on the waters. And I dreamed of a girl named Selene who lived on a high hill of trillium overlooking a valley of violets. She slept in a four-poster bed and ate rich cakes covered with cream and berries. I dreamed of Father. He propelled his way in the high skies toward the Pleiades, passing the moon, passing stars, even passing meteors that shot through the dark sky.

My last dream before waking was filled with birds of every color and every wingspan. They fluttered to a chestnut tree to learn songs from a lovely young woman in a green dress who sang and played a stringed instrument. Then the twittering and tweeting and songs of morning birds woke me just as the sun was rising over the lake.

CHAPTER 16

Bird Woman snored lightly as I stirred the next morning. A grey bird with a white chest perched on her shoulder preening its feathers. Other birds flew in with their beaks filled with berries, nuts, seeds, and leaves. They dropped them into a wooden bowl on the table then flew out again. I lay watching the birds. The puppies pressed their wet noses to my cheeks. They wagged their tails in my face, climbed and tumbled all over me until the bird woman awakened to struggle out of her nest.

"Good morning. Good morning. A fine morning it is," she sang as she shuffled her way to the table. Several birds flitted to perch on her shoulders. "Indeed, it is when one has such fine company."

I wasn't sure if she meant the birds, the puppies, or me so I just stretched and yawned. She looked into the bowl the birds had filled and invited me to the table. "Breakfast is ready," she said.

We nibbled the seeds and berries and told more stories of our lives. I was running out. My life had been so plain and uneventful, so I said, "I need to be on my way to find my mother's people—or my mother's portal. It would be so much easier if I had a canoe so I wouldn't have to worry about the farmer so much."

Bird Woman put her elbows on the table and held her chin in her hands. She was silent for such a long time that I feared she had fallen asleep again. A yellow and grey bird perched on her head and pulled at her hair until it loosened one long strand. It flew through the tangle of branches hanging from the ceiling to one corner and started to weave the strand into its nest.

"The way I see it," she finally said, "you need to find the canoe. Then maybe it will bring you to your mother's people where you'll be safe from the farmer."

"If only it were that easy. How I can I even find the canoe? It was so long ago since I was born in it. Maybe it doesn't exist anymore." I worried about wandering on my own again, confused, never sure of anything, and always fearful of the farmer. I hugged a puppy to myself and hid my face in its fur. It wiggled and licked my nose. I wished for a puppy, for anything, so I wouldn't always be so alone.

"Canoe or no canoe," I said, "I must be on my way. Thank you for feeding me and giving me a bed for the night." I tried to sound brave, but my voice was ragged.

"Oh, no. I'm not letting you go until you have bathed. And washed your hair. And put on clean clothes," she twittered. "You have a long journey ahead and it's best to start out clean."

The truth was, I couldn't remember when I last had a good washing. I reddened to think what I smelled like. The puppies hadn't minded last night, but then they were puppies. I didn't know what my travels held for me and I certainly did not want to meet my mother's people reeking of sweat, musk, stinks, and stenches of every kind.

Elizabetta Anastasia Maria Francesca led me down the backside of the hill she lived on to a twisting river. A pool had formed in one of the curves by a high rock outcropping. A branch of the river poured over the ledge in a streaming waterfall. Bird Woman pointed to it and said, "Take your time. Stand under the spilling waters to wash your hair and loll in the pool as long as you want. Use sands to scrub your elbows and knees."

I did as she directed while she waded in the river waters and picked crayfish and clams and tossed them to shore. I scrubbed myself from head to toe.

"Do you have a clean dress?" she asked.

"Only my mother's. I don't know if it fits or not."

"Makes no difference, we'll make it fit," she said as she took off her apron and handed it to me to dry myself. Afterwards as we sat in the bright sunlight. She combed her fingers through my hair untangling it gently. I imaged that the closeness I felt now must be like when a mother doe softly nuzzled her fawn. Or a mother fox playfully rolled with her kits. I felt a comforting warmth, not only from the sun, but from the tenderness and touch of bird woman's hands. I yearned to have a mother.

When my hair was dry, Bird Woman wove four braids and pinned them around my head like a coronet. "I wore my hair like this to one of those fancy balls I liked so much," she said as she tucked a few pink and white coral bells amongst the braids.

I unfolded my mother's dress and pulled it over my head. Bird Woman tacked up the hem with spikes from a thorn apple bush so I wouldn't trip on it. Other than being too long and too roomy at the chest and shoulders, the dress draped my bony body quite well, and I delighted in its softness. I breathed the lavender and chamomile scents that wafted from the fabric, and was glad I no longer had to wear the gunny sack dress.

"Spin around so I can see you front and back," Bird Woman said. She continued talking as I turned on my toes. "You have room to grow, but the color is perfect. Now scrub your other clothes in the pool and hang them on those viburnum bushes to dry. While you're doing that, I'll steam the shellfish."

After washing my gunny sack dress and underthings, I helped Bird Woman dig a hole in the sand next to the pool. She dropped in two potatoes then puckered her lips and whistled a little tune. Birds from every direction carried twigs in their beaks and dropped them over the potatoes. When there was a mound, she lit it and said, "Now we wait until they're almost roasted. Then we'll add the clams and crayfish for the last few minutes. No slurry for us today. We'll feast like princesses such as you and I!"

We sat on the riverbank watching the fire, listening to the birds, playing with the puppies. Curious, I asked, "Are these the puppies you saved?"

"The very same, but other than pulling them out of the water, I didn't save them. Now, they are here with me waiting. There were twelve. Three have already been called. Look over there. In the wild rose patch. I have markers to remember them."

I made my way to a tangle of roses. Three stones. Three names. Frisky. Nosey. Wiggly. "Lately I'm having trouble remembering," she said when I sat beside her again. "I no longer remember how long I've been here. Days? Months? Years? Decades? I don't remember what my mother and father looked like. I cannot sort memories from dreams. What is real. What is not."

Her skin was smooth and lustrous. Her hair golden and she looked quite young. "You can't have been here too long," I said.

"Oh, but I have. The puppy stones have moss on them. That doesn't grow overnight. I fear I will be here waiting forever. There must not be any demand for my soul. I was selfish and spoiled. I threw tantrums. I made life miserable for my parents. I always demanded more than my share of sweets and tarts. The only unselfish thing I ever did was to try to save the puppies, and I wouldn't have done that if I hadn't been so bored."

I stammered, uncertain what to say, "You've been kind to me. You fed me. Gave me a place to sleep. I've never had a mother, but I would want one just like you." It was all true, and I realized that besides her, I would have liked Lily or potato-cake woman to be my mother, too.

"I've enjoyed every minute with you," she said adding shellfish to the fire pit and spreading sweet grass over everything. Oh, the aroma! My mouth watered so I slid my hands into the pockets of my mother's dress hoping I'd find a handker-chief to wipe my drool. In one there was a smooth stone, and in the other was a paper. I wiped my mouth on my sleeve and unfolded the paper. The writing was the same as in *Alcyone's Dictionary*. My mother had written it!

"Read it to me," Bird Woman said.

I cleared my throat and read.

I lie upon fragrant cedar boughs
Above the shores of Kawishami
Beneath the warming golden orb
Resting upon soft forest duff.

I grow heavy with two babies!
I beg Polaris "Bring me to my mother's land."
My mother died in a roaring river.
My father burned in the awful fires
Before I was forced away by marauders,
But I hope someone survived that great tragedy.
I fear giving birth without my people near.

The moon already waxes from sliver to gibbous
We must leave soon, before the full moon
Polaris shakes his head saying,
"Too far and too dangerous."

I put his hands on my great and swelling belly.
"Feel," I say. "Two heads. Two babies.

I need my people."
Polaris just swallows another elixir.

I dream I will give birth to a brown-eyed daughter.
I dream I will give birth to a green-eyed daughter.
Twins to be born under the divine comet.
Twins of ancient prophecies.
Selene and Luna.
Moon daughters of my womb.
Polaris wants sons.
Castor and Pollux.
Or Altair and Rigel.
Names fit for star boys he so hopes for.

I breathe in the forest.
I listen to the birds.
A fox plays with her kits.
I pray to the gods of the woodland.
To Diana and Artemis: I beseech you,
Be with me at my time of birthing.
To Tapio and Mielikki: I entreat you,
Shelter me in your fragrant forests.

I shook almost uncontrollably as I read my mother's words. The bird woman took my hands in hers. I said, "Twins? I had a twin? He or she must have died along with my mother. But what if . . . What if my twin was born and lives? Where is he or she? A person at the last festival mistook me for someone named Selene. Is it possible? Did my mother really want me named Luna and not for the cursed weed Purslane?" Questions and possibilities and impossibilities tumbled in my mind. *What if? Maybe? Then what? And where?* I wanted to know!

Rubbing the stone in my pocket—my mother's moonstone—I looked to the sky as though the clouds could spell out answers to my questions. They swirled above me changing from tranquil white fluff to scudding, scolding gloom and back again. I felt as though I was being drawn up into the complexity of the universe, and that I was transforming with the clouds.

Deep within myself I felt I was truly Luna. I had washed Purslane away as I had bathed in the placid pool, scrubbing layers of dust and grime from my elbows, knees, from between my toes, from the back of my neck and from my hair. Then I slipped into my mother's dress and became Luna.

Singing birds and yipping puppies brought me back to reality. Bird woman smiled at me. "You look happy," she said. "A good cleansing and the dress have made all the difference. You look like a new person."

"I am a new person. I feel it." I said. "I *am* Luna!"

"Yes, you are." She smiled then added, "I remember a day—it must have been over a dozen years ago, maybe even fourteen or more—I saw a red canoe on the lake in a light mist. The mist suddenly thickened into a dense fog and covered the whole lake. In an instant, a mighty storm blustered. I couldn't see anything; the fog was so heavy, but I heard a woman call out 'Curse the pain. Curse the pain!' I remember that because I wondered why she was in such pain."

"*Curse the pain?*" I repeated. "*Curse the pain sounds like Purslane!* My mother never intended me to be named Purslane. Father! Why did he ever give me that awful name? A weed!" I withered for a moment then straightened up and asked, "After you heard the woman cry out, what happened to the canoe and the people in it?"

Bird Woman answered, "Like I said, I couldn't see anything because a thick fog covered the whole lake. It had been an eerie fog. It had dropped like a curtain in the blink of an eye, but when it finally lifted, and the storm calmed, there was no canoe. No nothing."

"What do you think happened to my mother? Did she tumble into the waters from the canoe?" Father had said that he and I were tossed to our home shore, and the canoe was upside down in the middle of the lake. I wondered about what potato-cake woman had said about some lakes giving back what they took away. Could that be? Could my mother and my twin be somewhere? In a portal of the dead? Or even alive?

Elizabetta Anastasia Maria Francesca poked the embers away from the clams, crayfish, and potatoes. "I don't know, but I hope someday you'll find the answers to all your questions."

With deft fingers, Bird Woman plucked the shellfish and potatoes out of the coals. "From the first moment you called *Hey ho!* I felt something wonderful about you in my bones. I have never known why I was left for so long here between the living and the dead. Now I know. Maybe I've been waiting for you. Someone I could care for other than myself. Maybe now the puppies and I will be reassigned."

"Are you Andromedan like Willem and Lily?" I asked.

"Andromedan? No. My ancients came from other distant stars. The stars of Magellan."

"How did that come to be?" I asked, curious.

"I don't know. I told you I didn't pay much attention to my lessons. I do remember my father and uncle talking about the long-ago people on our home planet fighting a great fiery battle against each other. Each clan was sure their beliefs about the Great Wisdom were right and all the others were wrong. The clashes became so deadly, that my ancestors saved themselves by encapsulating themselves in space armor, zooming into the universe in aeronautical discs and finally landing here on this earth. Generations of Magellans have been born here ever since. Or something like that. I wish I'd paid attention so I could tell you the whole story."

Again, her story sounded like a story Father would have told, but her story also seemed true because she hadn't embellished it with dramatic twists and turns. "Where will you go?" I asked. "When you're reassigned? Will you be with the puppies? Willem and Lily were sad because they were going to be separated and would no longer remember their life together."

"I don't know, but I hope to be wiser in my next life than I was in the last. You are the first visitor I've ever had in all my time here that seems like an eternity. I've learned about caring from the puppies, but when you came—hungry, hiding from the farmer, and needing a place to rest—I felt something new stirring deep within me. A feeling. It was compassion. To my surprise I actually cared about someone other than myself, and I didn't want to let you go. I wanted to share my meals with you and listen to your stories. I had had so much and you had so little, yet you never complained or fussed like I had. Maybe that's what I had to learn here in this tumbled-down hovel so far from everything I'd ever known."

"You not only fed me, but you led me to knowing who I really am. All because you made me take a bath." I couldn't help but to laugh at the thought. "I was like a tadpole in the pond transforming myself. I was like a slithery snake that sheds its old skin so it can grow."

Bird Woman laughed with me and said, "I like to think you were a caterpillar inside a cocoon waiting for the time to emerge as a lovely butterfly."

"A very dusty, grimy, dirty cocoon," I added as we laughed again.

"Now that I think of it and see the color of your mother's dress, you have emerged as a most beautiful Luna moth. Have you ever seen one?"

"I don't think so."

"Well, you'd remember if you had. They come out at night, so aren't seen often, but they are the largest moth, the most breath-takingly beautiful moths ever. Their large wings are the soft green of your dress. You are now Luna in more ways than one."

My cheeks warmed. I'd never heard such wonderful words. I picked up Elizabetta's apron that held the potatoes, clams, and crayfish in one hand, looped my arm through hers as we walked up the hill to her home together. As we got closer, I noticed that it looked even more ramshackle than it had before. Clay that had chinked spaces between jugs and wheels had fallen to the ground leaving gaps in the back wall. I worried if it could remain standing if more fell out.

Inside, we spread the apron on the table and sat next to each other on the bench. As we ate, the branches over our heads turned into a fine dust and wafted down. Birds no longer flew in and out bringing berries and nuts. The puppies had not followed us in. I listened, but could not hear them chasing and yipping outside. I looked at Bird Woman. My chest quaked with a deep sadness of what was coming.

"Don't be sad," she said. "I know what's coming. The puppies are already gone. Last night as I slept soundly, the voice of the Great Wisdom came to me. It said I would be rebirthed soon, and would walk this earth again."

"But, but . . ." I stammered unable to get any words out.

She patted my hand. I know she did. I saw her hand on mine, but I couldn't feel her touch. "In my dream," she said, "I stood tall and walked easily. I will not carry my painful brokenness into my next life. I know I'll be a better person. Rich girl. Poor girl. Maybe I'll even be given a beautiful voice like my mother had so I can sing with the birds. Most of all, I hope I'll be lucky enough to have a friend like you."

A lump formed in my throat as I watched a mist envelop Bird Woman. A heavy weight settled on my chest. Nothing seemed fair. Everyone I loved left me. A farmer pursued me. And now, disappearing before my very eyes was my bird woman Elizabetta Anastasia Maria Francesca.

CHAPTER 17

I slumped crying on the sandy shore of Kawishami. Crying because Father had abandoned me; Willem and Lily were gone; Bird Woman had vanished into a mist, and I was alone again. When I finally ran out of tears, I wiped my eyes and walked back up the hill. The earth didn't tremble. I didn't get dizzy. The portal was no longer there. Nothing was as it had been. No mud-chinked house. No buckets of sprawling squash and potato vines. No puppies tumbled and played in the sun. The rivulet, the little waterfall, and pond were just as I remembered. I found three stones in the tangle of wild roses, but no names were scratched into them. A blue and orange bird twittered and flitted from tree to tree, following me as I looked for any sign of what had been there. Finding nothing, I headed down the hill to the shore. The bird sang a beautiful melody. I picked up a blue feather that dropped as it flew away.

On the shore, I wrote.

My name is Luna.
I AM LUNA!

For days I had been carrying my boots, walking in the soft sands, and feeling the wet grains ooze between my toes. The ruffled shore had been pleasant to walk on barefooted, but then I stubbed a toe on some half-buried driftwood and cut my sole on a broken clam shell. Before leaving the shore to tend to the cut, I looked for the farmer. I was always jittery and wondering if he still looked for me. I headed for a wooded area where I could sit on a knoll watching for the farmer. I pressed moss to stop the cut from bleeding. As I massaged my sore feet, I spied a bit of red peeking out from between two trees.

Sticks, stumps, leaves, and lake weeds tossed by the winds, mounded the red thing I was curious about. I dug and tossed off flotsam and debris until I uncovered the bow of a red canoe layered with a thick filthy crust. The canoe looked like it had lain right side up under the heap of detritus for years. A surge of relief filled me. The red canoe was real, and I'd just found it! I hoped it wouldn't leak once I got it into the water, but my mood was lightened just knowing that paddling it would be better than walking the rest of the distance around the lake.

I slept on the shore that night, covered only by the rays of the waxing gibbous moon and the shawl Lily had given me. The next day, I exposed more of the canoe by digging away sands, twigs, and other debris. Constantly, I looked up and down the shore making sure the farmer wasn't coming. I jumped at the tiniest noise, even when a bird twittered unexpectedly from nearby. Every scaping of a tree branch in the wind kept me on edge.

That night I tilted the canoe to make a shelter and crawled under it to sleep, but a wicked storm shook the skies with thunder keeping me awake. The clamor and clashing of gusty winds rocked the canoe sheltering me. I traced the ribs of the canoe with a finger, feeling the roughness of the wood and wondered about my mother. I tried to draw an image of her lying there giving birth while my father paddled furiously trying to get to her people. I tried to remember her scent that had lingered on the dress I wore. What had I smelled? Chamomile and lavender, for sure. Basil and cedar, too? I rued that her scent had left the dress and now smelled like me, the lake breezes, and the woodsy duff I lay on. After the storm rumbled off into the distance, I finally slept.

That morning when I had the canoe completely empty and dug out, I found its paddle buried beneath it. In my excitement, I forgot all my fears. I dragged the canoe into shallow water and was about to get in to paddle a few feet from shore to check if it still floated when the farmer burst out of the shoreline woods.

"Ye not gettin' away this time!" he yelled. "I'll tie ye up like a hog going to butcher. Ye'll not wiggle yer way out!"

I tripped trying to scramble into the canoe. He clutched at me. My heart raced, my temples throbbed, I gasped. The world around me blurred and spun. I yelled, "I am not who you want. You bought Purslane. I am Luna!" I swung the paddle and missed him completely.

"I don't care what ye name be or ain't. Yer father took coins for ye fair and square." He grabbed my arm and tugged me so hard I fell face down in the sand.

I had gotten halfway up when he put a boot on my back pushing me to my hands and knees. My hair tumbled over my face. I drew my knees up and crouched. My stomach rumbled with hunger. How could I be hungry at a time like this? Humiliated, I thought of roasted chicken, eggs, and butter. My mouth watered thinking of all the good food.

"NO!" I screamed knowing the food came with a price—living with the farmer. I would rather join Mother, Willem, Lilly, and Bird Woman in the other world than join the farmer in his.

With a kick to my behind, he said, "Get yerself up and shut yer mouth."

Cowering, not wanting to be hit or kicked, I stood as straight as I could. I had a choice. I could go peacefully with him, have a life of milking cows and churning butter and who knows what else, or I could. . . . I didn't finish the thought. I kicked him right above a knee.

"Gaaah! Dammit!" He bent to hold his knee. I grabbed the paddle and hit him squarely in the behind. He flew forward, sprawling in the sands and spewed vile words along with threats. "Hang ye from the gallows! Ye just a mutton-faced cow. Ye should be glad I take ye. Lice bag!"

I threw my pack into the canoe and jumped in. The canoe stuck in the sands of the shallow water. Before I could push into deeper water, the farmer was up and hanging onto the canoe. He clutched my dress and yelled, "Wormy varmint, ye'll not get away!"

Bitter bile rose in my throat, but I would not let him have his way. I drew a deep breath, glared at him and yelled, "I'm Luna!" Then I jabbed him in the stomach with the paddle.

He fell back yelling and groaning. "Yer dead when I catch you! You maggot faced whore!"

With one big heave, I pushed the canoe into the water and paddled furiously toward the depths of Kawishami. Paddling for my very life and my heart pounding, I didn't look back until I was well into the middle of the lake. He still stood on the shore shaking his fist. For a long time, he bellowed words that the wind carried away. I thought of the magic man's disappearing box. I wished I could put the farmer in one and tap three times with a snake-carved cane. Poof, he'd be gone and I'd never have to worry about him again.

My muscles tightened as I paddled as far and as fast as I could. The last time I looked back, he still stood on the shore stomping his feet and waving his fists at me. Even though he was far away, I trembled as I thought of how close he'd come to grabbing me for good.

A light breeze whispered *He can't follow where the canoe takes you.* I wanted that to be true.

Far out in the water and away from the farmer's reach, I breathed deeply with relief. I stretched, loosening every muscle that had clenched in fear. A lightness filled my chest. I'd never hit anyone before. The worst I'd done was swing the sack with father's elixir bottles. I did that out of anger. I'd struck the farmer out of fear. I thought of the power that came with those two emotions and the feeling of strength they'd given me. Then I thought of the kindnesses of the potato-cake woman, Willem, Lily, and Bird Woman. I'd felt something different with them. And that gave me strength, too. I wanted to fill myself with that feeling again. I didn't like fear and anger.

The canoe rocked gently. I calmed as I floated on the waters. I traced the ribs of the canoe. I traced my own ribs. A breeze whispered to me. And I knew that cradled in the canoe, I could travel away from the farmer and a life I didn't want. The life of Purslane was behind me. Luna was ahead. My new name gave me strength. I would never again have to be like a weed to be trampled on and tossed aside.

The waves of Kawishami softly rocked me as a mother rocks her child. I choked back tears. This was where I'd been born. And where my mother died.

CHAPTER 18

As the darkening sky brought a chill, I wrapped Lily's shawl around my shoulders and folded my old burlap dress into a pad to kneel on as I dipped the paddle to travel further into the unknown. The almost full moon reflected on the waters making a silver path for me to follow across the lake. I pointed the canoe toward a small river opening where I would leave the lake and hoped to find my mother's people. The thought excited me, but I felt alone and afraid, too. I trembled slightly, not only from the chill, but from dread of leaving Kawishami that had been home all my years.

How I wished at that moment to be with Father in our hut or at a Harvest Moon Festival with the potato-cake woman. I imagined all the colorful booths with red, green, and blue banners. Hearing the sounds of squeeze box music, flutes tootling, pigs oinking, and even Father's voice encouraging people to have their fortune told. Feeling the hot sun and even the squish of mud and muck while catching a pig. Smelling ham hocks roasting, sausages frying, and most of all potato cakes. If I could have snapped my fingers and gone back to all that was familiar, I would have done so.

Even with the turbulence of my thoughts and feelings, the gentle waves of Kawishami rocked the canoe and sleepiness overcame me. I stowed the paddle and stretched out on the ribs of the canoe. With the moon washing its light over me and the stars twinkling, I fell asleep before I could find Polaris and the Pleaides.

I dreamed Father examined rare plants in a tangle of verdant jungle while chattering monkeys tossed his hat back and forth. He rejoiced as he plucked an exotic flower. He tucked it into his pocket and with a mighty jump, flew through the heavens to bring the flower to my mother. He ducked as meteors whizzed by him. Finally, he caught the tail of a comet, and he sped on his way out of my dream.

Then I dreamed of my mother wearing the very dress I now wore. She walked past me at a festival while I ate potato cakes. I wanted to catch up and tell her I was her daughter, but my feet mired in the muck of a pigpen. I called out, "Mother! Mother! It's me. Luna!" But she didn't hear because the clickity-clack of a puppet's feet was too loud. My own sobbing woke me from the dream.

The gentle light of dawn brightened the sky as the moon and stars slowly dimmed. I gripped the edges of the canoe and sat up. I was no longer on the lake, but following the currents of a river. I couldn't even see Kawishami behind me past the trees lining the snaking river. The canoe was headed toward a thick fog.

The damp mist webbed my face, my hair, arms, and dress. I peered through the haze as the canoe bumped along scraping against rocks and gliding under branches. The current carried me faster and faster as the waters foamed and tumbled over steep ledges. I held on as the canoe tilted this way and that.

The fog slowly lifted as the canoe swooshed along. Trees bent over the river. High stone ridges lined both shores. I tried to direct the canoe with the paddle, but the water whirled me along too fast. The rocky river sparkled as the sun rose. Wolves howled in the distance. A hawk silently floated on air currents above me.

Where would this river lead me? Was I in the land of my mother's people? Would I find the hills of trilliums and violets and feel Wind Song in my heart?

Nothing answered my questions. The canoe passed more rocks, ridges, and boulders. The desolate howling of the wolves drew closer.

The canoe scraped over more boulders and bumped into more ledges. I hung on for dear life as the canoe nose-dived down a cascade of plummeting water into a pool below. The canoe crashed to a stop and rolled over.

I spilled into the river from the canoe's cradle into which I had been born.

Stunned, I slowly moved my arms and legs to see if I'd broken any bones. A sharp pain shot through the shoulder I'd landed on. I felt a growing knob on the side of my head. I hurt all over, but unbroken. Not so for the canoe. The bow lay cracked and splintered against a huge boulder.

Knee deep in water, I struggled to pull what was left of the canoe out of the river. All around me, tall granite ledges reached to the sky. Clams covered the shallow sandy bed near shore, so I gathered as many as I could hold in my skirt before climbing the low bank. I was hungry and all alone in a land that was all hard rock and soft mosses. I dropped the clams into a depression between rocks that held a little water then went searching for wood, twigs—anything to start a fire over the clams so they would steam open, ready to eat. I headed into a wooded area to gather kindling.

When I returned, I found I was not alone. A humpbacked troll-looking man was busily scooping my clams into a pouch. He also had my canoe paddle, skunk fur pack, and boots at his feet. The thought that the farmer had caught up to me brought terror. I picked up a rock and shouted at him.

"Those are my clams! My paddle! My pack! And I'm not going anywhere with you!"

He looked at me from under a wide floppy brimmed hat. His eyes were the clearest blue I'd ever seen. His massive white beard reached mid-chest. His clothes were of the roughest bur-cloth. Rougher than the clothes the goat boy or pig man wore at festivals. Rougher even than the sack dress Father bought me. His trousers bagged, but looked clean and unpatched. He didn't look like the farmer who'd been chasing after me.

"Aav-iap," he said bowing to me. His voice sounded like gravel scraping—like he hadn't used it for a long time. *Aav-iap* made no sense to me, but despite the raspy sound, he seemed gentle enough and unlike the farmer. He had made no move to threaten or hurt me. He'd even bowed to me. No one had ever done that before. I calmed just a little bit.

"Good day," I said to be polite. Then pointing, I added, "Those are my clams."

Without saying another word, he handed me the sack with the clams. Then he hefted my back pack, turned up a steep path, and signaled to me. He had all my things. I was wet and cold and hungrier than I'd ever been so I followed him, but I held onto the rock I'd picked up. We climbed ever so high until we were at the face of a towering stone ledge. In front of an entrance to a cave, a glowing fire and a stump were evidence that this was the man's home.

He wasn't the farmer, but I was wary so I stood a distance away still gripping the rock. I relaxed a bit more when the man poured all the clams into a dented pot and filled it from a flow of water that trickled down the stone ledge near the cave entrance. He stoked the fire up a bit, set the pot of clams over it and sig-naled me to sit on the stump. I didn't. I could watch the clams from where I was.

Without another word, he went into his cave and came out with a piece of wood heaped with mushrooms. He pointed to the stump again. This time I sat. He handed me the mushrooms. As he went into the cave one more time, I studied the round-capped morsels. *Crimini* is what Father called them when we went mushroom hunting. They were firm and fresh. When the man came back with a handful of mushrooms for himself, he sat cross-legged on the hard stones close to the fire.

My fears lifted with each mushroom I popped into my mouth. He didn't look scary at all as the fire's flames danced shadows across his face, and he ate watching the clams steam.

"Thank you for the mushrooms," I said. Then pointing to myself, I added, "Purs . . . er, Luna"

The man nodded and pointed to me, "Purs-er-Luna," he repeated.

I shook my head and said "Luna." Then I pointed to him.

He pointed to himself. "Ossi."

"Ossi," I repeated not wanting to forget.

"Luna," he said smiling. All the while a melody of wolf songs reached my ears.

"I'm from Kawishami or at least I used to live there, but I'm going to find my mother's people—the Ice People," I said.

Ossi looked puzzled, then shook his head as he said, "Ne narami."

I didn't understand his language and he didn't understand mine so I said no more. As we ate, Ossi seemed content with the silence. I wondered about him. Who he was, and what was he doing way out here all alone? He must be wondering the same about me.

When the clams steamed open, Ossi brought out a wooden plate that looked like he, or someone else, had carved it. He divided the clams so half were on the plate and the other half still in the dented pot. He handed me the plate and sat on the stones again with the pot on his lap.

We ate not saying a word. The only sounds from Ossi were the cracking of the shells even wider than they were from the steaming. He scraped the clam flesh out with his fingers. Having no utensils, I did the same.

When we were done eating, I took the two potatoes from the potato-cake woman and laid them at his feet. He picked them up, smelled them, gently touched each bud that was forming in the eyes. "Potatoes," I said.

"Tanurep," he answered. Then he bent and gathered all the clam shells, piling them neatly away from his cave entrance. He put more wood on the fire. I was grateful for the warmth because my dress and boots were still wet from my fall into the river, and the sun was lowering in the sky. I had no idea what I was going to do. My canoe was shattered. I wasn't sure where I was and how I was going to get where I wanted to go or how long it was going to take. The canoe, at least, had been a place I could sleep and feel was mine.

The man, finished with the shells, went to the ledge. He cupped his hands to catch water that dribbled down the stone face and then drank from them. He signaled for me to do the same. The trickles took a while to gather, but soon I had enough to lap up like a cat. To me it was the best water I'd ever tasted. Father and I usually scooped water from the lake or the river that ran by our hut. Most of the time it was speckled with floating leaves, insect wings, or other debris. The water from the ledge was clear and cool.

"Good." I said wiping my mouth as I went back to my stump. An evening mist enclosed the rocky ledge. Shivering a bit, I pulled Lily's shawl tightly around me. I wished we could talk to each other. I had so much I wanted to ask, especially one burning question. "Where do I go from here?"

He pointed to my pack so I opened it. On top was the feather I'd found when I'd left Bird Woman's portal. I handed it to him. He blew on it and watched it waft in the air. It landed on my shoulder. He smiled an enormous smile. I couldn't help but chuckle. He looked at me with his pale blue eyes and laughed a laugh that sounded more like a gurgle. For that one moment laughter was our common language.

When I took Father's book from my pack, he studied the title that I found so incomprehensible. Nodding to me, he turned pages until he found illustrations of the plants Father had studied. He beckoned me to sit by him. He pointed to the leaves and berries of poison ivy and said, "Nay a-doys," as he shook his head and took a small stone and pressed an x on the upper corner of the page. He continued turning pages, marking many with an x and saying "Nay a-doys" over and over.

On other pages, he seemed happy, almost jubilant to say, "Ya! A-doys!" No x was etched on those corners. He was telling me which were good to eat and which weren't. They were the same as Father had pointed out to me. I started using his words, *ya, a-doys* and *nay a-doys*. He seemed pleased when I did. We looked at the book together until the setting sun made it much too dim to see, and our fire was almost out.

I stood, thinking I would salvage what I could of the canoe to make a shelter for the night. Before I could get more than two steps away, he gently took my hand and said something that sounded like *ai-piiv*. I didn't have the slightest notion what he meant so shook my head. He beckoned me to follow. Once again, I did. Not far from his cave was a smaller cave.

Inside, he pulled two stones from his pouch, struck them together until they sparked and lit a small torch that was wedged in a crack in one wall. On the other side he pointed to a tree trunk ladder that led to a high ledge covered with skins and furs. "Auk-kun. Auk-kun," he said while closing his eyes, tilting his head onto his hands, and snoring.

As welcoming as it looked, I was uncertain and a bit afraid. I didn't know this man although he'd fed me and been kind to me. I was very tired and the walk down to my canoe for the night in the dark was a bit frightening, too. Still, I'd rather sleep under my broken canoe. I shouldered my pack and made for the cave's opening.

"Nay. Nay," he said pointing to the darkness outside and then to the fur bed.

A blanket of weariness covered me. I looked outside. It was so dark. Finally, I pointed to the floor to show the man where I was willing to sleep.

He responded adamantly by pointing to the ledge saying "Auk-kun. Auk-kun." With that he left the cave. I watched as he headed for the other cave and entered. I watched for a long time, but he didn't come out again. I hugged my pack close to my chest. I felt a gentle vibration so I reached in deeply until I found the little round stone from my mother's dress pocket that I had forgotten about. I relaxed and felt close to her as I held the stone that she'd held at one time.

I thought about Father as I looked into the darkness and listened to the wolves in the distance. He had abandoned me. He had sold me. Here I was with a kindly man trying to decide if I could trust him. The stone warmed even more. Finally, I tucked the stone back into my pack and climbed the ladder. I was glad to be on the high ledge snuggled under the warm furs. I was lulled by the songs of the wolf pack and slept the deep sleep of the very weary that night. Only one dream came to me that I remembered when I awoke the next morning. In it I followed a pack of wolves through a rocky and mossy land. That's all there was to the dream. Nothing frightful to disturb my sleep.

A frosty coating covered the rocky land and ledges the next morning. My boots were still wet, so I didn't put them on. Cold nipped my bare toes as I walked on the flat rocks. Ossi was stirring something over the fire in the same dented pot. When he saw me, he pointed to the stump again. I gladly sat and pulled my feet up and off the stones. He handed me a carved spoon and the wooden plate with a mound of something mashed in the middle. A barely discernable aroma of earthiness arose from the mash. The man was scooping it right from the pot into his mouth and mumbling things like *ummm, aa-vih*.

I followed his example. The first mouthful was slightly sweet, slightly tart, and was greatly delicious. I repeated his words, "*Ummm. Aa-vih,*" and scooped and ate until the plate was clean. All the while, I dreaded the moment I would leave and head into the unknown to continue my search. After drinking drippings from the ledge and making a trip into a thicket of straggly bushes to relieve myself, I hoisted my pack and my wet boots Willem had made.

The man dropped the armload of bark and skins he'd carried from his cave and hurried to me as fast as his humped back would allow. "*Nay. Nay.*" He took the pack from me and pointed to my bare feet shaking his head.

We sat near the fire. Ossi showed me how to cut narrow strips of birch bark all exactly the same width. While I cut, he shaped and sewed an animal skin with a bone needle. I had no idea what we were doing until he had me stand on a large sheet of bark while he traced my feet with a sharp rock.

We didn't talk. How could we? The only word I'd understood was *a-doys* and maybe the one he'd said while pointing to the bed last night, but I didn't remember that word. The trickling of the water falling near the cave, the burbling of the stream below and the faint song of the wolves on the distant ridge were the only sounds that the breeze brought to us as we worked.

He showed me how to weave the bands of bark together. Little by little, I could see a woven foot piece taking shape. Then he poked holes with a pointed stone and sewed the skin to the bark making a boot. We stopped only to crack open and eat a pile of hazelnuts he'd brought out from his cave. When we'd finished one boot, he presented it to me with a slight bow and said, "*Luu-naa.*"

I smiled and nodded. "Yes, I'm Luna." I bowed to him.

The boot was much too big, but Ossi packed mosses around my foot. The soft moss made the boot snug and warm. I took his hands in mine and tapped my booted toe.

"Thank you, Ossi." I hoped he understood how grateful I was to have a warm boot with the cold weather coming on. The ones Willem had made for me were sturdy, but not warm, and they were still wet. The new ones were perfect for the coming winter.

I did not take the boot off until later that afternoon when Ossi pantomimed that he needed it to measure for a new one we worked on together. Before long, I was wearing two moss-stuffed bark and skin boots. Then Ossi wrapped a wide curl of birch bark around each of my legs from ankle to knee. Leggings for deep snow! I could take them on and off when needed. I was as happy to have them as

I was with the polished boots Willem had given me. But they reminded me that I would have to be on my way. I thought of Father and wondered if his boots had fallen apart on his journey.

I set about trying to make Ossi understand that I needed to leave. On the smooth sloping rock that led from river to his cave, I drew a picture with a soft stone. A big circle for the lake. "Kawishami," I said. Then I drew the river from the lake to a small circle. I pointed to the river below the ledge we were on and then to my drawing. I pointed to the little circle and then waved my arms at everything around us, hoping he'd understand that I meant his stone ledge where we were. "River and here," I said. Then I drew the river further and looked at Ossi and shrugged my shoulders. "What's beyond here?" I asked.

Ossi studied my map. He pointed to the little circle then patted the rocks we stood on. I nodded and said, "Yes, yes."

He took the soft stone from me and made my little circle much bigger, then he drew the river longer and even more twisted than it had been. He scratched a small circle. Then he sketched more river. After that he shrugged. Then Ossi pointed to the circle he'd enlarged and howled like a wolf. Wolves in the distance howled in reply. "Wolf Song." I said. I was in the land of Wolf Song, but that told me nothing about where my mother's people were.

I bowed to thank Ossi and even though the sun was past its high point, I picked up my pack again.

"Nay. Nay," he said taking my pack from me. I was glad to hear the words because I hadn't relished the idea of starting my journey in the coming dark.

CHAPTER 19

After Ossi and I fished from the river bank, we gathered clams and mushrooms. My new boots kept my feet warm as the sun settled lower and the rocks cooled. Stars began to twinkle in the darkening sky while we sat around the fire waiting for the clams to steam and the fish to smoke.

Under the shroud of night, Ossi began talking. I didn't understand a word, but I listened spellbound as his voice wove a story. At times he gestured, shrugged, pointed, and nodded speaking in a somber tone. At other times his blue eyes sparkled in the flames of our cooking fire and his smile was so broad I could see that his two front teeth overlapped just a bit. Toward the end of his story, his voice softened and his eyes darkened with sadness. He looked to the black skies when he reached and patted the hump on his back. Tears fell from his eyes. His voice thickened and broke as he told the last of his story.

I didn't understand a single word he spoke, but a lump formed in my throat and my eyes misted over. I looked to the skies. The moon shone through tall trees casting shadows on our rocky ledge. A star plunged through the darkness. I thought of my mother and father. Alcyone and Polaris. My chest tightened as I wondered what Ossi's misfortune and heartbreak had been. What had led him all alone to this barren ledge?

A chunk of wood on the fire crackled and spit a spark high into the air. Ossi stood and scooped the clams from the pot. As he set them before me, he said, "Aa-doys."

After we ate, I told my story. Ossi listened intently. When I came to the part about catching the pig, he must have heard the merriment in my voice and seen the laughter in my eyes because he chuckled as I described pinning it down in the slimy muck. Just as I had sensed when he told something happy and when his story turned sad, he responded to different parts of my story. When I told of Father selling me to a farmer and leaving to find my dead mother, he brushed a tear from his eyes as I did.

We didn't know each other's words, but we listened to each other's voices and watched eyes and smiles. I knew how he felt and was sure he was sensing the same feelings as I told my story.

Ossi and I stayed late at the fire taking turns telling our stories. The myriad of stars brightened as the night darkened. We pointed to the Great Bear that looked like a dipper and to the smaller bear. I pointed to the North Star and said, "Polaris." When I found the Pleiades, I said, "Alcyone."

Ossi pointed out other stars and said their names in his strange language. I watched as the soft moonbeams of the full moon shone on the man who'd made me boots. Why he was living alone in this rocky land on this ledge of granite was somewhere in the story he had told me. I wished I could understand it. A gentle breeze blew, and the wolves sang from their ridge.

Even though it was barely dawning when I awoke the next morning, Ossi was already stirring something in his dented pot over a small fire. I made my way into the small thicket to relieve myself. After washing at the river, I examined my broken canoe. Ossi had dragged the pieces higher onto the ledge. The bow lay on its side completely broken from the rest. He'd laid splinters from the ribs side by side. The back of the canoe looked sturdy enough, but putting the bow and broken ribs back together looked impossible. All it was good for now was firewood. I would be walking the rest of my journey.

After eating the mash Ossi made for breakfast, I led him to the map we'd made on the smooth slanting rock the day before. I pointed to the first circle and howled like a wolf. I pointed to the small one he'd drawn some distance down the river. I shrugged to ask my question. *What land is that?*

Ossi looked into the dim sky. The star that shines in the early morning still shone although dimly. He pointed to it then drew an outline of a star.

Father had taught me about that star along with so many others. "Morning Star?" I asked.

He bent to the map. Next to the little circle he drew some jagged lines. I didn't understand, so he went to our cooking fire and pointed to the flames. He drew the jagged lines again.

"Fire?" I asked. I pointed to the cooking fire and drew jagged lines that I hoped looked like flames. "Fire?" I said again.

He nodded and then drew an *x* over that small circle. "Nay," he said as he traced over the *x* making it darker. It was the same as he'd done with Father's book. If a plant was not good to eat, he'd etched an *x* in the corner of the page. I was more confused than ever. *What could be so bad or dangerous about a place with such a beautiful name that he was putting an x on it? And why did he make fire drawings next to the morning star?* I thought about what Father had told me about stars. I hadn't understood the big words he'd used like *thermonuclear fusion, gravitational collapse, and radiating energy,* but I'd nodded as though I did so he'd tell me more about the Pleiades and my mother.

Father had called the morning star Venus. Was Ossi telling me that it was also a ball of fire like the sun? Confused, I opened my mother's dictionary and turned to the Vs. Right after venomous, I found it.

Venus. Goddess of Love and Beauty.
Also, the morning star we see shining brightly in the early hours.
Venus. The bringer of light.
Also Lucifer.

Lucifer? I didn't remember reading anything about Lucifer, so I turned to the Ls.

Lucifer. Another name for Venus the Morning Star.
The bringer of light.
My people called fires lucifers.
Lucifer. The symbol of evil.

I must pass through the Land of Morning Star? Venus? Lucifer? Beauty and Evil. What could be more beautiful than the bright morning star at the beginning of day? But the name *Lucifer* was bad. I remembered Father cursing whenever he accidentally cut himself or stuck himself with a fish hook or stubbed his toe—saying things like 'Be damned, Lucifer!' I wished I could ask Ossi why he'd put an *x* on the Land of Morning Star or did he know it was also the Land of Lucifer?

I wished I could make sense of the morning star having two names like Venus and Lucifer. Maybe it was like myself. I had been Purslane, now I was Luna. Father had two names, too—Stere and Polaris.

It was a puzzle I couldn't solve. I needed to start my journey again. I wondered what lay beyond the land of Morning Star so I drew light lines in all directions from the small circle and shrugged my shoulders hoping Ossi would point out the direction I should take after that.

He shook his head. Disappointed, I picked up my pack, ready to leave. Ossi brought the fish we'd caught and smoked over last night's fire. He also brought mushrooms, some tender roots, and dried berries for my journey.

Before I could swing my pack—now overflowing—to my back, Ossi again stooped to the rock we'd been drawing on. He signaled me to come beside him. He drew two faces. Identical faces. On the first he drew a tall body. On the other, a shorter one. Pointing to me, then to the shorter drawing he said, "Luna." Next, he drew a circle around the tall one. Moisture like the morning dew sparkled in his eyes. He said, "Etta Carina."

I wished I could understand. I wasn't sure if the words *Etta Carina* were a name or just more of his words that were so puzzling to me. It was obvious he's drawn a picture of me, but who was the other? The bigger one? *Was he asking about my mother?*

I looked at Ossi. He looked at me intently with his blue eyes. He brushed away a tear. I found myself brushing tears from my eyes, too. Who was this man who had fed me? Made boots for me? Who I couldn't understand, and yet for whom I felt. . . . What did I feel? Curiousity? No, more than that. I didn't feel alone with him. I was no longer afraid or wary. His hard rock ledge home felt just like that, like a home. I needed to leave the comforts I'd found there to find my mother's people, but I didn't want to leave Ossi.

The wolves howled in the distance. I imagined them standing on a ridge of steep rock watching the Morning Star fade into the brightening sky. I wanted to say so much. I wanted Ossi to understand what I said. Finally, I said, "Thank you. Thank you for the food, the warm fire, for the bed of furs." I pointed to my boots. "Thank you for warm feet."

Ossi took my hand in his. At that moment, no words were necessary. He spoke to me in his gentle language. At the end, he pointed to the drawings of the two people. *Did I remind him of someone from long ago?* We let our tears fall together.

The wolves howled reminding me that I must be on my way. Ossi hung my wet boots onto one strap of my pack. He showed me two stones that when struck together made a spark for a fire. *Lucifer stones.* He tucked them into my pack.

Just as I was taking my first steps away from the stone hard ridge where I'd found softness, Ossi draped a beautiful fur wrap over my shoulders. In the nippy morning it felt good, not only warding off the chill, but also because I had found one more person who cared. I didn't know if I had entered a portal at the full moon, and that he—like Willem, Lily, and Bird Woman—would dissolve into thin air before my eyes, or if he was still of this world. I hoped he was of the living and that maybe I'd see him again even though that seemed unlikely.

Ossi walked me down the steep rock that led to the river I was to follow. At the place where I'd first seen him scooping my clams into a bag and thought he was stealing, we stood facing each other. He swayed from foot to foot. His eyes glistened. I swayed with him. My eyes filled with tears. No words were needed as he took both my hands into his and held them to his heart before turning toward his cave. I felt a thickening in my throat and a profound emptiness. The wolf song echoed through the stone ridges and ledges mournful and somber.

CHAPTER 20

For three days I walked alone, climbing over sharp rocks and stumbling along the river's bank. I wished for the canoe. I had no idea what direction I should be traveling to find my mother's people, so I kept following the river, not knowing where it would take me. I thought of Father, wondered if he was still living. I dreamed that he had flown through the skies and had found my mother. A great emptiness stirred within me. I wished to be with another kind, generous person. One like the potato-cake woman, or Willem and Lily, or the Bird Woman, or Ossi.

The moon shrank and waned into its gibbous phase, yet it spread eerie light on the land as I woke early to start my fourth day of walking. The huge boulders and majestic ledges of Ossi and Wolf Song were far behind me. The nights had been chilly so I was thankful for the fur wrap Ossi had given me. More than that, I'd felt at home with him on his rocky ridge. I'd felt a comfort unlike anything I ever felt with Father. I missed that feeling.

When I awoke on the fifth day, I followed the river, listened to its burbles and ripples, climbed over and around huge stones. A woodpecker rat-a-tatted in the distance. Before long I warmed, so I shed the fur and tucked it under my arm. At the same time, a pungent smell stung my nose. Even with Ossi's repeated *x*'s still fresh in my mind, I followed the river toward the smoky odor.

The smell strengthened. I heard laughter and a chicken squawking frightfully. Despite Ossi's warning, I hurried to see what was happening. And then I saw a half-naked girl chasing a chicken around steaming, bubbling, gurgling mud pots. The chicken flew and squawked. The girl jumped after it laughing and sliding on the muddy ground.

A huge area, as far as I could see, was covered with round sink holes of steam rising from the ground. The pocks were filled with turbulent hissing and boiling, bubbling mud. It truly could have been Lucifer's invention as it lacked the beauty of Venus the Morning Star. Watery mud spewed skyward at intervals from one or another spitting pot. Uprooted trees lay everywhere covered with grime. The shrieking girl slipped and fell as she chased the chicken. She laughed deeply and wildly as she got up, slipped again and continued her pursuit.

Finally, the girl snagged the chicken by a leg.

"Hey ho," I called to get her attention.

"Who you?" shouted the soiled and smudged girl who looked to be quite a bit younger than I was—about ten years old or so. It was hard to tell. She was so skinny, I could have counted all her ribs. What was she doing way out here all alone?

She scowled as she held the chicken upside down by its legs. It struggled, flapping its wings, and squawked an ear-shattering protest. Glaring through tangled hair, she strutted toward me shouting, "Who you an' what you doin' here?"

Remembering Ossi's warning, I said, "Luna. I'm Luna, and I'm just passing through on my way home."

She continued shouting. "Well, Luna. You here now. Gimme your pack!"

"Why? There's nothing good in it." That morning I'd finished the last of the food Ossi gave me. I looked hungrily at the chicken.

"Empty now!" She scowled.

"It just has an old dress, books, feather, shawl, withering potatoes, tree bark, and rocks inside."

"Now!"

I hesitated. I didn't like being shouted at. I should have turned and scampered away. Fast. But my stomach rumbled, and what danger could the girl be to me? She was much smaller and bonier. At that moment, she bent, picked up a knobby stick and bludgeoned the chicken. As she dunked the chicken in a steaming cauldron, she turned to me again.

"I said empty, *now*. Do it, or I pluck you like a chicken."

I put my pack down. By now she was plucking feathers and throwing them to the wind. One floated and stuck in my hair. I began to unload my pack. When I took out a potato, she laughed and tossed it aside. "Just dumb potato. Old. Wrinkled. Just like Grammy." Her laughter rang out.

Next, I showed the Lucifer stones and feather. "You carry potatoes, rocks, an' feathers? You dumb as big person."

When I laid out the bark leggings, *Alcyone's Dictionary*, my mother's letter, and my old burlap dress, she bellowed, "Junk! Jest junk! Why you bother with junk? Maybe I roast you with chicken." With that she took a knife and slit the chicken open and pulled out the entrails that she kicked into a rumbling mud pot. It sizzled and stank.

I quickly took stock of what other weapons might be lying around besides the bludgeon, knife, and kettle of hot water. Just then one of the bubbling cauldrons spewed mud. The girl jumped back, but not in time to keep from getting covered with mud. She guffawed as she wiped her face.

"What you name again?" she asked as she skewered the chicken with sticks and then hung it over one of the roiling mud pots.

"Luna," I said. "What's yours?"

"Name's Lamb-i-kins an' don't ask agin."

"Is that your real name?" I asked.

"Huh! Pap called me *Spoiled Rotten Ugly Gap-Toothed Brat,* an' tell me I born bad. Born bad cuz I born when moon cover sun an' make alla world dark. But after he beat me, Grammy hold me tight an' say I not born bad. She rock me an' call me her good little Lamb-i-kins."

Her voice cracked a bit when she said that last part, so she turned to the chicken and pretended to check it as it started to roast. The sticks she had poked through it rested on cross-legs she'd made of tree branches. Then she shuffled through the things from my pack again and started to turn pages in my mother's dictionary.

"Do you know how to read?" I asked.

"Little words," she said softly. "Mam teach me with words drawn on my hand. Grammy teach me with books. She read me many times when Pap not home."

Sensing a story behind her words, I asked, "Why did Mam draw words on your hand? Why didn't Grammy read when Pap was home?"

"Oooh," she scowled. "Too many questions. Pap get mad. Pappie say readin' waste a time. That I shoulda be doin' somethin' pro-duck-ive like pretendin' I lame an' beg for coins. Or I be pick pocketing uppity-ups or somethin'. Grammy have two books she hide. One *Tales and Mysteries from the Frozen Far Lands.* Stories like dreams."

Her shoulders slumped as she said, "Day come Pap catch me an' Grammy reading story 'bout beautiful queen who live in big fancy ice castle with magic ponies. I holdin' the book. Pap yell he gonna burn book. I hold on tight when he try take book from me, my arm get twisted. I in pain but keep holdin' an' he would've flung me into fire with book if Grammy hadn't pulled me away."

I heard her voice quiver. Her whole body trembled as she whispered, "Grammy tell me run. I run but hear awful things. Yelling. Hitting. I not even look back, but run, run. Last thing I hear Grammy screaming Pap to stop."

"What happened next?" I asked.

"Don't know. I run for woods. I hide some days under bushes. Then I hungry so sneak back one night an' peek in window. Pap there, but no Grammy. Then I run and run some more an' find here."

The chicken was beginning to smell good. Lamb-i-kins stood and turned it to roast the other side. "Where did you get the chicken?" I asked.

She looked at me. When she'd told me her story, her voice had softened, and she sounded sad and vulnerable. Now her eyes steeled again, and the set of her mouth frightened me. She shouted. "You jest like big people. Dumb! Ain't it easy to see? I borrow things. Like chickens." She jabbed the knife into the ground to emphasize each word. She scared me. She was young and small, but very angry.

The chicken smelled better and better. My stomach roiled with hunger. "Is there anything I can do to help?" I asked.

"I need no help. Never. An' don't go thinkin' you get to eat some of my borrowed chicken that you did nuttin' to get." She stood at the side of one of the many Lucifer fires holding the bludgeon in one hand.

I tried to keep Lamb-i-kins talking while the chicken roasted. She glared at me and played with the bludgeon. I decided I should have believed the x Ossi had put on the circle for the Land of Morning Star before I found out that it was better named Land of Lucifer and that referred to more than the bubbling mud cauldrons.

I started to collect everything from my pack that Lamb-i-kins had strewn about. I slid the moonstone into my pocket. Lamb-i-kins stalked toward me holding the knife and the bludgeon. "Oh, no! I not say you leave yet." With that she gave Father's book a quick kick with her bare feet. Then she picked up the boots Willem had made.

"Borrowing good. Gets me what I need. You hungry. I make trade this time. Only this time. Two neck bones an' rib meat for boots."

She dropped the knife and bludgeon and began measuring the boots against her feet. I felt brave so I said, "The boots are worth more than that. Even one boot is worth more than the scanty bits you offered. For both boots, I get half the chicken."

"Huh!" she snarled. "I holdin' boots. You not holdin' chicken. I swap all neck bones, all rib meat, burned skin, and other chewin' bones. That a deal! No other choice, or I get boots an' you get long knife cut down yer arm an' bludgeon bump on head!"

The chicken pickings weren't much, but I savored each bit. When the meat was gone, I sucked and gnawed the bones and ate every bit of gristle. I was still hungry after we threw the last of the bones into one of the fires. I told Lamb-i-kins that I'd scout the surrounding woods to find berries, mushrooms, roots, or leaves.

"No!" She shouted. "No go nowhere past dead trees over there an' there an' there." She pointed out a circle around the cauldrons.

"Why not?" I asked.

"Cuz I say so! Stay here! Where I see you."

"I'm still hungry," I said and started out anyway. Before I got too far, Lamb-i-kins grabbed me by an arm and my hair. "Owww!" I complained as she walked me back to the bubbling and steaming mud.

"No goin' til I say!"

"I'm just passing through," I said. "I have to get to the land of my mother's people."

"I say *no!*"

"All right," I said, "but I'm leaving tomorrow." I didn't feel so sure as I thought about the chill settling over the land signaling winter. It was warm here among the churning cauldons of mud and fire. Lamb-i-kins had found a good place to live. While I thought, I walked around investigating her camp site. Lamb-i-kins followed wearing my boots. By the trunk of a downed tree, I found a heap of dented pots, a huge pile of clothing and rags, coils of rope, the skull of a large animal, a tattered book that was no longer readable, and a few shards of broken mirror.

"Not be thinking to borrow my things," Lamb-i-kins yelled. "Hard finding em an' lugging em here. Unnerstand? Hands off. No touch. I boil your liver if'n you mess my things."

I was getting tired of hearing her yelling, so I quit looking. I thought it best to change the subject—and Lamb-i-kins' mood—so I said, "Tell me about your grammy again. Tell me about the good times you had with her."

Lamb-i-kins locked her eyes onto mine with a cold stare. "She only good big person, so no talking about her." She scooped up the chicken feathers and lay them in a pile. Not having anything to do—but get yelled at—I found a spot next to a dead tree that leaned against another and sat next to it.

Harsh as Lamb-i-kins was, I felt sorry for her. She was so young and alone and trying to survive. Her life had been harder than anything I'd endured. She needed a family. Even as I felt sorry for her, I still thought about getting away from the wild girl and her bludgeon. I watched her stir a stick in a boiling mud pot and wondered if she'd always be alone, or if someday she'd find a family who'd be kind and take care of her. Tired from days of walking, I relaxed in the warmth of the spewing Lucifer cauldrons. Without another thought, I fell asleep.

I awoke to a tugging. Lamb-i-kins was binding my feet to a mud-covered log. I buckled my knees and tried to kick free. Lamb-i-kins picked up the bludgeon she'd killed the chicken with. "You be needin' this," she shrieked and bonked me on the head.

When I came to, it was dark. I was lashed to the tree; my hands and legs tied. My head ached something fierce. I called out to Lamb-i-kins. No answer. I stretched around as much as the ropes would let me. Lamb-i-kins was nowhere to be seen.

I squirmed and twisted in the ropes trying to find a weakness, a slack, anything that would allow me to unravel the binds. The tethers held. My wrists bled. My ankles too. I tingled all over. Numbness spread from my toes through my legs. Fear seized me in an instant. *Where was Lamb-i-kins? How was I to get free?*

I'd escaped the farmer, but I couldn't escape what a little girl had done to me. I'd walked far. All for nothing. No matter how I tugged at the ropes, I couldn't loosen them.

Two or three days passed yet Lamb-i-kins did not return. I lost count of the days and nights. My head ached all the time. I feared she had been captured "borrowing" food. Or was she like Willem and Lily and had turned to dust? Been reassigned? Was I left here to starve, soil my clothes, and die, never to be heard from again? Why hadn't I paid attention to the *x* Ossi had inscribed over the circle of Land of Lucifer?

Hunger clawed at my stomach. My tongue stuck to the roof of my mouth. My head ache worsened. I wondered how much longer before I fell asleep and didn't wake, so I refused to surrender to sleep. I struggled to keep my eyes open and shook off a drowsiness when in the distance, I heard a scraping on the river rocks and a splash of water. Then I heard branches snapping and plodding footsteps coming closer. I shrank behind the tree to which I was tied. Was it Lambi-i-kins returning? Or worse, had the farmer found me? I wouldn't have the strength to fight him. I wished with all my might that I had paid heed to Ossi's warnings. I hoped it was Lamb-i-kins. What was in store for me if it was the farmer was too painful to even imagine.

Petrified, I tried to make a plan to escape when whoever it was hopefully untied me. If it was Lamb-i-kins, I'd grab my pack and run, if my legs would still carry me. If it was the farmer, I'd grab the bludgeon that lay not too far from me. I'd use it if I had to. The footsteps sounded close. I twisted my neck to catch a glimpse of who was coming. A two-legged furry creature zigzagged between trees. Each heartbeat thudded in my ears. It wasn't Lamb-i-kins. The farmer? Someone else who'd do me harm? A cold chill swept over me. I quivered in the ropes that bound me.

I felt the moonstone warming in my pocket. I wished I could reach it, hold it in my hand and stroke comfort and hope from it. I twisted my neck to see again. The creature crashed through branches and slipped on the muddied ground. A tiny ray of hope filled me like the ray of light that pierced through the tree branches and glowed on the rock beside me. The fur-covered creature walked bent over with a hump on its back—like Ossi. My moonstone warmed even more.

Gathering all my nerve, what could it hurt even if it wasn't Ossi? I needed help. I called out as Willem and I had once greeted one another, "Hey ho!" The fur-covered creature stepped out of the trees into the warm mud-covered Land of Lucifer the Morning Star.

"Aa-vi-ap," the creature replied. Ossi's voice! Ossie's language! I swelled with relief. I'd never heard anything so beautiful in my life.

He untied me. I cried. He held out a hand. I clasped it and looked into his soft blue eyes. A smile broke on both our faces. Ossi's eyes. Ossi's smile!

He shook a sack from his humped back. In it were dozens of small dried fish, clams, handfuls of mushrooms, shelled nuts, and dried plums. Ossi and food! I was so happy I reached into my pocket to rub my moonstone.

"Ossi," I said peering into the sack, "how did you find me? I have missed you every day since I left you by the ridge of the singing wolves."

His eyes brightened and in his beautiful language he told about a dream he had after I left. In his dream, I was imprisoned in the land of bubbling, spewing mud pots, so he'd come to save me.

My moonstone pulsated with warmth against my leg. I didn't know how, but I understood every word he said. *Was this really happening?* Or was I so thirsty and hungry, I just thought I understood?

The stone warmed even more so I slid it from my pocket. Its blues and whites danced and swirled. Ossi looked at it. Then he loosened a pouch hanging at his side and took out a small white stone. As it whirled with yellows and pinks, much as my own did with blues of every hue, he told me how he'd hurried to fix my canoe so he could catch up to me and give it to me. Could it be that the stones magically, fantastically, and impossibly were the connection we needed to understand each other? Father had told me that plants communicated with each other and if we paid attention, we could understand them and animals, too. Could stones do the same?

Words tumbled from my mouth. "Our stones look so much alike. Maybe they're parts of a bigger stone. Is it possible?"

Ossi smiled his big warm smile. "I don't know. There are many things I don't understand, but it is good that our stones are giving us word-understanding."

As we drank river water and ate dried fish and plums, we held our stones and talked. I told him about Lamb-i-kins. He told me how he had woven strips of bark together and had attached them to where the bow of my canoe had been. What had been the stern was now the pointed bow. It no longer looked like a canoe with its squared-off back, but he'd patched it so well that only a little water had seeped in as he'd followed the twisting river to find me.

When we were done eating, he handed me the paddle. "Yours to find your people," he said.

I didn't want to leave Ossi again so I searched for the right words to thank him. "I have been so alone. Many years with my father, yes, but still alone. With you, I feel safe. With you, I feel wanted and cared for. With Father I was a weed, a burden, a curse. Your warm soft words even when I didn't understand anything you said, filled me with something I've never felt before. Something I could never have imagined." I paused as I touched the moonstone. A feeling of calm and belonging came over me. "I hope to find my mother's people, maybe even a portal to my mother. I might even have a sister. I need to find her if she lives, but I fear none of that will happen because I don't know which way to go, and I'll be alone again."

Ossi held his moonstone and listened as I talked. His blue eyes were almost hidden beneath his bushy brows. When I stopped, he nodded. Then he began to speak. Through his words and eyes, both gentle as a song, I tried to look into his world, into his thoughts. At the end he repeated, "I-sass-nak. I-sass-nak. He was promising to travel with me on my journey. "Together," he said. "Together."

CHAPTER 21

Ossi and I walked the land of seething mud pots. I told him how wild and blustery Lamb-i-kins had been—had to be to survive on her own. The piles of kettles, clothing, and other things she'd borrowed were still there. We found a chicken bone, feathers, and her footsteps in the mud. My pack was still there. The boots Willem had made were gone. So was Lamb-i-kins.

"I don't think she's coming back. It's been three days." I said wondering where she'd gone and why she'd left me tied. Cruel as she had been to me, I wanted her to be safe. She was too young to be alone, finding food, taking care of herself. I wanted her to have found a home with someone like Ossi or the potato-cake woman, but I feared that had not happened.

Ossi and I paddled as the sun reached its highest point in the sky but gave no comforting warmth. The river wound around stones and steep banks. Its icy water told of the cold nights ahead. Frost had shriveled grasses and bushes. No berries hung from branches. No mushrooms poked through rich duff. I watched a fox weave its way through the edge of a forest, nose to the ground, sniffing for prey. If it had kits, they were already grown enough so they could hunt for their own food just as Lamb-i-kins did, but sadness filled me because she had no one to go home to at night. The fox kits did.

We paddled in unison, finding a rhythm of reach, dip and pull. We paddled until the sun sank low. Then we hoisted the canoe onto shore, ate from Ossi's sack, and settled for a night's rest. Even wrapped in furs and sheltered by low branches of an ancient cedar, whirling winds chilled us to the bone.

In the darkness, owls hooted, and a fox yipped. When I heard a chorus of wolf howls, I thought of the stories Ossi had told when my stone had been lying in the bottom of my pack, and I hadn't understood a word of his language. So, I asked, "From where do you come, and who are your people?"

He answered in a song. As I listened, I breathed in the gentle aroma from cedar boughs he'd laid on the flickering flames of our camp fire.

I am Ossi.
Long ago of the Ice People.
Now I am Ossi of no people
For so long. Alone.
Until Luna came. You, Luna.
Your eyes are eyes I know.
Your smile is a smile I know
From long ago.
Together we paddle a stony river,
Looking for your people.
Looking for a home.

It was so beautiful that I felt my eyes mist. "What do you mean?" I asked. "You know my eyes and smile?"

He said, "Long ago when I lived with my people—a girl, a lame girl named Etta Carina—well, your eyes and smile were like hers."

"What happened to her?"

"I don't know. It was long ago. Now it is your turn to tell me who you are and who are your people."

I was stumped. Who I was? I had shed Purslane, and was just beginning to know myself as Luna. I knew little about Father. All I knew about my mother was her name Alcyone, and that she wanted to be with her people when she gave birth and to feel Wind Song in her heart again, but most of the time Father said she came from the Pleiades. I began by singing as Ossie had.

> *Named by my father*
> *I was Purslane.*
> *A weed. A curse or a blessing.*
> *Most likely a curse*
> *because*
> *I took my mother's breath so I could breathe.*
> *I took her life so I could live.*
> *As I entered this world, Mother died in the red canoe*
> *On the waters of Kawishami.*
> *Now I'm Luna.*
> *Sold to a farmer.*
> *Abandoned by Father.*
> *I look for my mother's people and maybe a sister.*
> *I look for home.*

There was so much more to my story, but I choked on a lump in my throat. The fire had died down. Ossi said, "Alone, both of us, but now together. I will not leave you until you find your people and your maybe sister. Sleep now. I'll keep the fire burning."

During the night, I awoke countless times to hear the hollow hooting of an owl and to see the comforting silhouette of Ossi bent over the fire.

When the sun woke us, we got up, broke our fast, and paddled through the day again. This became our ritual for several days. The river seemed endless. I hoped for a hamlet at every bend. I wished for the sight a hut in the distance—anything to show this land was inhabited. Each day grew colder. Each day the wind blew with a foreboding chill.

We ate in silence the day that Ossi emptied the last dried plums and a small fish from his sack. For days after that, we gnawed the soft, tender part from inside the bark of trees. We dug for worms, slugs, and tender roots—anything we could make into a mash.

One frigid day when we had paddled far, Ossi pointed to a building shadowed by a high rocky peak. We dragged the canoe onto shore and headed toward the decaying building that leaned with the wind. Birds flew in and out a door that hung on one hinge. As we neared, Ossi said, "Food and shelter."

The building had once been a stable. Rotting saddles, reins, and other straps of leather hung from the walls. Networks of spider webs draped from beam to beam. The only signs of life were mice scurrying in the mounds of straw that filled the stalls, and birds that flitted in and out of nests tucked into crevices beneath the roof.

Behind the stable was a building that had toppled over. We carried armloads of its well-weathered boards for firewood.

I chased doves and pigeons toward Ossi. He swung a board and stunned them. After we had caught and plucked five birds, we rigged a frame over a fire. Soon the roasting birds dripped fat onto the sizzling and spitting flames below. My mouth watered as I smelled the welcome aroma. For the first time in many days, we ate our fill as we rested and warmed ourselves around the fire.

After the meal, we pulled our fur wraps around us and sat by the dying embers. Ossi put more wood on the fire and stoked the flames. I remembered that Father always told his best stories while we sat around a fire after eating, so I said, "Tell me more about your people. Tell how you lived."

Ossi cleared his throat. "In my long-ago home, I lived with my mother, brothers, father, grandparents, aunts and uncles, and cousins in our beautiful land. As was custom among my people, when I entered my fifteenth year, I began searching for my spirit animal. I headed to the woods every day seeking one that was special. I peeked into fox dens and rabbit warrens, followed the wolves across fields, plains and into woods, and even tamed the little gray mice of the fields. Despite all my efforts, none spoke to me. None invited me into their world. None followed me into mine.

"I was near desperation. If I didn't find a spirit animal by my next birthing day, I would be declared spiritless and would be shunned. I hunted out the bear and spoke to it boldly. I swam with the salmon and whispered into the waters. I climbed high trees and mimicked the birds. All was in vain. None joined their spirit to mine."

A flame spit into the night air. An owl hoo-hoo-ed.

"The day before I was to announce my spirit animal at a great ceremony, Mother and Grandmam prepared a huge feast. They hung stew pots over fires. Father risked angry bees by harvesting honey from their nests. Grandpap tended the stone and clay oven while Mother ground rye and tender roots to make flatbreads. Father also wrapped freshly caught fish in clay, ready to bake when the breads and cakes were done.

"I helped skin rabbits and pluck grouse to roast. All that night I tossed and turned because I had no announcement to make. The next day would be a disaster. All the feast food would be thrown, uneaten, into the river when it was discovered that I had no spirit animal. I cried into my arms as silently as I could."

I felt anguish for Ossi when he'd thought he would be a great disappointment to his family. It was like Father's dashed hope that I would have a gift from the comet that would bring riches to him.

"In the morning, the sun taunted my deep sadness by shining brightly. The sky was the loveliest blue. Birds sang and flit from tree to tree as my mother, father, grandpap, grandmam, aunts, cousins and whole families—even neighboring clans—came to celebrate. I wished for dark skies and torrential rain. Such was my mood. I considered running away rather than enduring the shame and shunning. I planned what I'd take with me. My knife, a pouch of seeds, a stone to spark fire, and the clothes on my back. Nothing else. But I couldn't run. I had to face my people and their disappointment."

Again, my heart squeezed thinking of Ossi not having a spirit animal.

"Father and Grandpap stood by me as each of the visitors greeted me and offered a gift. A new hunting sling. A skinning knife. A leather pouch. A fur wrap. Gifts I would never use when I was declared without spirit and had to leave my people forever.

"When the flautists put their flutes away, and the dancers twirled a last twirl, I sat on an oak stump with everyone circled around. They lightly tapped their drums. Thrum. Thrum. Thrum. I felt the vibration of the steady rhythm as it pulsed through me. I should have calmed and felt the pulse of everyone breathing with me. But I could not. My heart raced tat-tat-tat and tumbled instead of beating with the steady thrum, thrum, thrum. My own breath strangled me. Grandpap knelt behind me, put his hands on my shoulders, and sang the ancient song joining the earth and sky spirits. It told of how everything in nature sings."

The Sun and Moon shine and sing.
Mother Earth turns as the Winds sing.
The Waters murmur gentle songs.
All the Trees of the Forests sing.
They sing. They sing.
Lau-laa. Lau-laa.

Ossi sang the song softly, his voice murmured as gently as the waters. I found myself wanting to sing with him, but my own heart raced rat-tat-tat wondering if he was alone because he'd found no spirit animal.

He continued, "I hung my head low and closed my eyes. Grandpap would sing one more time, then everyone would look to me for my announcement. I wondered how I would ever hold my head up and tell everyone that no animal had chosen me. Clenching my hands, tears filled my eyes. A huge lump rose in my throat as I prepared to disappoint my family, to stand with dignity and say my goodbyes, to hear my mother and grandmam cry and beat their chests as they watched me walk away. Just as Grandpap sang the last *lau-laa*, I felt a soft whir of air, then the prick of talons gently grasping my shoulder. I opened my eyes. There, perched close to my cheek, was a beautiful great gray owl.

"Taika! A most celebrated spirit had come to me! I looked into the eyes of the owl. It looked deeply into mine. Father and Mother hugged each other, happy that the spirit of owl was bestowed upon me.

"Grandmam said, 'Aye! The owl brings you wisdom. How fortunate you are!'

"I was speechless. Owl of the Moon was on my arm preening its feathers. My heart rose beating joyfully. Deeply, I breathed in air reviving my spirit. I heard the murmurs of delight from all my people. Stroking the owl's ruff, I stood, bowed, and led everyone to the feast table."

I shook myself from my listening reverie. I was happy the owl had chosen Ossi, but still wondered why he'd lived alone on the tall stone ridges. He told a good story. A real story. His memories were good. He'd had a big family. A family that followed the ways of their ancestors. "I wish I had a family that big and a story that good," I told him.

He answered, "Not all my memories are good. It is late. We should sleep now."

That night I crawled into a mound of straw. Ossi did the same and was soon snoring softly as I drifted off to sleep.

CHAPTER 22

We sheltered in the stable as a windstorm roared outside. The birds that roosted overhead provided us with the food we needed to regain our strength before we traveled on.

That evening I told Ossi about my life with Father. How we foraged in the woods, fished the lake, dug for clams in the river. I described our hovel. He laughed at the story of Father and his fight with the skunk that was now the fur lining of my pack. "In the spring," I said, "we often sat around a small fire at dusk and ate dandelion flowers fried in a bit of grease and finished our evening by chewing on wild chives or mint leaves. Sometimes Father told stories. Sometimes we sat in silence listening to waves lap on the shore and to frogs singing in the bog." So much of my time with Father had been worrying about his moods. Now I realized we'd had many good times, too.

When I finished, Ossi picked up the thread of his story where he'd left off the day before.

"Another three years went by. I was now a young man. On the first full moon of the vernal season, I would have to leave my people for three full wanings and waxings of the moon. I would travel alone with only my spirit animal as a guide. While on my journey, I hoped to discover if I would become a dreamer of dreams, a tender of the fires, a hunter, a fisher, or a keeper of stories. When I finally returned to my people, I would be changed. I would be a man. A man ready to seek a bride. Oriina, my friend Gromske's sister, interested me the most.

"Taika watched as I packed a sleeping robe, knife, stone for sparking fire, a needle, and a kettle into my bundle. I also packed the moonstone that Taika had plucked along a streambed and dropped into my lap the day before."

Late that afternoon, the sky darkened and heavy snows fell. We carried arm-loads of wood and piled it in the stable. I looked to the sky. So did Ossi. It had changed to an ugly green. "We need more wood," Ossi said. "A big storm is coming."

A wolf howled in the distance. A whole pack answered with hollow echoes. I plucked and gutted two birds then huddled close to the fire while the birds roasted. Questions tangled in my thoughts. *How long will the storm last? What will happen to us after we eat all the doves and pigeons?*

Ossi must have heard my thoughts or he was having the same. He brushed snow from the door to the stables and said, "We need to move along before the snow gets deep and we've eaten all the birds. We need to take down as many as we can. Not all of them, but enough to feed us until we find a village. Perhaps tomorrow or the next day, the storm will die down, and we will go."

More birds flew into the stables seeking shelter as the snow thickened. The straw trembled with little rodents doing the same. The sky became dark as night, and snow changed to a steady sleet. The winds blustered so hard I was afraid the boards and roof would fly off our shelter.

While we ate, I told Father's story about how my mother had come to him from the Pleiades. As I told it, I thought of how different Father's stories had been from Ossi's. Father's changed with each telling and depended on his mood. Ossi's were solid; stories one could believe. I moved closer to the fire when Ossi started his telling again.

"As I packed for my separation journey, I thought how much I'd miss Oriina. When I returned, I would ask her to join me in the uniting ceremony. She was unlike the other girls. She could hurl stones from a wooden sling and take down a hare with a single try. She also came home carrying more trout and graylings than I ever caught on three fishing trips. She'd make a good wife.

"My friend Gromske was to take his separation journey at the same time. The elders pointed us off into opposite directions—Gromske to the east. I headed west.

"On the day of my leaving, I hoisted my rucksack and traveled away from my family and our cooking fires with my back to the barely-rising sun. Taika followed. My empty stomach growled. Gromske and I were allowed nothing to eat before we left. We had to find our own food. I wasn't too worried because Taika was a good hunter and always brought me a squirrel or rabbit dangling from his talons. Gromske wasn't so lucky, his spirit animal was a ptarmigan."

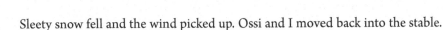

Sleety snow fell and the wind picked up. Ossi and I moved back into the stable. We crawled into piles of straw to keep warm. Soon he began his story again.

"My heart jolts when I remember what happened. It was broad daylight. Taika slept in the hollow of a nearby tree. I was halfway through my separation journey and had overcome all the challenges of surviving on my own. That day I was lost in my thoughts about Oriina, when a band of marauders crept through the woods. My first warning was when, as if on cue, they ran into my camp and encircled me.

"All my fighting skills were for naught. There were eight of them—all carrying clubs and knives. I tried to talk reason to them as they circled closing me in. Over and over they chanted, 'Blood. Gore. Bludgeon. Death.' The throb of each word beat with my heart and frightened me to the core.

"They'd streaked their faces with red berry juices and circled their eyes with ashes. Their hair was long and twisted into a single braid that looped behind one ear. The skull of an animal was tied to the top of each one's head. Beaver, fox, wolf, and one with a bear skull.

"Trembling, I offered them everything in my sack to go away. The chant swelled louder and louder. Their circle tightened around me. They banged their clubs together. The menacing sights and sounds frightened me to a paralysis I had never known.

"I begged and pleaded. Then I heard a screech and a flurry of wings. Taika flew straight at the murderous one with the bear skull. He clawed the man's eyes and then swooped to claw another. The marauders staggered in shock. Three of them had been blinded before they knew what was happening. I gained my senses and clawed at the eyes of the one nearest me. That's when I felt a tremendous blow to my back. Stunned, I struggled to stay on my feet. I heard bone-chilling shrieks as Taika attacked one after another. The bludgeon bashed into my back again. I buckled to the earth barely conscious. By the time I got to my knees, the marauders had stumbled away, leaving a trail of blood. The shrieking stopped. The stillness was as deafening as the shrill screams had been.

"I struggled to my knees and whistled for Taika. I expected him to come swooping. Then I heard a soft wheeze. I crawled to the sound and found Taika lying on the ground. He'd been clubbed, too. His breath came ragged and rapid. I held him to my chest murmuring *Don't leave me. No! No!* I willed him to live, but it would not be. One of his wings drooped. Blood soaked his feathers. He gasped. His eyes fixed on me, seeing nothing. Taika had joined the spirit world. Now, he would only fly in the world beyond the star sky."

Ossi's voice trembled and faded as he recounted that day. I could not imagine his grief. I thought of Ossi alone, mourning his owl. I thought of myself alone, always alone, even with Father at my side by our crackling fires. I closed my eyes and saw a vision—a woman with long dark hair wearing the same dress I now wore. I felt a longing and tears came to my eyes.

As the storm raged outside, I took out my moonstone. Blues swirled as if in motion. The pearly translucence brightened and faded. Shadows hid the blues. Yellows and pinks appeared in gentle waves, and then paled. The blue wisps arose again against the whites. Mesmerize by the stone, I made a wish. *Help me find my mother's people.*

Ossi held his moonstone too. He brushed the tears from his eyes and simply said, "We will go when the storm dies, and the sun shines."

CHAPTER 23

All afternoon the winds gusted and shook the stable. We stayed buried in mounds of straw. I felt a mouse crawl along my leg and settle by my knee. I smiled. "Don't bite, little one," I said. "I'll share my bed with you, just don't bite." The critter quieted—to sleep, I hoped. Ossi chuckled.

"Good time to continue your story," I said as the wind rattled the boards.

Ossi thought for a moment before saying, "I decided to return to my people even though my separation journey was not over. I feared the marauders would return and club the last breath out of me. I also wanted to warn my people about the mauraders, and finally, I ached to be with my family while I performed the ancient burning ritual for Taika.

"My wounded back pained tremendously with every step I took. Hunched over in agony, I looked forward to my mother soothing poultices on my back and the *naiga* calling for the healing spirits to undo the damage that had me in agony. Everyone would dance the healing dance and chant the words that the *naiga* whispered over me. These thoughts kept me moving onward despite the pain."

I thought of my own journey, my fear of the farmer and the anger I felt toward my father. Ossi's journey had been much worse.

He continued. "But it was not to be. At first, the smoke I smelled told me that my village was nearby. When I got closer, the smell turned acrid and stung my nose and eyes. It was not the aroma of cooking fires that welcomed a weary traveler. When I made it to the edge of the woods surrounding our encampment, I stopped.

My heart stood still. Gone! Our bark and sod homes were rubble. Charred trees reached to the sky like ghastly skeletons. The gardens ruined. Smoke rose from the very ground. Nothing stirred except for vultures flying overhead."

Ossi stopped. I couldn't see him, but I imagined how this memory stung him. Sleeping rodents or not, I crawled from my straw bed and went over to the mound where Ossi huddled. "I'm sorry. I've never imagined something so wrenching could happen."

He reached out to me. In a muffled voice filled with pain, he said, "Wrap yourself in furs. Stay warm." Ossi patted my hand.

"There isn't much more to tell," he said. "The ravages of my village caused me such sadness that I vomited until my throat was raw and burning with acids. I wanted to die.

"I found the remains of my home. I chased vultures away while I carried rocks from the river and built cairns over the many mutilated bodies. Most were so badly burned I had no idea who they'd been. The heavy work gave me something to do. I was afraid if I quit, I would just lie down, cover myself in the ashes of my previous life, and beg the vultures to carry me away.

"The only solace I had was that my friend Gromske was safely away on his separation journey. My back slowly healed as the days went by, but I was aware of the great hump that remained. I was no longer able to stand straight. I put all my pain and grief into that hump and still carry it every day. It reminds me of my people, good as they were, yet the marauders who destroyed them. It is a burden that I lived, and they died.

"The first night I went into the forest to hide and get away from the ravages of my home. I made my bed on soft boughs. The scent of fir trees, mosses, and forest duff filled my lungs—so clean and needed after the smoke and ashes of my devastated village. Unable to sleep even though I was exhausted, I followed the arc of the near-full moon and was comforted by its ancient beams watching over me even as I grieved for my family, Oriina, Taika, and so many others.

"The day I finished covering all the bodies with piles of stones, I held a ceremony of farewell to all who had died. In our tradition, the oldest of the surviving family was the one who lead the ceremony. Young as I was, I was now that person. In the shadows of a late evening, I walked from cairn to cairn. I sang words of mourning for the spirits of the people. I sang words of hope for a new life for them. As I walked, I heard ghostly rustlings, murmurings, weeping, and pleas. I wasn't afraid. It was as it should have been. The voices of my people—alive in spirit.

And then I walked the whole village in silence. My shadow—if I had turned to see it—was that of an old man with a hunched back.

"As I lay down on deep forest mosses that night with the full moon above, I thought of my separation journey. Taika was dead. I was alone. On my journey, I always had the assuring thought of returning to my family, to my village, to Oriina. I was only eighteen years old. I had not received any dream, message, or call to what I would be. I had hoped for so much. Without a guiding spirit, without a calling, I was nothing, Just alone."

Ossi became silent for a long time. I waited, hollow inside, feeling for Ossi and knowing his story wasn't over.

"Each day I walked with the ghosts of my people, and at night I slept on soft forest mosses. I did that while hoping Gromske would return from his journey at the end of the summer, but the appointed full moon came and went. I waited for one more full cycle of the moon. He still didn't return. I feared the marauders had found him. I did not want to spend the winter in my burned-out village with all the shadows, wavering images, and voices of my people following me each day. I didn't know what to do or where to go. Spiritless and without direction, I hefted my pack and twirled with my eyes closed. When I started to stumble and fall, I opened my eyes and headed in the direction I was facing.

"I walked far and wide until the next full moon. Ahead of me were tall stone ridges, a river, and several caves carved into the ancient stone. Wolves sang in the distance. There I made my home. For twenty years I've lived in solitude and loneliness. It seemed fitting to me that I should live on the cold hard ledges of barren rock. The forest around me and the river than ran at the foot of my ledge provided all I needed. I mourned and lived in seclusion. Until one day, a canoe crashed into the rocks of the river near my cave. And Luna, there you were."

I reached for Ossi's hand. I remembered that day. Ossi with the long beard and floppy hat. Ossi with the soft eyes and gentle voice. Ossi who fed me. Watched over me. He'd given me so much when I needed someone. It must have painful for him to remember the destruction of all he'd loved. Yet he'd told me. Devastated as I was to hear it, he'd trusted me with his story. He'd been alone for so many years. I wondered. *Did he need me as much as I needed him?*

A bird softly cooed from the rafters. No mice scurried. Outside the wind silenced as though to honor his story.

CHAPTER 24

In the morning, we went out into the bright sunlight. The storm had given its best. We needed to leave. Our on-the-wing food supply was running low. We batted down as many birds as we could and roasted them. I tended the fire and wondered where we would go. Winter was already showing its fury. I worried how far we would wander in these strange lands in the midst of cold and snow having no idea how to find paths that led to my mother's people.

I stuffed the roasted pigeons and doves into a canvas bag we found in the stable. It was time to go. The sun sent glimmering streaks across the snow as we carried our packs and furs to the canoe. The river had frozen and was covered with snow, so Ossi unwound a length of rope from the stable and tied it from the canoe to his waist. As Ossi towed the canoe with our packs through the snow. I walked beside him.

We followed the river and sometimes walked on the frozen waterway where it had been wind-swept of snow. The only sounds were the crunch of our footsteps and the whisper of the canoe as it slid along behind us.

At night, we made camp under the sheltering branches of a spruce tree. In the morning, we melted snow for drink and ate one of the roasted birds. An owl hooted and snow drifted down on us from branches above. We slept.

Late on the fourth day of slogging through deep snow, a sharp wind howled out of the north. Ossi pulled the canoe under some trees, and we settled down for the night. The wind whistled and twirled great quantities of snow. We shivered in the piercing cold.

The next morning, we ate the last pigeon. We sucked the bones and chewed on the gristle. Then we set off along the frozen and heavily snow-covered river again. Struggling through knee-deep snow and towing the canoe tired us quickly so we made little progress. Ossi rubbed his back when we stopped. I asked if it hurt. "Not much," he said, but I didn't believe him.

My legs tingled and turned numb. Ossi often stumbled. We trudged that way, cold and out of food. I was afraid we'd soon be so completely exhausted and we'd crumple down into the snow and never get up again.

When I could barely lift my legs high enough to walk in Ossi's tracks, he stopped and pointed to the canoe. "Uutsi! Sit," he said.

I refused because I didn't want to add to Ossi's burden. Nevertheless, he insisted, led me to the canoe, and wrapped all the furs around me except for the one he wore around his shoulders. "Soon," he said trying to reassure me, "we'll find a place for food and shelter."

Or we'll both freeze to death.

After Ossi stumbled for about the fifth time, I called for him to come into the canoe to rest. He did. We huddled together hoping the storm would pass quickly.

I was trembling uncontrollably when a strong gust of blustery wind began whirling the canoe along the snow. Snowflakes swirled around us. I became dizzy as the canoe spun faster and faster.

In the eerie howling of the wind, I held Ossi close. For what seemed a long, long time, I wavered between sleep and a numb wakefulness as the wind spun the canoe through ever-deepening snow. When the storm finally calmed, we slid to a stop on a sloping drift. The canoe tilted. Once again, I fell out of the canoe into which I had been born. I shook myself to a new reality.

A stout woman stood above me saying, "Oh, me lordies above. What 'ave we 'ere?"

CHAPTER 25

The woman shivered and said, "Help me drag that man in from the cold. And ye. Come ye in too. I've a roaring fire. Sit by and warm ye-self."

Inside, she bent over Ossi saying, "Give me a hand an' let's git him in front of the fire. Wha' in the stars above are ye doin' out in this satanly weather?"

I stammered, trying to bring words to my frozen mouth, as the woman laid a shawl over Ossi. To me, she said, "Ye look frozen 'alf to death yeself. Keep an eye on yer pap there. Try an' rouse him a bit while he warms."

I thought to tell her he wasn't my pap, but the warmth of the fire comforted me, so I reached my hands and feet closer to thaw them.

"M'name's Huldor. This 'ere is my wayside inn. An' ye are?"

"I'm Luna," I said, the name still new to my tongue.

Before I could explain who Ossi was, she said, "Well, Luna, I be in the kitchen fixin' some spiced cider to warm yer innards. Ye keep warming yeself."

When she left, I sank to my knees next to Ossi. He lay so still I wasn't sure if he was asleep or on his way to the nether world of the dead. I pulled off his boots and birch bark leggings, then my own, too. I watched Ossi's chest slowly rise and lower with each breath. I was thankful he still lived.

Huldor brought mugs of steaming cider. Bits of spices I'd never tasted floated on the juice. Sweet and flavorful as the cider was, my stomach cramped. I tried to cheer myself as I sipped and thawed in the warmth of the fire.

After I finished the cider, I tapped Ossi on the shoulder. He did not waken. I lay my head on his chest. His heart beat unevenly and faintly. His breath rasped.

I begged him to open his eyes. Huldor tried to spoon warm cider into his mouth. At first he swallowed, but then sputtered and his mouth fell agape.

Huldor cried, "Oii, oii! Whatever shall we do? This man will surely die. Oii, oii!"

The moonstone warmed in my pocket. I held it hoping and wishing I could help Ossi. I held the stone to his chest. As I did so, a buzzing swarm of tingles came over me. The fireplace with its crackling flames and Huldor vanished as if a dream. The room around me glowed with swirling colors. I was in a realm of floating lights and gentle winds singing. Words came to me. From where I do not know, but I sang them into Ossi's ear.

> *Glow like moonlight*
> *Sacred stone.*
> *Blessed stone.*
> *Thaw the frost.*
> *Melt the ice of winter's claws*
> *That binds Ossi to the frozen realms.*
> *Bring breath song on warm winds*
> *Bring heart song from drumming of phantom wings.*
> *Warm frozen flesh.*
> *Send coursing, reviving life-blood through his veins.*
> *Heal all wounds.*
> *Draw pain from every limb. Fling it to the deeps.*
> *Glow like moonlight*
> *Sacred stone.*
> *Blessed stone.*

I tapped his chest, willing his heart to find an even rhythm. I breathed deeply, willing his breath to come easily. My fingers and toes tingled. I saw images of him as a young man. Strong. Vital. Brave.

Everything I had whispered to Ossi, everything I had done, had come as naturally as if I had done the same every day of my life. As I said the words, I felt each one. Songs of healing filled me. Gentle winds led my hands. A steady, surreal buzzing washed over my body. My whole being felt charged with the energy of life. I smelled summer forests and flowers. I tasted sweet saps, pungent herbs, and golden honey.

Like lake mists on an early autumn morning, I saw the cold dissolve and rise from Ossi's blood and bones. I felt the bite of ice leave him. I saw his breath come easier. I saw, as if I was looking into his chest, his heart warm and beat stronger, sending life-giving blood throughout his body. I held my hand over the moon-stone on his chest feeling his heart beat as strongly as ever.

My head cleared of the buzzing. The realm of floating lights and gentle winds faded, and I became aware of the hard floor beneath me; the crackling of flames in the fireplace, and Huldor pouring cider. One of Ossi's eyelids flickered. I slid the moonstone back into my pocket as a wincing pain cramped my own stomach.

CHAPTER 26

Ossi slept by the fire. I stayed by his side watching each breath he took until Huldor insisted I sit at a long plank table. A white tablecloth with embroidery of blue and violet flowers formed a circle in the middle where a large bowl of nuts sat. I'd never seen anything like it.

Huldor fascinated me as she waddled about making sure I was warm and fed. She was as kind as the potato-cake woman had been. Her cheeks were rosy and her nose a bit lopsided. She was no taller than I was. Long dark braids were pinned around her head. She peered over a pair of thin rimmed spectacles. Over her nubby wool dress, she wore a white apron.

When Father and I had gone to the Harvest Moon Festivals, I had tried to imagine what the houses in the hamlet were like inside, but I never could have guessed anything this wonderful. Ten chairs stood around the table. Smaller tables had lacy white things under oil lanterns. An orange cat slept on top of yarn balls in a basket. A picture of sheep in a meadow hung on one wall.

Huldor came out of her kitchen carrying a bowl of barley soup with root vegetables and a mug of pungent tea. "This winter has been harsh," she said, "I've not a guest 'til ye arrived."

Despite the goodness of the soup Huldor set before me, despite the warmth of the fire crackling in the stone fireplace, despite the cheeriness of the inn woman, I was feeling sharp spasms in my stomach. I felt increasingly queasy and out of sorts. I thought the cramping was caused by the hunger and cold I'd suffered for many days. Finally, all the strange goings-on in my body were too much to bear. I stood—my soup only half-eaten—wondering where to find an outhouse.

I found Huldor in the kitchen, but I didn't know the right words to use. At the festivals, I'd heard people say things like pot closet, biffy, toilet, pee pot, outhouse, latrine, and shat shack. I fumbled for words. Huldor took my hand and led me to a small room at a far corner of the house. "Ye be needin' to spend some time in the biffy?" she asked. I breathed a sigh of relief.

Huldor closed the door. "I be right out 'ere if ye be wantin' anything."

It didn't take long before I noticed something unusual. I panicked. My heart raced. Was I dying? I cried out in distress. Huldor was instantly there asking, "What is it, me darlin' girl?"

I pointed and cried again.

"Oh, lovey girl. Tis as natural as the moon in the sky." She took my hand and asked, "Never 'appen before?"

I shook my head and groaned.

She led me up some stairs to her bed chamber as though she did this sort of thing every day, and it was the most ordinary thing ever. She explained, "We'll get ye fixed up an' feeling better in no time. First of all, let's tear ye up some moon rags from this old bed coverin'. I spose ye be wonderin' what's this all about. Ye's now turnin' into a woman and ye needs to know about womanly things."

Her warmth. Her kindness. Her caring. All of it eased my suffering. I was greatly relieved to learn that I was not dying and this was a natural happening. As we tore strips to make the moon rags, she told me to note the phase of the moon when this all happened, because it very well would happen every time the moon was about in the same phase. She told me what herbs to use for teas during that moon phase to ease the aching, "bad humors or just plain old grumpiness."

She asked how old I was. "Fourteen," I said, thinking of the slashes Father carved in the log wall of our hut.

"Well, that be about right. Any age betwixt twelve and thirteen. Ye being so skinny, and not fed well for a long time—maybe even fourteen is when the moon bloods begin."

Huldor also explained something she called the "sweetly singin' birds and the bumblin' bees." She ended by saying I was now a beautiful flower that—if I didn't behave myself and spurn lazy drones that would buzz around me—could turn into a plump fruit. Most of what she said made no sense to me, but then I thought of the mayor's daughter. Maybe? Still, I didn't really understand it all. It seemed impossible. Like a Father or All-Seeing Eye story. She also told me about all the changes to my body that'd happen as I grew into a "proper young woman". *Oh, so that's how I'll get breasts.*

As Huldor fussed over me, she told me about a celebration her kinfolk held when the moon bloods began for a girl. "We called it *moonflow*. The elder women who no longer experienced moonflow took the girl to a pond encircled by seven ancient cedars. The trees exuded a heady aroma. When it was me turn, the women gave me a quaff to drink then directed me to bathe in the pond waters. While I washed me-self, they sang throaty songs an' danced a circle aroun' the pond. I felt the waters cleanse me as I breathed in the deep cedar fragrance. I soon felt a swirlin' an' a tinglin' through my whole body, and then a feelin' of leavin' the pond an' floatin' in the ether of the eternal skies. When I returned to me senses, I had a white robe made of the finest lamb's wool wrapped around me. The women then served me a tea brewed of burdock root."

She raised her eyes to look at me and chuckled. "Don't ye worry. I have no burdock root, an' the nearest pond be frozen."

After I returned to the table, Huldor set a plate of warm tarts before me. "Here ye are. Sugar-plum jam tarts, they be. Picked the berries, made the jam with bee honey, an' now they is tarts on the platter. Eat as many as ye be likin'."

I was feeling much relieved but still crampy.

Huldor leaned over Ossi and said, "He sleeps like a bear in the deepest winter," and then she hustled to her kitchen to brew a special herbal broth for me.

"Sip it slowly now," she cautioned afterward. "Let it warm ye an' relax yer woman innards. Better yet, sit again by the fire an' let the dancin' flames mesmerize ye into a different world."

I carried the broth to sit by the fire. Ossi still dozed. My pack was close by, so I opened it and took out my mother's dictionary. I turned the pages until I found words like moon, moon tide, and then moonflow.

> *Moonflow: Oh, how I suffer with cramping and pain.*
> *My mother called it the curse women must bear*
> *In order to birth beautiful babies.*
> *Why can't be we have a blessing instead of a curse?*

I had been puzzled by so much of what Huldor said. At least I now knew that the moonflow was connected to babies.

Ossi groaned in his sleep. I worried that he slept so much. I asked Huldor, "Do you think Ossi'll be all right? He worked so hard pulling me in the canoe and toiling through the deep snow."

Huldor stopped clearing the table and asked, "What did ye call 'im?"

"Ossi," I said. "He's been so good to me. I hope he'll get better."

Huldor removed Ossi's big floppy hat and looked closely at his face, mostly covered by his huge bushy beard and eyebrows. "He being yer father?"

"No, but he fed me and took care of me after I crashed my canoe. Even though we speak different languages, our moonstones are magic or something, because if we both have them close, we understand each other."

Huldor nodded. "I knew an Ossi way back when I was a girl an' lived with me people." She wiped her eyes as she told how she'd liked him and always tried to get his attention. She looked at his ears. Were they the same? Could she even remember after twenty some years? Huldor wondered how he got the huge hump on his back or if he'd always had it. If that were so, he was not the Ossi she'd known. She examined his hands. "They look different," she said, but then she put her hands next to his to show how hard work could change one's youthful hands into knobby ones. "I wish he'd open his eyes. Those wouldn't change, would they?"

"They're blue," I said. "A warm blue."

Ossi snored quietly.

"Do ye remember eny of the words he spoke?" Huldor asked. "I spoke a different language as a child, too. If he spoke that same language, we'd know fer sure." She chuckled, then added, "If he's that same Ossi, he'd never know me now, jest like I don't know if he's the Ossi I liked so much."

I thought back, trying to remember Ossi's strange words. One he'd used many times came to mind. "The word he used when he wanted me to eat was something like od-ys, ol-ys or an-ys," I told her. "I don't think I'm saying it right."

Huldor shook her head. "He must not be the Ossi I knew."

CHAPTER 27

I stayed by Ossi throughout the night dozing on and off. I awoke at times to hear Huldor humming and chanting in a low voice. I didn't understand, but to me, her words were filled with goodness and healing. Her hum swirled with the warmth of the fire. I relaxed and swayed as though I was a branch in the breeze.

In the morning while Ossi still slept, I got up to stretch my sore muscles. I tip-toed to look out the window. No snow fell. A raven perched in a tree.

As I put a log on the dying fire, Huldor brought out mugs of tea, and Ossi awoke. The tea wafted aromas of mint, chamomile, and something else. Ossi swallowed the liquid and stretched as though warding off stiffness.

Huldor smiled as she helped Ossi to a chair. "There. There. That's better now, isn't it? Ye'll be up an' dancin' afore ye know it."

I myself must have been smiling from ear to ear as I took one of his hands and words of relief tumbled from my mouth. "Ossi, look where we are. In a real house. We made it through that terrible storm. This kind woman thawed us by her great fire. I was so worried when you slept the sleep of the dying. What would I do without you? You were frozen half to death and that was my fault. I'm glad you live."

Ossi patted me on the shoulder and then bowed to the Huldor and said, "So-ti-ik."

Huldor looked at him. "Ye speak me old language," she said. "The language of m'ancients." The she said words in the language I didn't understand.

Ossi's eyes opened wide. I took out my moonstone so I could hold it while he spoke his strange and beautiful words. "My name is Ossi. My home was destroyed by marauders when I was away on my separation journey. It is twenty years or more since I have encountered anyone who speaks my language."

Huldor looked deeply into Ossi's eyes and said in that same language, "My people, too, were destroyed by a band of brigands. Ossi is the name of a young man I liked very much. He was a friend of my brother." And then she sang her story as Ossi had sung his.

The full moon and the beauty of the stars
Belied what happened that dreadful night
When young Aivo screamed and cried,
"They come. They come."
Aivo died there in the center of our village
With a piercing blade in his back and
The alert still in his mouth.

In the dimness of the night
A rabble, a fierce horde rushed our village
Gnashing their teeth. Torching everything.
Father yelled, "Run! Hide!"

I ran but before I could hide,
Strong arms grappled me to the earth.
A booted foot on my chest held me down.
A blade to my throat kept me silent.
I heard screams. Agonized cries.
The thud of bludgeons.
The cracking of skulls.
I prayed for death to be sudden there
Under the boot of the marauder.

Captors tied me and Etta Carina to trees.
From there we watched the destruction of our families,
Our hopes and dreams.
The fires that burned our homes burned indelible images into my eyes.

The raiders hefted the bodies of our loved ones onto flaming pyres.
The fires burned my heart, leaving it smoldering in my very chest.
In the end, our village was but ashes.

The wind picked up and swirled the ashes
They landed on me.
They landed on my friend.
The barbarians smudged ashes on their faces
And danced a horrific dance in the glow of the dawning sun.
I retched—tasting ash and smoke—the remains of my people and my life.

Our captors carried me and Etta Carina to their far-away village.
They tied us to wooden stakes on a wooden platform.
Many came. They poked and prodded.
Stripped us of our clothes and dignity.
Looked into our mouths. Felt our teeth.
And then the bidding started.

Etta paled with fear,
But she stood tall and looked over the crowd to the skies.
Some laughed and pointed at her saying,
"You'd have to pay me to take her.
Her with the twisted leg!"
The seller called out, "Never mind her leg.
Look at her face. Her strong teeth and back.
And she's of the age to bear a child when the comet comes!"
The bidding stalled. No one wanted to buy one so lame.
Then a young man came forward.
He dressed, not like a scallywag, as so many were,
but in a fancy robe.
He bid, not silver or gold coins, but the horse he rode.
He untied Etta Carina, removed his robe, and wrapped it around her.
Then he took her hand and they walked away together.

When it was my turn,
I cringed with fear shrinking before all the eyes.

Quaking until my legs no longer held,
I fell to my knees.
When it was over,
I was forced to go with a stinking man
Who tied a rope around my neck and led me away.
He had black teeth and spit gobs of tobacco upon my feet
Laughing. Hooting and hollering,
"I soon be father to a Comet child!"

As Huldor spoke, Ossi shut his eyes as though he was trying to block the horrific images of his tortured people. His brow furled. His jaw clenched. A soft moan escaped his lips. My breath caught, and I, too, groaned as I remembered the story Ossi told of returning to his village to see everything destroyed and his family dead.

My life with the wicked man was all pain, injury,
Beatings and hard work.
In the year the great comet passed our night sky
With its luminescent tail glowing, portending the birth of a child.
Child of the Comet. Child of the prophesies.
Child born special to have great gifts.
I wanted no child of the rotted-toothed man.
So, I swallowed potions.
I was no longer Oriina of the Ice People.
I became Huldor of the odious man.
When Huldor finished, Ossi wiped his eyes and said, "Your story is my story. I am
Ossi of your childhood. You are Oriina—my friend's sister."

Huldor replied, "That dirty man who led me away on a rope ne'er asked m'name. Jest called me Huldor. Made me talk his language. Took so much from me. The Oriina of my young years is long gone. I am Huldor now."

Ossi reached to hold her hand. "You are Gromske's sister. I hoped to take you as a bride when I returned from my journey."

Huldor clasped her other hand to her heart. "After so many years! I never dared even a little 'ope to ever see you agin. An' now ye be 'ere."

My heart warmed as I listened to them recount good memories. Memories of their days in the sunshine picking berries, fishing in clear streams, and watching the stars and moon drift along the night skies. Ossi told Huldor his whole story. I half listened while turning pages in my mother's dictionary. I found the word *marauder.*

A painful memory stabs me as I think of the day intruders attacked our village.
Marauders: They stole. They burned. They clubbed and killed.
Nothing remained, but ashes and ruin.

I fingered stains on the page. Tear stains? Had my mother cried as she wrote that? Her village had been plundered and people killed, the same as Huldor's and Ossi's. Could it be . . . ? I closed the dictionary as Ossi said to Huldor, "I have no idea what happened to Gromske, your brother. I waited at our destroyed village for him to return. I even waited a full moon cycle past when he should have returned. He never did. Maybe marauders killed him too. You and I and Etta Carina are maybe the only ones who survived."

CHAPTER 28

For an instant I had hoped, but it wasn't so. If Etta Carina, Ossi and Huldor were the only ones from their village to survive, then my mother hadn't been from their village. Ossi and Huldor dabbed their eyes and nose, and I wondered how many villages the marauders had destroyed. I, too, was sad thinking of how many lives had been lost, and how many years Ossi and Huldor had spent apart with just their memories.

My stomach grumbled in hunger. Huldor laughed and said, "Oo-ee. We need a bite of vittles to fill our bellies. Fine inn keeper I am." She shuffled into the kitchen and came out with bowls of ground oats cooked with cream and maple syrup, a dozen hard-boiled eggs, tarts left over from the day before, and a pot of steaming tea.

As we ate, Huldor said to Ossi, "Your eyes are the same, but I never would have recognized you. Your long beard covers so much of your face and your eyebrows have grown bushy."

Ossi laughed. "There wasn't much reason to scrape off my beard when I was alone those twenty years. Maybe I will now."

"And 'ave I changed so much that ye didn't remember me?" Huldor asked.

"I haven't been alive enough until now to consider the possibility," Ossi said holding his moonstone so I could understand. "But now, I see your smile hasn't changed, but you used to find more use for it back when you were playing pranks on me and your brother."

"Ooof! Don't remind me. I was envious that me brother 'ad such a good friend. I wanted to be part of yer adventures rather than stuck doin' the chores Mother found for me. The only way I knew how to get yer attention was to play mischief around ye." Her eyes sparkled as she looked at Ossi.

We were clearing the table when Huldor said, "I wonder what ever happened to Etta Carina. I 'ope that fancy man in the robe was good and not a stinkin' beast."

I perked up to listen. When Ossi had drawn the two pictures on the stone, I hadn't understood the words *Etta Carina*. Now he and Huldor were saying it was the name of a childhood friend. *Could it be? No, my mother's name was Alcyone.*

Ossi looked at me, then he said to Huldor, "Have you looked at Luna? It's possible that my memory isn't so good after being clubbed on the head, but I still remember Etta Carina, and Luna looks just like her."

Huldor stopped brushing crumbs from the table and came to me. She peered at me, her eyes above her spectacles. "I don't know," she said. "Me eyes aren't so good anymore. These lenses help, but everything is still fuzziness."

"From the first moment I saw her, I have been reminded of Etta Carina. Not only does she look like Etta, but she smiles like her, and her hair is the same color. Her father was a professor with a fancy robe. It can't all be coincidence."

"Well," Huldor said, "that would be wonderful!" She turned to me and asked, "What of yer mother? Was her name Etta Carina?"

I brushed the hair out of my eyes. If that had been her name, Ossi and Huldor would be of her people—the people I was looking for. Wanting to believe that I'd found two of my mother's people, yet doubting, I said, "Father never said my mother was lame. She died when I was born. Her name was Alcyone."

CHAPTER 29

The wind picked up, and more snow fell. Huldor looked out at the storm and said, "With these drifts, the lads from down the lane not be comin' to do me chores. I have chickens, rabbits an' goats. I be needin' to wade through the snow to feed them soon."

Ossi said. "I'll do the outdoor work."

"Oh, no, you be needin' to rest and heal."

"I'll help," I said remembering that Father had sold me to be a milkmaid on a farm. I had run from the farmer, but I wouldn't mind helping Huldor and Ossi.

I gladly carried armloads of wood from an outdoor shed and filled the box by the door while Ossi and Huldor went to the barns so she could show him what chores needed to be done.

After all the meals and chores were done, Huldor said, "Tonight you'll have a real bed. No more sleeping in front of the fire." She looked at my pack made of birch bark and skunk fur. "I'm sposing ye not be 'aving a night dress in there. Jest a moment an' I find ye one." She came back carrying a long dress. "Sheep's wool. Warm as can be."

I made a last trip to the biffy and washed in the basin of warm water Huldor set out for me. I had never slept in such a bed with a frame that raised it off the floor. And a quilt filled with feathers for a covering! I had slept in a loft on corn shucks, in a tree trunk, in a puppy nest, in my canoe, on a fur-covered ledge at Ossi's, and in piles of straw. Now a real bed! I sank into warmth, softness and glorious comfort.

After a huge breakfast the next morning, Huldor applied a thick poultice to Ossi's skin before he went to care for the animals. Huldor sent me to straighten the beds while she washed the dishes. When Ossi came in with a basket of eggs and a jug of fresh milk, Huldor said, "Time to put up our feet an' 'ave some tea."

When we were comfortable in chairs around the fireplace, I opened my mother's dictionary to the Es where I had found words like eternity and ethereal. Now I looked for and found *Etta Carina*. My heart beat faster. I held my breath as I read.

Etta Carina
A star in the constellation Carina.
Brighter than most stars.
Brighter than the sun.
Dear husband did not like that I was named for such a distant star.
He renamed me Alcyone, a star closer to Polaris in the sky.

Excited, my heart beat faster. My mother had been Ella Carina! She had been from the Ossi's devastated village! He and Huldor had known her. She had been lame. She had died giving birth to me, and my twin must have died with her.

Showing the page to Ossi and Huldor, I said, "My mother was Etta Carina."

Ossi said, "It had to be because you look so much like her. I'm happy to have known your mother, but I'm sad that she no longer lives."

Huldor held me in her arms. Her warmth, her softness, her gentleness brought tears to my eyes.

"I want to know about my mother. How she became lame. And everything else." I was with her people. The people I'd sought. I felt as though I'd been swept off my feet. I wanted to inhale everything they knew. I was thrilled. I had found two of my mother's people!

"One spring when Etta Carina was very young," Ossi began, "she and her mother were swept downstream by sheets of frozen ice that had broken loose during the thaw. Jagged wedges of ice crushed Etta's mother to her death and twisted the life from Etta's own leg."

The crackling fire and hiss of the kettle brought us to the present. Huldor rose to pour more tea. We nibbled leftover tarts. Huldor and Ossi tried to sort out the jumble of their memories. Ossi continued my mother's story. "Her grand-pap carved braces for her leg—each one larger than the last as she grew. Even though she couldn't climb trees, she was quicker than anyone else when it came to learning lessons."

Huldor interrupted. "And much quicker than meself. She used to teach me new words. Hard ones. An' remember, she knew the names of all the plants below our feet an' of all the stars above. Her grandmam and pap taught 'er everything, all the time. She could've been a professor 'erself. Smart, she was. Right smart."

"Didn't she ever have fun playing with the rest of you?"

"Oh, we all had fun all right," Ossi said, "but she couldn't run and tumble like we did. When we gathered reeds in the wetlands, we brought armloads home. We all sat while our grandmams taught us how to weave mats, baskets, and shoes. Your mother's fingers flew while she wove. Her weavings were beautiful. And she was the best at making up songs with beautiful melodies. Her father made her whistles and flutes from the willow tree. She could tootle tunes as quick as a wink. When we made up guessing games and riddles, Etta was the best again."

Huldor added, "An' ooof, she could 'ave been a poet. She knew lots of fancy words an' could recite 'er whole family lineage back enough generations to count on all my fingers an' toes."

As I listened to stories of my mother, images formed in my mind, and she became real to me. It was as if I could see her and peek into the days of her life. I was happy beyond anything I'd ever felt! I was with my mother's people. Ossi and Huldor were the only ones of her village who still lived. I looked at Ossi and my heart warmed. I looked at Huldor. Her kindness filled the whole room. While the storm roared and raged outside, I was warm, safe, and as contented as could be with them.

CHAPTER 30

The wind blew furiously. Tree branches slapped the windows. A raven huddled with his back to the trunk of a tree. I felt sorry for him and all the animals suffering in the storm.

We stayed warm by the fire. Ossi asked Huldor what life had been like with the man who bought her. She stirred honey into her tea, then spoke.

"Oh, woe was me that day. I 'ad thought the worst thing that could 'appen 'ad already when I saw me mam an' pap bludgeoned before me very eyes an' the whole village burned. Little did I know that an unholy 'ell was yet in me stars. That 'orrible day, he walked and dragged me for a long distance. I begged for 'im to untie me. As we plodded along, and for all the rest of his days 'ere on earth, he shouted names to me like rag bottom, flea bitten, ugly-muggly, rubbish brain, an' worse that I shan't repeat. He spat chewy tobakky to the wind in such a way that it spattered me hair an' clothes. Soon, I was a sweaty, stinkin mess, just like 'im.

My heart sank as I listened to the pain and humiliation Huldor had suffered.

"Every day I planned me escape. Decided that as soon as he trusted me enough to untie me, I'd bolt. Well, months an' years went by. He never left me alone untethered. I worked 'is farm. Slopped 'is pigs an' cleaned the sty. I shoveled chicken droppings from the hen house. Cooked 'is meals. Spat in 'em every noontime when he wasn't lookin'. I learnt to talk 'is language like I do now. One day, he insisted we go to the river an' scrub ourselves shiny. He said a travelin' preacher man had come to our village and we was goin' an' get all legal an' married."

Huldor put down her knitting and cleared her throat. Her furry orange cat jumped onto my lap at that moment. It circled, lay down, and purred as I stroked its soft fur. I imagined the horrible man and was reminded of the farmer who'd bought me from Father. I clenched my hands and was glad I'd clobbered him with the paddle.

"On our way to the village I decided to be all nice an' go through the ceremony. Then he might trust me enough to stop tyin' me up. The preacher man looked twice at me all roped up aroun' the neck, but he still went on sayin' the words to marry us in the eyes of 'is god. After we said *I do*, mister preacher man looked at the rope aroun' me neck. He smiled as he said, 'You are now bound together until death do ye part.'

"Those were me favorite words of the whole thing. They gave me an idea. Death would part us. An' it wouldn't be mine."

Huldor crossed her arms over her chest. "All's said an' all's done." With that she picked up her knitting again.

I wondered what had happened to the man who'd tied the rope around her neck and led her into his life. I wondered how she'd come into possession of such a fine inn. Those were stories I hoped she'd tell us, but Ossi didn't ask, so neither did I.

"Time to get some vittles ready," Huldor said.

"I'll help." I wanted to cook and bake along with Huldor to learn the secrets of such delicious foods and teas. Besides being with Huldor, I liked the warmth and glorious smell of her kitchen.

"Thank ye. I do be needing help. Come along."

Her kitchen and scullery were something I could never have dreamed. Gleaming copper pots hung from hooks along one wall of the huge room. Not a single one was dented. A twig broom stood in the corner. A big iron stove took up much of the wall across from the pots and pans.

"We's be needin' some provisions. Follow me an' I'll show you where they are." Huldor led me to a separate room off the kitchen that was cold as could be. "This 'ere be me cold-storage larder."

A skinned rabbit and chunks of meat hung from hooks. Bins held rutabagas, potatoes, and beets. Cabbages lined a shelf, as did baskets of carrots, apples and plums. On a higher shelf was a tin lettered CORNMEAL. Another RYE, a third

OATS, a fourth BARLEY. Clay jars labeled BUTTER, HONEY and MOLASSES rested next to each other. I never could have dreamed such an abundance of foods. Huldor dropped a cabbage into my arms then filled her own.

"Now to the scullery," she said after we stacked everything on a table. In a room off the other side of the kitchen, there were a dozen or more knives in a rack as well as a saw and a cleaver hanging from nails. My mouth gaped at the sights.

"Me tools of cookin'," she said with a proud smile. "Ye'll find none better fer miles around."

A grinder. An apple peeler. Rolling pins. A dough box. A clay jar for yeast. Butter churn. Bowls of every size were on shelves alongside pitchers, tureens, ewers, mugs, plates, platters, and a basket of tableware. I touched everything and repeated the names after Huldor.

She handed me a big knife and a chopping board and showed me how to shred the cabbage. While I chopped, she took down a deep pot, filled it with water from the barrel she and Ossi had carried in from the pump while doing chores. She put it on the stove top. With a cleaver, she whacked three pig knuckles in half and put them in the water with some garlic cloves and whole onions she'd taken from a bag hanging from the wall. Then she cut carrots into big chunks and added them.

Soon the cabbage, carrots, and onions bubbled in the pot and the pig knuckles stewed. The kitchen air filled with steam and aroma. My mouth watered as I thought of the delicious feast we'd have that evening.

"Now we make some biscuits to sop gravies," Huldor said. She showed me how to crack an egg. "We be needin' two more, so ye crack 'em into that bowl while I see to the flour."

I was dipping my fingers into the slippery cracked eggs, trying to catch pieces of shell that had fallen in when Huldor noticed. "Never snag 'em that way," she said showing me how to use another piece of shell to scoop up the little ones. I helped stir the flour, baking powder, salt, eggs, and milk together in a blue crackle-glazed bowl.

When that was done, Huldor taught me how to knead in some pork cracklin'. "Fer flavor, pork can't be bested." I helped her grease a flat baking pan with a slab of bacon and we dropped spoons of biscuit dough onto it.

When those were baking, the pig knuckles stewing, and the cabbage simmering, I thought we were done, but Huldor said, "Now let's get some corn puddin' on the stove. Spoon on some honey an' we'll have a perfect sweet to end our sup!"

All the time we worked, Huldor explained why she did things the way she did and why she added certain ingredients. I listened eagerly. Father and I had roasted rabbits and squirrels over an open fire outside. We'd made teas from leaves and roots. We'd made mushes from ground oats and ryes, but we'd never had a kitchen, a cold larder, or a scullery with peelers, grinders, and scrapers with which to do all those things.

As I breathed in the heady aromas of Huldor's kitchen, I thought of the potato-cake woman who had crouched beside a fire on the ground to made delicious fried cakes. When her cakes turned from grey globs into crispy golden delicious-ness, it had seemed like pure magic to me.

CHAPTER 31

The next day the wind still buffeted and rattled against the window panes, and snow fell constantly. Huldor kept me busy in the kitchen before mealtimes explaining more to me about cooking and baking. In between meals, Ossi cared for the animals and Huldor tried to teach me to knit. She gave me two big wooden needles with a ball of yarn and showed me how to hold the needles, cast on the yarn with hopes of knitting a muffler. My hands refused to grasp what I needed to do. One needle or the other fell. The yarn rolled across the floor. The orange cat chased it. My cast-on stitches were uneven. I wasn't knitting. I was knotting. My hands cramped and rebelled. I was thankful when it was time to start the evening meal.

"Maybe if I had a loom, ye'd find yer talent with weavin' like yer mother," Huldor said. "For now, fetch the rabbit hanging in the cold larder."

I hurried to make up for the complete failure I'd been at knitting. She'd been ever so patient and kind as I dropped, knotted, and made big snarls. I thanked all the moons of Jupiter, as Father had often done, that I was better in the kitchen. "An' bring a couple rutabagas, carrots, an' onions," she called to me. "After we get them roastin' in the oven, we'll git some sweetness ready too. I'm goin' to jist sit 'ere on this stool while ye do all the choppin' an' mixin.'"

Excited that Huldor trusted me, I went into the scullery to crush dried bread into crumbs with a rolling pin. Next, I washed, cored, peeled, and sliced apples. After spreading lard on a baking pan and mixing the bread crumbs and apple slices with cranberries and raisins, I added a handful of brown sugar. Then I stirred in a

163

quick pour of cream and three eggs. I spread the dough on the baking pan, drizzled it with melted butter and sprinkled the top with more crumbs and a spice I thought was absolutely heavenly—cinnamon.

"Perfect as a summer day with wild roses bloomin.'" Huldor patted me on the shoulder and smiled. "Now we 'ave time for some tea while we wait fer it all to roast and bake."

We settled by the fire. I took out the letter my mother had written so long ago. I read it over and over, wondering about the twin I might have. And if I did, how would I ever find her? Wearing my mother's dress, holding her dictionary, and reading her letter brought me sorrow. I was touching things she'd touched. I didn't have any of my own memories of her. I tried to imagine her living in the hut with Father, traveling to the harvest festivals, and singing under the chestnut trees. And, most of all, I liked imagining her being friends with the potato-cake woman, Huldor, and Ossi.

As the harsh winter roared outside, Huldor, Ossi, and I sat together by the fire. I leaned my shoulder against Ossi's because I noticed that Huldor was doing the same. Ossi's skin healed with the poultices Huldor gently daubed on his face morning and night. Ossi didn't like the poultices, but I noticed he did like the closeness of Huldor while she dabbed his skin. She always smelled of wood smoke, fresh bread, onion, garlic, basil, cedar, or whatever else she'd been cooking up in her big kitchen. I even liked that.

When not busy in the kitchen, and to avoid the knitting needles, I began helping Ossi with the outdoor chores. There were three nanny goats to be fed and milked. I poured some of their fresh creamy milk for the barn cats and the stray dog that slept with the cats in the haymow. A busy warren of rabbits needed daily cleaning, as did the goat shed and chicken coop. Ossi did the cleaning while I fed and watered the rabbits and chickens and collected eggs. Together we spread fresh straw for their bedding.

The goat shed, the rabbit warren, and the chicken coop offered shelter for the animals and a second haven for me. I stroked and tickled the cats—there were four—as they purred and rubbed against me. Little by little the stray dog got used to me and Ossi, and soon he was coming to lie next to me in a pile of straw along with the cats.

When we were done with all the chores, we'd go to the goat shed. There, we'd sit in the straw to talk. The goats maa-aa-ed and nuzzled us. One nanny tried to chew on my clothes like potato-cake woman's goat had.

One day, Ossi split some wood into thin sheets. I held the pieces while he shaped them with a plane. Then he put the pieces together to make little huts that looked almost like the brood boxes the chickens used to hatch their eggs.

"Why are we doing this?" I asked.

"Nestings for baby bunnies," Ossi answered.

My eyes opened wide. "Are there babies?"

"Not yet, but come the melting of the snow, you can count on it."

A warm feeling came over me. I was happier with Ossi and Huldor than I'd ever been. They were my mother's people. When I tried to remember Father, my chest squeezed. I'd imagine him, not sitting around our fire telling stories, but zigzagging around stars, trying to escape the farmer.

That evening I paged through *Alcyone's Dictionary* as we sat together. I flipped to the pages with words starting with *w*. In between *wife, wild rose,* and *wish,* I found what I was looking for.

> *Wind Song is harmony in the heart. Contentment.*
> *It is a place to carry with you wherever you go.*
> *If not, it is something to seek.*

Wind Song was a feeling. I read the words again. Here, at the inn, with Ossi and Huldor, I felt wanted and cared for. Was wind song what my mother hadn't felt with my father, and why she wanted to be with her people to give birth?

Ossi was so many things my father hadn't been. He never tired of my questions. He never scolded if I spilled water. His words were always gentle. He never had impossible moods. One day when we were resting in the straw, he asked, "What was your father like?"

What was he like? Complicated and unpredictable, but more, too. "When he was in the right mood, he told me fantastic stories. We fished together, scoured the woods for food. He taught me about the plants beneath our feet and the stars over our heads. At other times, he became stony cold and distant—like he was far away in another world. He wouldn't talk. He drank his elixirs and didn't eat. I didn't think he really cared about me.

"I was shattered when he told me he'd hoped my birth in the year of the comet would bring me great gifts, and he was unhappy because I hadn't shown anything that could be used to enrich ourselves. He grieved for my mother greatly and maybe even wished that she'd lived and I hadn't. When he sold me to the farmer and left to search for my mother in the stars of the Pleiades, I felt like the weed he'd named me for—purslane—something to be trod upon and pulled up by the roots and tossed aside.

"Maybe he's still wandering and looking for a way to propel himself to the skies. I wish he'd always told me the truth instead of making up stories. Despite all that, he was a good man in some ways. Mother was lucky he led her away, rather than the man Huldor suffered."

I took a deep breath. I'd said words I didn't think I'd ever say out loud. Ossi nodded. He was gentle in his ways of handling the animals and teaching me. I could depend on his stories to be true. Even though he stooped with a huge hump on his back and his skin wept from being frozen on our journey, he didn't complain or drink from bottles of elixirs and tonics to soothe his aches and pains. He must have been lonely and missing his family for many years. I was glad he and Huldor had found each other again.

A sudden thought came to me. *Ossi is so steadfast and reliable that he could be the North Star—the Polaris who my father wanted to be, but wasn't.*

Another day while we were resting in the straw, I asked, "What are the prophesies of your people—our people? The ones about children born when the great comet passed through the night sky?"

"Why do you ask?"

"I have a letter my mother wrote when I was still in her watery womb. She said she'd give birth when the great comet passed through the skies."

"The comet! On the year you were born. . . ." Ossie paused and scratched his head. "Yes, the Ice People, my people and yours, told prophecies and stories about the comet."

"Tell me what you know. I want to hear the prophecy. What does it mean to be born of the comet? Father hoped I'd have special skills, but was disappointed when I didn't show signs as I grew. How am I supposed to feel? How am I supposed to know?"

CHAPTER 32

Ossi lay back in the straw and began telling me what he remembered. "Our people repeated the prophecies over the evening fires. We sang, too. Songs about heroes of the past who'd done good deeds. And of scoundrels who hadn't.

"My father told me, 'You have the owl for your spirit guide, but you must listen and learn from the ancients, too.' That was one of the prophecies. By honoring our ancestors and their ways and wisdom, we would always have a guiding light. Another was that we should care for and live softly on Mother Earth. If we didn't, her beauty would fade and she would have no more to give us.

"After my village was destroyed, it was too painful to recall what I had lost—my family's faces lit by evening fires and their songs rising in evening mists. I never again let the prophecies, the stories, or the songs linger in my memories until now you asked."

I felt his sorrow. His family and spirit animal had been killed. He was doomed to walk hunched over in pain, carrying the huge burden of his wound and his failures.

The moonstone warmed in my pocket as Ossi continued, "Another prophecy was to beware of those who use trickery or enchantments to enrich themselves or to gain power over you. And if I remember rightly, the final prophecy was about children born when the great comet was seen in the star sky. You could be born knowing songs of healing or with visions of foresight. As you get older, you could become a dreamer of dreams, a seer into the past and future, a healer, an enchanter of words, or you could ply any of the mystical arts or so many other things I can't remember."

My moonstone warmed more. For a long time, I sank into a reverie thinking about what Ossi said. When we first arrived at Huldor's and Ossi lay wavering between life and death, a song had come to me. A song willing his heart and breath to strengthen and bring life to him. I hoped my gift would be one that helped others in some way. Then I thought about entering portals to the other world to see Willem, Lily, and Bird Woman. *Were these things part of my gift?* I held onto my moonstone and sank deeper into my thinking and wondering.

In my reverie, a world of soft breezes and gentle songs opened before me, and a spectral woman appeared. She raised her arms to the sky; she bent to the earth and plucked two flowers, and held them to her swollen belly. A fox, a coyote, a rabbit, a squirrel, a hawk, and a bear encircled her, caring for her. Even an otter slipped from the waters and wound itself around her twisted leg.

The woman then lay on soft mosses writhing in pain. An otter rubbed its cheek against hers and a fox brushed her forehead with its tail. With a moan, a gasp, and a final struggle, the woman gave birth. She took the newborn into her arms. With the hem of her dress, she wiped the baby dry, then held it to her breast. While the woman slept holding the baby close, the animals slept at her side except for the bear who stood at the edge of the woods watching and guarding her.

Maybe my mother hadn't drowned in the waters of Kawishami. I took a deep breath and remained as still as I could, unwilling to let go of the surreal images. Was seeing images part of my gift, too? Or just my deep desire to see my mother?

Licks from the stray dog brought me back to reality. Ossi was milking a goat and the cats pounced in the straw. Wind rustled leaves. I heard the soft whirring warble of a raven. I held on to the memory of my mother, so happy to have seen her, alive and well.

Done with caring for the animals, Ossi stacked an armload of wood to carry into the inn. I stayed behind savoring the peaceful images while petting the dog's soft belly. He thumped his tail and nudged my arm.

When I was ready, I headed to the woodpile to carry in wood, too. The raven I'd heard roosted on an overhead branch softly fluffing its feathers. Watching the raven, I almost stumbled over the canoe. Instead of leaning it back against the shed, I climbed in. The raven fluttered away. Flakes of snow fell on me from the branch where he'd roosted. As they melted, trickles of icy water slid down my face.

I wiped the droplets away and thought of how I'd paddled the canoe fiercely across Kawishami's blue waters to escape the farmer. Then I thought about my mother and the vision I had just seen. Wistful and calm, I didn't want to let go of the memory. The hair on the back of my neck tingled as I realized that she had not drowned after I was born. It was supposed to be good that I was born when the comet flew overhead, but yet a strange twist of fate had deprived me of my mother. She had lived. Maybe she still did.

Thinking and reliving what I'd seen, I sat in the canoe that had whirled and twirled in a storm separating me and Father from my mother so long ago. Picking up the paddle, I pushed it deeply into the mounded snow. The canoe propelled along the path toward the woods. I dipped paddle over and over again wishing I knew more about the day I was born. The canoe skimmed along the crusty snow.

As I paddled, I remembered entering portals and finding Willem, Lily, and Bird Woman. The vision I'd had of my mother was so real, so I held my moonstone, closed my eyes and whispered to the wind and to the canoe, "Take me to my mother. Take me to my mother."

With each stroke of my paddle the canoe crunched through the snow. I kept my eyes shut and wished with all my might. After a while, I began to feel queasy. The canoe shivered and quaked as it slid along. When I finally opened my eyes, my vision was hazy, but I was in the midst of a glade surrounded by snowy skeletal trees that had lost their leaves for the winter. The wind picked up and began to whirl and swirl the canoe, circling time and again. My stomach churned with the spinning of the canoe. Tree branches spun. The whole world twisted and blurred. When the wind subsided, and the canoe stopped spinning, I felt lightheaded and dazed.

Soft green moss instead of white snow covered the ground. The surrounding hillside bloomed with trilliums and violets. A glimmer of floating lights—blues, yellow, and greens—drifted and hovered.

When the eerie lights dimmed, a woman with long dark hair sat before me at a great wooden loom. As she bent to her weaving, I heard a gentle whoosh of the shuttle as she thrust it between threads. The thud of the beater bar and the creak of the treadle echoed in the glade as she thrust the shuttle again, weaving threads into cloth. I shook my head to clear the sounds. I shook my head to clear the vision. Still the woman weaving at a loom remained. *Moss instead of snow? Flowers blooming? Had I crossed another threshold? Entered another portal?*

"Hey, ho!" My voice barely scratched out the words. The woman turned. "Selene!" she whispered and held her hands over her heart.

"I'm Luna—not Selene." I paused, then asked, "Mother?"

CHAPTER 33

The woman rose slowly as a glowing light shimmered around her.

Even though the woman no longer sat at the loom, her shuttle still whooshed through the threads; the beater bar still thudded, and the treadles still pumped up and down.

"Selene?" she whispered again.

"I'm Luna." I wanted to run to her. To hold her. To have her hold me, but she looked as hazy and translucent as the morning mists that rose from Kawishami as the sun rose. Panic swelled; I didn't want her to disappear.

"Selene, that's unkind. You saw how I grieved for my first-born child that I lost before I'd ever held her."

"Mother, I am Luna." I trembled. My mother was no longer of the earth world, but I'd just seen a vision of her living on after I was born. She had lived and given birth to Selene. My twin sister!

"Luna died in the waters of Kawishami. I've told you that, Selene."

"Mother, I am not Selene. Father always told me that you died giving birth to me, but he and I lived. He grieved mightily. I have your dictionary. And, look! I'm wearing your dress. In the pocket there was a letter and a stone. I have the stone here."

"Can it really be? It *is* my dress you wear. Selene would not know about the letter, my dictionary, or the stone. Luna? Are you truly my Luna?"

"Yes, Mother. I am Luna. Father named me Purslane, but when I read your letter, I knew you would have named me Luna." I took the moonstone from my pocket and held it out to her.

"My stone. An otter gave it to me one day long ago when I couldn't keep up with the others while they played a game of tag. Feeling left out, I sat on the shore of a river that ran near our village. I watched the sun dance on the ripples and listened to the burble and murmur of the waters flowing over stones. An otter left the water and shook herself on the shore close to me."

My whole body hummed.

"We looked at each other for a long while. The otter was sleek with long whiskers. I thought how wonderful it would be to tame her or have her be my spirit animal. I reached out a hand, but she turned and slid into the water again. I thought I'd frightened her, but soon she glided to the shore again, came right up to me and dropped that stone on my lap."

The stone warmed in my hand. Its colors swirled. "This stone is magical," I said. "If I have it in my hand or pocket, I can understand the language Ossi speaks." And then I remembered. "Mother, Ossi is of your people. I am with him. Huldor, too—the friend you knew as Oriina. They survived the marauders. And now they're together again."

Mother smiled. "Ossi and Oriina. I remember." Then she noticed. "The canoe! You were born. . . ."

Before she could finish, I said, "The canoe brought me to Ossi. Then when he and I were almost frozen to death, it brought us to Huldor—Oriina. And now it brought me to you." There was so much I wanted to tell her. So much I wanted her to tell me. Most of all, I wanted her to hold me in her arms. I wanted to feel the same warmth that I felt when Huldor embraced me, but Mother was a mist, a wavering vision. Not flesh and blood like Huldor.

"Come closer so I can see you. Selene's eyes are brown like mine. Yours are green like your father's. Otherwise, you two are as identical as can be."

"Tell me more," I said, longing to be filled with her story. "Tell me about Selene. Where is she?"

The image of my mother wavered as in a breeze. I feared she would disappear as Willem, Lily, and Bird Woman had. She stood by the loom and unrolled the cloth she'd been weaving. Without speaking, she spread the weaving and pointed to the story it told. The first was an image of her very young, toddling and holding her mother's hand at a river's edge. In the second, tumbling waters and surging ice swept them away. The next woven images showed her limping, using a crutch. In others she grew, played, and sang. Finally, woven into the cloth were horrible flames of reds and oranges burning a village.

All the while, the loom kept weaving a new story. The shuttle whooshed through the threads; the beater bar thudded, and the treadles pumped up and down. In the freshly woven cloth, I saw the comet—a fiery ball with a long trail of light following—passing in the darkened sky. As the treadle lifted a web of threads, and the shuttle passed through, and the beater bar pressed them into cloth, a red canoe appeared spinning in the glow of the passing comet. The whooshing, creaking, and thudding of the loom continued. The weaving showed two babies curled together, then growing apart. They were alike in every way except for their eyes. As the threads wove, two girls grew taller. One was shown one by a mossy log hut; the other sitting cross-legged by a loom.

I examined the whole of the weaving. It told me a story, but nothing of what the prophecy would mean. I asked Mother again. She looked high into the sky as though looking for the comet. I felt a chill. The moss rippled beneath my feet, chilling me as it turned to snow again. "Please," I begged knowing that my time with her was nearing an end, "do you have anything to tell me about the prophecies? What I can expect?"

The loom kept weaving a new story; a story not yet told. "Stop!" I cried out loud, wanting the moss to stop turning to snow; the warmth from turning to chill. I wanted to the see the story of my future and the prophecies. I wanted more time with Mother.

Glimmering and floating lights faded, and snow once again covered the branches of the skeletal trees surrounding us. The trilliums and violets disappeared. I shivered, but Mother held her arms out to me. Her embrace enveloped me. I felt as comforted as being enfolded by a feather quilt. Soft. Gentle. Great warmth and serenity filled me.

Mother spoke no more as she faded into a wisp of mist and left me.

A whisper as though from a breeze came to me. *Great gifts have been bestowed upon you, but beware of those who....* The rest of the whisper was carried far from my ears as the breeze sighed and left.

The warmth and mosses were gone. The loom disappeared. Mother was but a mist floating beyond my reach. Bereft, I stood alone in the cold and snowy glade, trembling and in awe of what had just happened.

CHAPTER 34

I told Ossi and Huldor about the canoe spinning into the glade where it had been warm with sunshine in the midst of winter. I told them about the two visions I'd had of my mother, the story the weaving revealed, and how the wind whispered to me. Huldor said, "Oh, me, oh, my. You have the gifts of vision seeing and of traveling to the world beyond."

My heart jolted. *Huldor said I had gifts from the comet.* Would Father have concocted a way to make riches from those gifts? Maybe even telling pretend fortunes. And if Huldor was right, were my visits in the portals of Willem, Lily, and Bird Woman part of the gift? I asked, "Do portals and phases have anything to do with my visions?"

Ossi answered, "That may be. Either way, you have a great gift. Our stories tell of a man—a man who lived many passings of the comet ago—who had visions of past and future. Sometimes they were brought to him on the wind. At other times, he could invoke them by playing melodies on his flute or while beating his drum."

I pondered and worried about what the visions would mean to me. Would I enter more portals? And if I did, what or who would I find? And what about the whisper that had seemed to come from the breeze but had faded away? *Beware of those. . . .* I shivered not knowing what I should beware of.

Spring came into full bloom. Leaves burst open on trees. Grasses showed through the patches of snow. Birds returned. The rabbits had their babies. One of the barn cats curled in a pile of straw with her litter of kittens. I turned to face the sun, closed my eyes, lifted my hands to the skies and rejoiced for the warm weather. In the evenings, Ossi, Huldor, and I sat under the huge oak tree behind the inn and warmed ourselves by the pit fire. We listened to the spring peeper frogs sing themselves out of hibernation.

During the day, we planned our garden. Two neighbor boys came to help with the planting. Huldor called them The Lads. When I asked their names, she laughed and said, "Oladd is the older, and Eladd the younger." I liked the lads. When they finished planting the rutabagas, they put their arms around each other's shoulders and sat for a moment in the shade of the oak tree. Sometimes they played a game they called I Dare You. Then one or the other would have to hang by his knees from a branch, or have to catch a little goat and kiss it on the nose. Their games made me wish for a sister so I could dare her to do something silly. Before the games got too out of hand, Ossi would set them on the task he wanted them to do next.

In the evenings, when I was finished with my chores, I slipped off to play with the kittens and bunnies so Ossi and Huldor could have time alone. My thoughts often ran to the lads and how they laughed so easily together as they worked. I dreamed of finding my sister, of us giggling together, kissing kittens on the nose, or picking wild flowers to pin in our hair. I wanted to find her but knew to do so, I'd have to leave Ossi and Huldor and travel alone, along roads unknown. I could do it. I wanted to find Selene.

One day, Ossi called me to help dig a new bed in the garden. "What are we going to plant here?" I asked.

He showed me the two potatoes the potato-cake woman had given me at the last festival. Green buds dotted the brown skins. "Time to get these into the ground so they can grow. It's just two potatoes, but at harvest time, we'll probably have enough to make those potato cakes you like so much. We'll keep four to plant the next spring. In a few years we'll have a huge garden of potatoes. All from just two. All to remind us of that kind woman who fed you potato cakes."

I was flooded with memories of the potato-cake woman and festivals. They had been my only door to the world outside our little hut and the woods around it. I thought of Father as he pretended to be the All-Seeing Eye, of the man with the magic box, and of being afraid of the click-clacking puppets. But mostly, I remembered eating buttery potato cakes with honey made by a good woman who gave me more than food. I chucked remembering her goat that had chewed on my hem. The memories warmed me. I wanted to stay and to be there when it was time to harvest new potatoes. I didn't want to leave Ossi and Huldor, but I also wanted to find Selene. The dilemma tore at me.

When I told Huldor and Ossi about wanting to find my twin sister, Huldor said, "Now that the snow is melting and the roads opening up people be movin' and travelin'. Guests be comin' soon. Time to get ready for them. Then when the muds settle, it be time enough for ye to find yer sister."

After that, she and I had not a spare moment. "Let's shake out the feather beds in a brisk breeze first and let them air in the sunlight."

After that, we scrubbed windows, mopped floors, and beat rugs. "We be needin' supplies afore the guests be comin' this way wantin' a bed for the night and vittles for their tummies. Take ye this rag and dust everything ye can reach while I take stock of the larder."

I was dusting a lamp when an ugly black spider jumped onto my arm, "Yee-eeek!" I screamed in panic and tried to shake it off. I kept screaming. I struck at it with the dusting rag. I hit so hard that my arm bumped the lamp, and it crashed to the floor.

Huldor ran in, "What be 'appening. Ye be hurt?"

I trembled, sweat beaded on my forehead and under my arms. Ossi held me as I shook. "You're as white as ashes in the fireplace. Come sit."

He settled me in a chair and started picking up the pieces of the shattered lamp. "I'm s-so sorry. There's a s-spider. It j-jumped on me. I was afraid it'd bite me. It was scary."

"Now, now, me dear. Nothing to worry about. Ossi'll find that spider. We be happy ye're not hurt. I'll have ye a soothin' cup of tea in a jiffy. Ye just sit an' calm yerself."

It took some time to settle myself. Still jumpy and sorry that I'd broken the lamp, I got back to all the cleaning and shaking out with Huldor at my side. While we finished our chores, Ossi and two lads began building a bath house.

"We're setting it around the well so there'll be no more carrying in water for baths. It'll have two rooms. One for dressing. The other'll be for washing. It'll have a stove to heat water and to keep the whole room warm." His eyes sparkled as he held Huldor's hand. "We'll move your big copper tub in there so no more carrying hot water up the stairs and lugging that big tub from room to room for guests who want baths. Better yet, in the bath house, the pump won't freeze up in the winter. No more carrying snow to melt for water."

Huldor hugged Ossi with delight. Ossi hugged her back. Right in front of me! "Oh, me be the luckiest woman in this world. No more meltin' snow. No more luggin' water for baths!" She and Ossi hugged each other again. This time they drew me into their circle of arms, too. I felt warm and happy, and never wanted to let go of the two of them, yet I was drawn to finding my sister. And to do that, I'd have to tear myself away from Huldor and Ossi. That wouldn't be easy.

Two days later, under a cloudy sky, guests arrived while Ossi and I tended to the chickens. We heard the jingle jangle of a team of horses, a voice calling *Whoa,* and the creaking of a carriage stopping. I gathered the eggs but was unhappy to think of the commotion of guests. I wondered if he or she would disrupt my time with Ossi in the barns and in Huldor's kitchen that swarmed with aromas of onion, garlic, roasting meat, baking bread, frying pork-back fat, and apple-wine vinegars.

As I carried eggs to the house, a raven perched in a nearby tree. I wondered if it was the same one as I'd seen and heard before and if it had a family. It looked at me intently, tilting its head to one side. After preening its feathers and making soft throaty sounds, it flew to a branch closer to me. I wished I had time to watch it longer, but Huldor needed the eggs.

When I entered the kitchen, Huldor told me about the guests. "A woman travelin' with a girl. I didn't get so much as a look-see at the girl because she was still out in the carriage collecting 'er things, when I 'elped the woman in. They must be rich because they 'ave a coachman to 'andle the 'orses."

My skin tingled. Horses and a carriage? They must be richer than I could imagine. I was curious to see those guests.

"Her clothes be of every color! All fancy with laces, shiny buttons, an' ruffles. She even be wearing a fur wrap though it be too warm for one. She a different sort, that's for sure." Huldor said beating her chest, "By Jove an' all the stars above, I do 'ope they be on der way tomorrow. Already she's snooping in every corner, checking to see if there's any dust that hasn't been wiped up. Good thing I dusted away that spider's web. Guests are already here an' we still be needing a trip to town to get supplies."

Ossi came in with a pail of goat milk. The carriage driver who'd been in the stable settling the horses followed him. He introduced himself as Tegla. Huldor and I brought the two men big bowls of soup. Even though Ossi had already had his supper, he readily finished another bowl. I brought them platters of cheese, bread, and apple scones.

When Huldor and I carried trays of food to the dining table, the girl slouched in a chair by the fire, and the woman didn't pay any attention to us. She had her eyes half-way closed and flit from corner to corner waving a bunch of smoldering herbs in a clay pot. She ended by spinning and twirling in the middle of the room. Her red, yellow, and orange skirts and scarves spiraled in a dizzying swirl. She lifted her arms with her eyes closed and said, "Arise good spirits. Let no harm come to us. Let evil have no power here. Let only goodness enter and purify this room and all about."

Back in the kitchen, Huldor began brewing a chamomile and mint tea. She chuckled as she steeped the leaves. "Chamomile and mint," she told me. "A perfect combination to relax weary travelers and to make 'em sleepy. Sleepy—as in they will go to bed early an' not be smudgin' an' purifyin' any more of me rooms."

Something about the woman twitched my memory to a time when I'd seen a woman with swirling, twirling skirts and scarves. "I might have seen her or someone dressed like her before." I scrunched my forehead and thought. "At the last festival Father and I went to, a woman set up a fortune-telling booth where Father had earned coins as the All-Seeing Eye. She danced and spun in colorful clothing just as our guest is doing. Magda was the name on her sign. She said something strange to me that day as I hurried away to follow Father. I wonder if she's the same person."

"She might be," Huldor said. "She introduced herself as Lady Magda."

CHAPTER 35

Huldor carried a slab of smoked bacon from the larder and put it next to the eggs for the coming day's breakfast. "Do ye know what time ye'll be leaving tomorrow?" she asked Tegla.

The coachman scratched his beard. "We'll be on our way as soon as I inspect the carriage wheels and axels in day light. A bit back, we hit a muddy hole in the trail and almost tipped the whole caboodle over." He lowered his voice and looked at the door. "Scared the lady, that's for sure. You shoulda heard her scream. I didn't think I'd ever get my hearing back." Tegla shook his head and patted his ears. "I hope no damage was done, but the carriage rocked so much after that, I'm afraid something twisted or broke."

"There are plenty tools in the shed if you'll be needing any, and I'll lend an extra hand or two if it comes to that." Ossi offered.

I filled dishes with cream pudding and raisins for the men and then filled two more to bring into the dining room.

Lady Magda sat at the far end of the table. Her travel companion had her back to me. When I set pudding in front of the lady, her eyes opened wide, and she clutched my arm. Her long nails bit into my skin hurting so much that I almost tipped the puddings over. "Oh, praise all the moons of Jupiter. Selene! Look!"

Selene? I looked right into the face that looked just like mine. She—shocked as I was—dropped her mouth open to match mine own. We both stared. Hair, tilt of chin, nose. All alike. She rose from her chair to face me full on. I stepped to do the same. I looked her up and down as she did to me. She wore a blue dress. I wore mother's green dress. Our only difference—eyes. Hers were brown. Mine green.

Stunned, I could only say one word. "Selene."

I stood before my twin who until a short time ago, I thought had never been born, and I couldn't think of a thing to say. In my dreams, I imagined us rushing into each other's arms, hugging and laughing with joy at having found each other. But that's not how it was. We both stood still as stones—paralyzed, bewildered, speechless.

She finally scowled and blurted, "Who are you?"

"Luna. Your sister. Twin sister."

"Impossible! Mother said you'd drowned in a terrible tempest on your day of birth. She mourned for you every day of her life. Every day!" She looked me up and down again.

"Selene." I said again as though saying it again would shake the numbing amazement from me. My voice quavered. "Father told me that Mother drowned after I was born."

My thoughts tumbled, trying to think of ways to chase the stiffness from the air. *Hold out my hand to her? Say something welcoming? Tell her I had always yearned for a sister?* I wished Huldor was beside me. Ossi, too. They'd know what to do. The very air thickened with Lady Magda's pungent herb smoke and muddled my thoughts.

Selene stepped away. She clenched her fingers nervously and looked everywhere except at me. I stepped toward her wanting to touch her hand, wanting to search her face to find mine, and wanting to be one with my sister. "When I learned about you, I planned to come looking for you. And now you're here. I'm so happy." I meant my words, but they sounded wooden even to me. I hoped they'd soften Selene, but she just frowned and stepped further away.

Lady Magda broke the tension as she rose from the table. "This is wonderful! Twins" Separated at birth! Selene and Luna! You haven't been together since you curled as one in your mother's womb. Both born under the blazing comet! What great fortune! Only goodness can come of this! Greet one another. Be one again. Daughters of the Moon! Sisters of the Comet!"

She took our hands and pressed them together. Selene's hands were icy. Mine warm. I thought to warm hers, but she let go and held her hands to her head. Magda whirled and twirled around the room exclaiming, "Oh, the joys. Oh, the wonders! The curse of the broken carriage brings the blessing of twins born of the comet together!"

All the while, Selene held her head, and Lady Magda kept swirling her skirts and saying things like *auspicious, propitious* and *providential*. I was sure none of them were even in my mother's dictionary. What she said next, I did understand. Father had yearned for the same.

"Riches! Riches galore! Abundant, profusely, copious riches!"

Now I was the one to take a step back. *Riches?* That's what Father had hoped for if I had been gifted with clairvoyance. Now Magda wanted to use me and Selene for them, too. Tears welled in my eyes, and I grew dizzy. I squeezed myself in a hug and raced back to the kitchen where no one whirled and twirled or used big words. Where it was warm, and where Huldor and Ossi were.

"Selene is real. She's here!" I blurted and told about the girl who looked just like me. My sister. And that Lady Magda wouldn't quit whirling, making me dizzy. I wanted to feel excited. I wanted to bounce up and down, but Selene hadn't been at all friendly, and I had been too bewildered to know what to do. I was upset— as upset as I'd been when the spider jumped on me.

Huldor folded me into her arms. "It be a miracle. Ye always wantin' to find yer sister. And now she be here. I 'ope she be stayin' here with us. With you. Together. Maybe. . . ." Huldor paused. Her voice darkened. "Maybe they be on their way in the morning. And ye be wantin' to go with them. At least, now ye know that there be no more need 'oping to find yer sister. She be found!"

What if Magda and Selene wanted me to leave with them? Magda had said *Riches! Riches galore!* The thought scared me. I'd been afraid of Lamb-i-kins and the farmer. But this was a different kind of fright. And unknown one. At least with Lamb-i-kins I knew it was the club I had to look out for. The fear I had for the farmer was being dragged off to his farm to milk cows, churn butter, and do a whole lot of other things I didn't want to think about—like marry him. I didn't want to leave Huldor and Ossi, but I didn't want to lose my sister again either. "I won't sleep a bit tonight." I told Huldor.

"Ye don't have to be making decisions tonight. Give it time. It'll all sort itself out and ye'll know what's best for ye."

CHAPTER 36

That evening Huldor did my kitchen chores so Selene and I could spend time together. We sat by the great fireplace where Ossi had stoked up the flames to ward off the chill of the night.

"How can it be," Selene asked, "that my mother said you and Father died, yet you say our father told you that Mother died after giving birth to you?"

I thought back to Father's story, but it didn't help answer that question, so I said, "All I know for sure is that at the time of my birth, a huge storm blew up while they were in the middle of Kawishami. Perhaps the wind blew Mother out of the canoe and onto a far shore where she gave birth to you. And maybe the storm blew Father and me away to another shore."

"That sounds possible and impossible at the same time. Didn't he even look for us?"

"He said he walked the shores of the huge lake for many days searching, but never found Mother. Every day, he was deeply sorrowful and mourned for her."

"Just think how different everything would have been if Mother and Father hadn't been separated. Mother mourned because she'd never even held you, and I never knew that you still lived."

"I didn't know I had a twin until a short time ago. Father was miserable missing Mother all the time. He tried to drown his sorrows with elixirs, drinking himself into a stupor. He'd forget to eat, to do the simplest chores, and he raged around in an awful state."

The whole time we talked, Lady Madga twirled around smudging all the corners while chanting and invoking names I'd never heard before.

> *Veiled Ones.*
> *Lilith, Freya, Isis*
> *Come.*
> *Be of aid.*
> *Cast your shrouds aside.*
> *Now is our time.*
> *Open my eyes.*
> *Let me see.*
> *Arise!*
> *Louhi and Yaga.*
> *Be by my side.*
> *Come.*

"What is she doing?" I whispered.

Selene narrowed her eyes and rubbed her forehead. "She conjures spirits."

⸻

At sunrise, Huldor nudged me awake. "Guests means no more sleepin' in. It's time to stoke the fires up, and breakfast needs to get a-stirring."

Tegla and Ossi were already in the kitchen. They'd tended to the fires, and Ossi was setting water to heat.

"Is the carriage travel worthy?" Huldor asked.

"It will be if Ossi and I can fix the part that twisted and replace the one that fell off. Probably into the mud hole. We're looking to make one, or find one in the village. If not, we'll have to go back and dig around in the mud. Might take some time to do that."

Ossi added, "We can maybe send one of the lads to the village for the part if need be."

"If that time comes, I 'ave a list of things for the larder we be needing, too. I was 'oping to get to the shops meself afore long. If more guests be coming, the lad'll have to take my list for me."

The talk of the neighboring lads perked my ears. If they came, I could introduce them to Selene. She could see how they teased each other as they worked. Maybe she'd warm to them and me. I hoped the lads would be helping with chores all summer. Now that I'd found Selene, maybe she'd stay and I would be there to see the gardens grow. Then we could joke and tease with the lads together. But . . . but what if Selene wouldn't stay and wanted me to go with her? The idea bothered me. I had thought finding my sister would be joyous, not filled with more problems.

Ossi and Tegla didn't find anything in the shed to fix the carriage. Lady Magda and Selene would not be leaving that day. Huldor told me, "It's a fresh day. Don't go bothering about 'elping me with meals today. Spend yer time with yer sister. By Jove and all the heavenly bodies! Ye've wanted to find her and now she be 'ere. Yer very flesh and bone. It be wonderful if she be wantin' to stay here with us as family." Huldor paused. "Just Selene; not Lady Magda. Our rooms not be needin' anymore spirit chasin'."

I laughed agreeing with Huldor. All that evoking spirits seemed senseless to me, too.

After breakfast, Selene and I settled underneath a large cherry tree in full bloom. I was full of questions, so I started, "How did our mother die?"

Selene blinked back tears as she said, "It was awful. A bad man beat her. I couldn't help her. She weakened and died."

I couldn't imagine anything so terrible. Huldor had endured beatings and batterings, too. An acrid taste rose to my throat. My mother had been brutalized to death. Selene and I were silent for a long time—each in our own thoughts. I finally broke the silence by saying, "Tell me more about your life with Mother."

Selene scowled slightly. "I don't want to talk about Mother and what happened now. Tell me about Father first."

The delicate cherry blossom aroma filled the air as I told her about Father having been a professor and how he knew so much about plants and stars. I told her about scavenging in the woods for mushrooms, wild apples and plums. And about the fanciful stories he'd told around our fire at night. And our trips to the festivals.

"You had a good life," Selene said softly.

"It wasn't good all the time," I said. "Sometimes we didn't have enough food.

Our shoes fell apart. I wore a dress made from a sack. And . . . and . . . and. . . ." I didn't know if I should tell her or not. Outrage swelled in me as I thought of our last days together. My words snagged on the lump that clogged my throat. "Father sold me to a farmer—to be a milkmaid or worse. Then he abandoned me so he could travel through the skies to find Mother in the Pleiades."

Selene looked at me sideways as though she didn't believe me, then she shrugged and said, "At least he didn't beat you."

I was surprised she didn't think it strange that Father sold me and abandoned me so he could travel the skies looking for our mother. I changed the subject. "We were born the year that a comet appeared in the sky. Did Mother tell you about the prophecies?"

Selene scowled and narrowed her eyes. "Rubbish! Of course, Mother told me all that nonsense. Yes, she told me. Over and over again. She said as I got older, I'd show signs and grow into something wonderful with gifts from the comet. She said that the whole time she carried us in her womb, she hoped we would grow to be great healers, clairvoyants, mystics, or alchemists. She made me memorize all the names of those who had notable gifts. It was useless. I don't care who did what long ago."

I was eager to know more about our people and their gifts, but Selene continued, "Every day as I tended to my dismal tasks, she watched me. Hoping I'd show signs of a gift. Something that would take us out of our squalor. But nothing. I just grew into a great disappointment for her." Selene slumped and plucked at the grass.

"It was the same with me." I started to tell her that Father had been disappointed with me, too, but just then Lady Magda found us outside. "Oh, it's so nice to see the two of you together. Twins! Twins of the comet. Tell me, Luna, what gift has been bestowed upon you?"

On the breeze, I heard a whisper. *Beware of. . . .* I felt a pricking in my thumbs. My scalp tingled. Lady Magda tapped her foot and repeated, "What is your gift?"

"I'm not sure." I wanted to shift her attention. "Maybe I won't have any. Selene, you memorized lots of ancestral names. Maybe that's your gift."

Lady Magda didn't let Selene answer. "That would be useless. No more of that ancestor stuff, now. I'm teaching Selene how to use the crystal ball to tell fortunes. She catches on fast. It must be her gift. She just needs to concentrate harder and not get so impatient. Once she learns, she'll do just fine. We're on our way to a May Day Festival in Allaton. I'll read palms. Selene will use the crystal ball. We'll dress as fancy as can be. Together we'll gather in lots of customers."

Selene's shoulders drooped, and she closed her eyes. I asked Lady Magda, "How did you and Selene meet each other?"

"The first time we met, Selene came to my booth at a festival with a man and woman. She was clean and well-dressed that time, although rather skinny. I tried to get her to let me tell her fortune, but the man and woman hustled her away."

Selene frowned, picked a dandelion, and pulled it apart little by little.

"The second time I saw her was at the festival of Hansberg, right after the Harvest Moon Festival. She was alone, traveling from town to town looking for work. Poor thing. She was ragged, unbathed, and hungry. She asked if she could rest in the shade of my booth for a while. Well, we got to talking. She told me about being born when the comet flew the skies. I knew she would be special, so I invited her to travel with me. Now we'll be a team and earn twice as much."

"I don't have any gifts." Selene threw the dandelion to the wind. "And I'll never have any."

CHAPTER 37

Selene puzzled me. She was like Father. At times, she seemed bored and reluctant to talk or get to know me. At other times, she livened up and even smiled a bit. No matter her mood, whenever I asked about Mother, she changed the subject and asked me about Father. She was most interested in stories about when he put on his robe and became the All-Seeing Eye. "Was he a real fortune teller? Did he have a crystal ball?" she'd ask.

How was I to answer? That he was as phony as the man with the magic disappearing box? That he told people what he thought they wanted to hear? That he made it all up? "I don't know," I said. "I don't even know what an *All-seeing Eye* was supposed to be like, but that's how he advertised himself."

That afternoon, before Ossi and Tegla left for the village with the neighbor lads, Huldor had me to write a list for the grocer and another for the dry goods store. When I questioned what the lengths of calico and muslin were for, she said, "Haven't ye noticed? Ye be filling out all nice and round an' be needing a new dress or two and some aprons mighty soon."

I looked at my dress. It was no longer a beautiful green, but dull—almost gray— from so much wear and many washings. It fit me snuggly almost everywhere. I hugged Huldor. "Thank you. I've never even dreamed of a new dress that isn't burlap."

Huldor stayed busy in the kitchen. I wanted to help, but she shooed me out telling me to spend time with Selene. Lady Magda chanted the strange names again, then smudged the rooms before bringing out her crystal ball. Because Huldor didn't like the smudging, I didn't either. So, I asked Selene if she'd like to go out to see the farm and animals.

We started at the barns. She had fun with the kittens, bunnies, goats, but not the chickens. "You're so lucky to have such cuddly animals to play with," she said. Her eyes shone as she smiled.

We laughed as one baby goat hopped all around his pen and another chased after him. Selene picked up the third one and said, "I've never seen anything so cute."

When we got to the river, Selene asked, "Don't you just love the sound of rushing water?" She stood at the very edge of the bank watching the swollen waters tumble over rocks. I thought of our Mother whose own mother had died in a river. At the same time, her leg had been crushed and twisted leaving her lame.

Selene must have had the same thought because she said, "Our grandmam died in the rushing waters of a river." She and I stepped back from the edge.

I found a patch of wild leeks and was picking them when she said, "You're just like Mother. Pulling up whatever you can find in the dirt to eat. You should have been the one living with her, and I should have been the one living with the Professor."

I reddened. I felt I needed to defend the mother I never knew.

"The professor—our father—and I pulled a lot of our food out of the dirt, too. In fact, he named me Purslane—an unwanted weed."

Selene's voice was cheerless as she said, "At least I wouldn't have had to listen to how much she missed the baby she'd never held in her arms. And other rubbish. Rubbish about the Ice People. Rubbish about comets. And whenever her twisted leg pained her, I had to do extra work."

I began to understand Selene's reluctance to talk about her life. Maybe this was our chance to learn to be real sisters so I said, "Father wasn't so easy all the time either. He was often morose. He drank elixirs. He mourned for our mother something fierce."

"He didn't mourn for me like Mother mourned for you? Of course, he didn't. No one cared about me. I was just good enough to do dirty jobs. The comet didn't even bestow any gift upon me. I wish I'd never been born."

"I'm glad you were. I'm glad I have a sister." I held her hand.

Selene looked at me closely, her eyes narrowed. "As long as I can remember, my life was terrible. Horrible." She let go of my hand, went to stand at the edge of the river bank, and looked into the swiftly flowing waters.

I felt sorry she'd had such an awful life. I wanted to be with her. To be family. I wanted us to be close. I took her hand again and led her to a willow tree whose branches swept low to the ground. As we sat listening to the burbling waters, Selene began her story—singing it as Ossi and Huldor had when telling theirs.

I am Selene
Named for a moon goddess
Born under the passing comet.

Father paddled the canoe
Taking Mother to find the Ice People
Hoping she'd give birth there.

After my twin was born in the canoe
A thick fog covered the lake
A tempest arose,
Winds swirled the canoe
Churning the waters.

When the storm subsided
And the fog faded
Mother lay on the sandy shore
The canoe floated upside down
In the middle of Kawishami
Alone, she gave birth to me
On the soft mosses of the shore
But forever mourned
My father and sister
Who'd been taken by the waters.

It was just the two of us.
Me, bound to Mother's back,

And her, wincing with each step
Of her lame leg,
We wandered from village to village
Seeking shelter
Seeking work.

Finally, Mother found a
Weaving shop.
The owner
Sat her at a loom
Surrounded with baskets of wool.
From dawn to dark she wove.

We lived in that weaving hut,
Sleeping on its hard and unforgiving floor.
Eating watery gruel and crusty bread.
The weaving hut was our only world.

As a child barely able to walk or talk
I picked briars from
The newly shorn wool.
As I grew, the owner set me to scutching flax.
For hours I scraped a knife along woody stalks
And pulled the long fibers from the straw
So Mother could weave beautiful lengths of cloth.

As we worked
Mother told me stories
Of the Ice People, of their prophecies,
Of the gifts of the passing comet
That I would grow to have. Our only hope,
A gift that would save us from that hut.
From our toil.
From the man who demanded so much from us.

I grew to hate that hut.
The never-ending work.
Sore muscles.
Bleeding fingers.
The incessant pounding of peddles, heddles, beater bars.
The stuffy air.
The enclosed space.
The cold gruels and crusty bread and moldy cheeses.

The man took Mother's weavings away.
To sell. To enrich himself.
I hated him, his unpatched clothes,
His shiny shoes.
He stroked my hair. My arms. My throat.
And more, saying, "My dear, you grow lovely."

One day—hating his lingering touches
That grew more frequent and frightening—
I ran.
It wasn't so long ago.
Just at the beginning of last summer
When buds leafed out on trees

I ran until I was hungry.
I ran until I was lost.
I didn't know where to go
Didn't know what to do
I missed Mother.
Worried about her.
Sorry I'd run leaving her with all the work.
And the man.
So, after just a handful of days, I retraced my steps
Found the weaving hut
Found Mother.

Her eyes were swollen—bruised black and purple.
Her lips crusted with blood. Three teeth cracked.
One arm shattered. Her lame leg bruised.
Her dress ripped.

The man.
I hated him.

I took Mother's place at the loom.
Surrounded by heddles, peddles, and beater bar.
She sat in my corner surrounded by baskets of wool
Picking burrs as I had once done.

Every night Mother twisted and moaned.
Every day her pain worsened.

I tried to work harder.
I tried to learn her skills.
But no rhythm came from the loom.
Peddles and heddles resisted my touch.
No intricate weavings blossomed under my fingers.

When the man came to collect my weavings,
He ripped them from the loom.
He stomped and roared.
He yelled and screamed terrible words.
He beat me.
He beat Mother.
Again and again.

Mother and I ran. For days.

She writhed from pain
In her arm, her whole body.
Her lame leg.
When she couldn't walk one step further.

I set her to rest near a river where otters played
While I went about pleading for work.

One day I scrubbed soot from a chimney hearth
In exchange for a withered apple and a grisly chunk of meat.
The next day and day after that I mucked out a chicken coop.
I plucked horse tail hairs for an artist,
Salted pig knuckles for a butcher,
Gutted a fisherman's catch.

I endured slaps.
Insults. Dirty names.
I was chased with a broom.
I escaped a gang of hooligans intent on no good.

Each day I brought what little I'd earned to Mother.
Each morning she'd try to rise
Insisting she was better
That she'd work with me.
Each morning she'd stumble and fall.
I'd find a shady resting spot for her.

One morning she did not open her eyes with the sun.
She did not hear the mourning dove sing.
She did not feel a beetle creep onto her arm.
Alone. I cried.

The hooligans found me weeping over her body.
They whooped with pleasure and set upon me.
They poked and jabbed.
Pulled my hair. Ripped my clothes.

I kicked and scratched and yelled.
Fearing for my very life.
There were four of them.
Only one of me.

Just when I thought I would be joining my mother,
A horse-pulled wagon happened by.
A man and woman jumped off.
"Begone or ye be tarred and quartered!"
The man yelled and swung his horse whip.

The good woman wrapped me in her cloak
Gave me water to drink.
The good man lay Mother in the wagon on a bed of sacks.
They took us to their home.
Bound my wounds.
Set bath water for me.
Fed me.
Gave me a dress and shoes.
All the while I mourned.
The man made a wooden box
And dug a grave on a sunny hill top.

The air was fragrant with sweet clover
As we lowered the box into the soft earth.
The woman sang a song I'd never heard.

May your body
Become one with the earth
May your spirit
Fly with the birds
May the stars welcome you.
To the forever sky.

Selene and I held hands joining ourselves in sorrow. I understood my sister better now. Her life had been much harder than mine. I hoped we could be a family together. We rocked back and forth as our hearts beat together. A bird sang from a branch above us. Leaves fluttered in the breeze. When we'd spent our tears, Selene stood on a boulder on the river's shore. Her fists clenched and unclenched. She kicked at little stones. Her voice was jagged as she spoke.

"There should only be one of us, but the comet's passing brought two. Good and bad. A gift and a threat. You and me." Selene's voice rasped rough and raw as she sobbed, "Because I ran. Because I thought only of myself. Because I tried to escape, the man beat Mother. I caused her death. I cannot live with that."

She looked to the sky, spread her arms, and plunged into the cold and rushing waters.

I jumped in after her.

CHAPTER 38

Selene fought me in the rushing waters, but the current carried us to a fallen tree that lay across the river. I grabbed on and pulled us both to shore. Shaking off the shock of the cold water, I realized we both thought we'd caused our mother's death. I, as Father had told me, when I took her breath and heartbeat when I was born. Selene carried a greater burden. She'd run, leaving our mother to the hands of a cruel man.

As I half-carried Selene back to the inn, she told me how the man and woman from the horse-pulled wagon had helped her, fed her, even brought her to the festival where she'd first met Lady Magda. Living with them had been idyllic until the day the man walked with her to the woods and began groping her roughly. She'd struggled as he grasped her. She clawed, hit and kicked to get away, and ran once again.

Numb from the cold water and even more so from Selene's story, I held my twin close as we stumbled into Huldor's warm kitchen.

Huldor set stools for us near her big stove. We were wet and so cold our teeth chattered. She gave us mugs of warm tea. While she rubbed our hair dry, she tsk-ed and clucked her tongue. "River be dangerous this time of year with snow melt an' rains. Ye be careful by it."

I wanted to tell Huldor what really happened, but Selene had begged me not to. I stirred biscuit dough and chopped carrots, beets, and turnips with Huldor while Selene kept warming herself by the fire.

By the time Ossi and Tegla got back from the village, it was almost dark. We'd already served Lady Magda and Selene their evening meal and had eaten our own. The men brought in the provisions before sitting to eat. They'd found the parts they needed to fix the carriage.

"We should be ready and on our way before high sun time tomorrow," Tegla said.

My thoughts were a muddle. I wanted to be with Selene longer. I wanted to protect her. Our lives had been filled with guilt, yearning and loneliness. Together, here with Ossi and Huldor, it would be different. I wanted us to be together. I wanted us to be like sisters as the lads were brothers.

I also had an uneasy feeling I couldn't shake. A pricking in my thumb—a warning Father said to pay attention to. That part of me wanted Selene and Lady Magda to be on their way. To leave me with Ossi and Huldor and our life with the animals, the building of the new bath house, the garden, and Huldor's wonderful kitchen. But Selene needed a home, too, and to be safe. I wanted Selene to stay.

That evening Lady Magda asked that I sit with her and Selene as Huldor hustled about setting the kitchen to rights. "You and Selene are so beautiful together," she said reaching to hold my hand. "You belong together. You've been apart for too long."

I scratched my thumbs. They pricked again. I glanced at Selene who just stared into the fire. I thought about what Lady Magda was possibly meaning. *Did she want to leave Selene at the inn—with me, Ossi, and Huldor? Or did she want me to go with them?* I looked at Selene again. She'd folded her shoulders inward; her face was drawn and stony. At that moment, I shivered. I wasn't sure I wanted to share my life with her, but she needed a home. She was my sister.

Lady Magda turned my hand over and began to study the lines. As she ran her finger along my palm, I felt sharp pricks, not only in my thumbs, but my whole hand. I tried to pull my hand away. She held it tightly. The pricks sharpened, like needles jabbing. "That hurts," I said and pulled my hand away.

"I'm only reading your palm," Magda said. "It shouldn't hurt. Come, give me your hand again."

The pricking turned to stinging. I looked at my hand. It looked the same as ever. Little by little, the sensation subsided to tingles, but I felt like spiders crawled all over my skin, and the hair on the back of my neck stood on end.

I tucked my hands into my pockets. The moonstone was cold to touch. I took it out to look at it and hoped it would warm and swirl its beautiful colors calming me.

"Oh, you have a moonstone." Magda plucked it from my hand.

Selene perked up. "Let me see it, my mother talked about one she used to have. Is this Mother's? How did you get it?"

Magda handed her the stone, saying, "You know, don't you, that moonstones are magical? They're akin to crystal balls."

I thought about how it let me and Ossi understand each other's language, but I just said, "I found it in the pocket of Mother's dress."

I reached to take the stone back. Selene clenched her fist over it saying, "If it was Mother's, then it's as much mine as yours."

Lady Magda stepped in. "Be nice now, Selene. Give back her stone."

Selene raised an eyebrow, gave me an unsettling smile and tossed the stone at me.

Magda held her crystal ball and closed her eyes. She chanted and swayed gently in her chair. At times she lifted one hand from the ball and held it into the air as though reaching for something. She cupped her hand and slowly brought it to her chest. Then she leaned back and moaned.

Selene wrinkled her nose and whispered, "She wants me to learn how to do that, but the ball doesn't speak to me like it does to her. If it speaks to her at all. Maybe she just makes it up like she wants me to. She tells me how to act and what to say to get money from the festival goers. She says people are entranced by magic. It takes them away from their dull lives. She's teaching me how to create illusions of mysterious powers."

When Magda opened her eyes, she looked at me directly and exclaimed, "The spirits have spoken! They have revealed the future. You! Traveling with me and Selene! What an attraction the two of you will be. Beautiful twins! Twins born of the comet! I'll dress you in gowns with layered skirts that flow in the breeze. Skirts of reds, greens, pinks, purples, blues, and oranges! Ruffles around your shoulders. Your hair will be piled high. Or curled close to your face. At times, one will wear black—all black except for bits of white lace. The other will wear all white except for dashes of black."

Magda painted a fascinating picture of how we'd look. I was much taken in by it, so I glanced at Selene. She slumped in her chair and rolled her eyes.

"Just imagine! People will flock to my booth to see you! They'll pay silver coins. Maybe even gold. I'll read their palms. Selene will work the crystal ball, and you, Luna, we'll get you a drum. You'll hold the drum to your chest. You'll feel the vibrations and evoke the spirits who bring messages from the other world with the steady thrum-thrum as you tap it. We'll call it the Drum of Destinies! Oh, this is so exciting! It will be pure magic to have the two of you with me."

CHAPTER 39

Stunned, I couldn't say a word. Lady Magda made it sound exciting, but my thumbs pricked again. She had my life all planned according to a message from the crystal ball. Had she really read my future there? She offered a life of traveling. I just had to pretend to tell fortunes as Father, the All-Seeing Eye had. That would be easy. I'd heard his messages often enough. There'd be no more burlap dresses. Selene and I would twirl our colorful layered skirts in the breeze. I pictured it as something wonderful. Maybe I'd even find the potato-cake woman again at one of the festivals.

Selene changed in an instant from gloomy to excited. She jumped up from her chair. "It will be so much fun, and we'll be together. Do come with us. Please. Just think, we'll have new and fancy dresses all the time. We'll eat all the best foods. Meet lots of exciting people. Oh, Magda, can we get lamb skin shoes, too? Just to wear at the festivals? And pierce our ears for dangly earrings? And wear rubies on our fingers?"

Lady Magda laughed a merry tinkling laugh. "Of course. Of course, all of that and more, too. We'll be a perfect family together. We'll have an artist paint a huge poster of the three of us. And a sign to hang at our booth.

Lady Magda
Palmist
Seer of the Future
Teller of Fortunes

The Beautiful Twins of the Comet
Selene and Luna
Reveal the mysteries of the Crystal Ball
And the Drum of Destinies

"We don't have to be Selene and Luna, do we?" Selene twirled around the room. "We could have some exciting and exotic names. Sybil and Sylla. Or. . . ."

"Venus and Vesta. Iris and Isis." Lady Magda turned to Selene, "What a good idea. You'll have new names filled with mystery and mysticism."

I caught the excitement. "How about Delphine and Delilah?"

Selene held her hands out to me. "Or even Celeste and Circe. Gisellee and Gaia!" We twirled and laughed together. I could be with my sister! We'd travel. We'd enjoy each other like the lads did. Then a chilling thought came to me. *What about Ossi and Huldor? What would they do? Would they want me to stay? Or would they be happy to see me go with Selene and Lady Magda now that they'd invited me— wanted me? Selene was my closest family. The family I'd searched for. Longed for.* I stopped twirling and laughing with Selene.

Huldor came in just then carrying butter biscuits for our evening tea. "I'll help you," I said jumping up so I could tell her and Ossi about Selene and Lady Magda's plans while helping Huldor in her warm and wonderful kitchen.

Lady Magda insisted that instead of helping Huldor, that I sit with her and Selene to drink my tea so she could tell me and Selene all about traveling to festivals, how we should act, and how we could lure customers to part with their coins to hear their fortunes.

Selene even lay her hands on the crystal ball and showed me what she'd been learning. "The most important thing is to create the illusion that something very important is happening within the ball. I have to focus on it. I have to be very intent. I summon the spirits to come forth and carry messages to the person sitting before me. Magda taught me how to pretend I've entered another world. I close my eyes and moan a little. I describe what it's like to be among the dead— to bring back a message. Then I have to slump in my chair and pretend I'm very tired from the long journey into the ethereal world." Then Selene laughed and added, "I can't wait to try all this at the May Day Festival."

Lady Magda scowled. "Remember. It is important to believe it yourself. Believe every word you say. Festival goers are looking to find relief from their dull lives. They seek some escape from toiling in the fields, shoveling shat from barn gutters, and being up to their elbow in dirty dish water and snotty-nosed crying kids. They need magic in their lives! It's up to us to give them that image. We offer a distraction from their daily drudgery, but we have to make our show real to them, otherwise they won't tell their friends and neighbors, and we'll be penniless."

The whole time she and Selene spoke, I thought of Father and how he'd tried to act the part of the All-Seeing Eye and of the magic man who pretended to make me disappear. When Selene told of pretending to enter the world of the dead, I thought of the portals I'd entered. I wondered. *Had all that really happened or had I just imagined it all in my hunger to escape my own harsh realities?*

That night my thoughts tumbled as I tossed for a long time thinking about everything Lady Magda said and how warm-hearted and eager Selene had been all evening. It was like she'd forgotten about her whole life with Mother. I wondered how she could change so fast. Then I wondered if I could change and forget about Father, Ossi, and Huldor while enjoying the thrills of a new life.

When I finally slept, I dreamed of myself and Selene dressed in sleek layers of silk. We twirled so festival goers would stop to gawk in wonder at our lavender, orange, and gold swirling skirts. We wore our hair loose so it swooshed with our every turn. Bells on our ruffles jingled. Our eyes sparkled. And our smiles invited. The crowds of people oohed, aahed, and rushed forward opening their pouches and laying money in our outstretched hands.

My dream continued. The festival was in full swing. A girl in a yellow ruffled dress came to me to have her fortune told. The pouch at my waist weighed heavy with coins. I tapped my drum and asked spirits to arise and be with me. A wavering apparition floated before me. "Speak, Spirit, Speak," I said.

It whispered, "Look above and behind you." Then it faded into the gloom.

I looked as it had said. Behind me was an almost invisible cord tied to my waist. Above was another tied to the top of my head. Cords tugged on each of my wrists and on my ankles. Lady Magda scolded, "Turn around! Never look back!"

Before I turned away, I saw she held the ends of many cords attached to both me and Selene. She pulled on a cord. My arm raised. She pulled on another. Selene and I danced with clacking feet, just like smiling puppets.

I awoke. Sweating. My heart pounded. Blood rushed through my veins. My heart beat wildly.

CHAPTER 40

I couldn't sleep anymore. Shivering, I waited for the dark of night to turn into the gray skies of the dawning. I was up and dressed before Huldor was. I even stoked the fire in the big kitchen stove before Ossi and Tegla came in.

"You're an early bird," Ossi said with a big smile.

"I couldn't sleep," I yawned.

"Well, tonight you'll rest easy. We'll get that carriage fixed as soon as possible, and they'll be on their way."

"They want me to go with them," I said. "They want me to be part of their fortune telling booth at festivals—beat the Drum of Destinies, and be with my sister. I'd have great adventures. We'll make lots of money. I'd wear fancy dresses."

Ossi's face turned the color of the stove ashes he swept into a pan to carry outside. "Have you decided to go, then?"

"What do you think I should do?"

"Well, you'd be with Selene." Ossi's voice was but a rasp.

"I like being here with you and Huldor. You've been so good to me, but Selene made it sound exciting."

Huldor came into the kitchen just then. "They've invited ye to go with them?" She gave a big sigh, wiped her eyes, and took down the tea mugs. "I was hoping she'd stay here with us."

"Ever since I found out that I had a twin, I've wanted to find her. Last night we were so excited to be together. Planning our life together. The possibility of ever finding Selene had always been just a faraway dream. Now the dream has come true."

Huldor wiped her eyes often as she crushed cedar buds into the steaming water then poured us each a mug of tea.

"Let's take these outside and watch the sun come up," said Ossi. His voice was thick and soft. "The morning birds are singing already."

In the yard, delicate violets bloomed. The goats maa-aa softly, and the barn cats scrambled through the dewy grass—maybe chasing a mouse. The stray dog nuzzled me. I stroked his ears as he put his chin on my knee and looked at me with his soft brown eyes. A raven perched on a branch. I breathed in the wonderful cedar aroma as I sipped my tea.

"You have a big decision to make, and only you can make it. We could beg you to stay and promise you all kinds of things, but it wouldn't be right. You have to know what's in your own heart and follow that." Huldor's jaw quivered.

She was right. The decision, hard as it was, was up to me and me alone. I sipped more tea and pondered my situation. I frowned as I thought. Stay? Go?

Gentle breezes fluttered the new leaves above us, and the branches swayed. A gentle melody made by wind and fluttering leaves reached my ears. A song made by the wind. Wind Song! I looked at Ossi and Huldor who sat side by side holding hands. They made no fancy promises. I didn't have to be Iris or Giselle, or Vesta. I was Luna! Happiness filled me as the sun peeked above the horizon and shone through the trees.

Ossi and Huldor were my people. They were my family—like the family Lady Magda, Selene, and I could never be. I didn't have to pretend the Drum of Destiny brought me messages. I didn't have to tell phony fortunes just to get money from people who probably couldn't afford to give up their silvers and coppers.

I had been entranced by images of whirling, twirling colors and promises of exciting travels. Lady Magda and Selene had lured me in—made a believer out of me—as they would any festival goer. Fortunately, I'd watched and learned from Father. It was all hocus-pocus and make-believe. I breathed deeply. The brisk spring air filled me with elation and a certainly as the sun rose higher. I thought of *Alcyone's Dictionary* and what she written about Wind Song . . . *a place in the heart.* I had found my own Wind Song.

Lady Magda was furious when I told her and Selene that I would not be leaving with them. She pointed a finger at me and scowled. "One does not defy the crystal ball without dire consequences. You *must* come with us. It is your future. You cannot just decide not to come! Whatever are you thinking? You'll stay here? A scullery maid? An upstairs maid? A run-and-get-whatever-fussy-guests-want maid? What kind of life will that be besides dirt under your fingernails and your hands becoming calloused and hard? I offer you a life of travel, of excitement, of riches! No more hand-me-down-worn-out dresses. You and Selene will live like princesses!"

Selene did not enter the rant. She scowled, slumped in her chair, and stared past me as though I was invisible.

"Selene, tell your sister how I took you in and have been training you, and what a good life we have. Tell her!"

"You tell her." Selene shrugged and chewed her fingernail.

I wondered how she could change from the twirling and excited twin of last night, to the moody and stony person of this morning. She and Father were alike in that way. I wondered if she would turn to elixirs as he had.

"After her mother died, Selene escaped from a life of drudgery," Magda started. "Her mother worked as a weaver. Ever since Selene could toddle, she had to do hard and tedious work with hardly anything to eat. I took her in, fed her, gave her a place to sleep, bought her dresses and taught her how to tell fortunes. I've done everything for her. Everything! As I would for you. The crystal ball has revealed all."

I understood why Selene wanted to travel with Magda. It would be an easier life than what she'd had. She'd have plenty to eat and beautiful clothes. On her own, she'd have to find work. Maybe with a farmer. Maybe with someone who'd beat her, and touch her in ways she didn't want to be touched. Then I thought of my dream. Of Magda pulling my strings, controlling my every move—like the puppeteer I'd seen at festivals.

My heart felt like it still had strings attached and was being pulled in two different directions. One with Selene. The other with Huldor and Ossi. Then I remembered the potato-cake woman and how the big troupe had taken over the whole festival grounds so she and her goat were so far on the fringes that no one came to buy her delicious cakes. If I went with Lady Magda and Selene, I'd be part of that troupe.

My answer was definitely no. I was not going to pretend to tell fortunes with the Drum of Destiny. Tegla even nodded and smiled when he heard that I would stay with Ossi and Huldor, the dog, cats, bunnies, and goats.

While Ossi helped Tegla replace the broken parts with the new, I asked Selene if she'd like to help me do Ossi's chores with the animals. She'd scrunched her face and held her nose as she sneered, "I'm not, and I will never be some poor goat girl who cleans shat for her supper."

My mood dampened. I didn't want our last hours together to be sour. "You know where I'll always be," I said. "When you and Magda travel near here for the festivals, you can come back to visit. We'll see each other then."

"Maybe. Maybe not. I don't care if we ever pass this way again." Selene turned away and bit at her nails again.

When Tegla hitched the horses, I watched him put bits in their mouths and attach harnesses, bands, straps, and reins. The thought came to me that Tegla was like a puppeteer, and the horses his puppets. I hoped he was kind to them.

"Now we can be on our way and not bothering you all," he said to me and Ossi. "The carriage is fixed good as new thanks to your help." He smiled and shook Ossi's hand. Then he looked at me and said, "You are with good folks here."

We said our goodbyes. If I had a qualm or second thought about not getting in the carriage with Selene and Magda, it didn't last but a blink of an eye. At the last moment, Selene said she'd forgotten something and ran back into the inn. A few minutes later, she hurried back looking a bit sweaty. She jumped into the carriage without a wave or a proper goodbye.

The horses stomped restlessly. They were eager to be on their way. I think Magda and Selene were eager, too. I was torn. Was I glad I'd met Selene? Or did I wish she was still a dream sister that I would one day meet, and we'd be happy together? We didn't linger over any more goodbyes. Lady Magda didn't look at me and didn't say anything. It was as though she'd already forgotten about me because I wasn't going with her. When I said goodbye to her, she just flicked her hand as though I was a pesky gnat—or a weed like purslane.

Tegla nodded and tipped his hat as he picked up the reins. "*Gee-up,*" he said and the horses started forward. Huldor called out, "We be happy to see you if ye be passing this way. It be good for the girls to see each other agin, too."

CHAPTER 41

As we watched the horses and carriage drive away, a cloud covered the sun. A chill ran up my back. I hoped Selene would be happy. I hoped she wouldn't blame herself for our mother's death anymore. I hoped . . . I hoped so much for her. But mostly I hoped I'd see her again someday. Maybe she'd become tired of traveling and pretending to be something she wasn't; then she might be ready to stay with me.

Ossi and Huldor wrapped their arms around me in a warm embrace. In the tangle of their strong and gentle arms I felt safe and alive. "We're your family now. We're glad you be staying and hope ye be happy with us even though ye have to work ever' day. An' some days be long and hard when guests come."

I melted into their hugs and drew in a big breath of cherry blossom aroma.

The no-longer-homeless dog bounded to us carrying a piece of wood in his mouth. "We need to give him a name," Ossi said. "He's a good dog. He's already chasing deer out of the garden. And he helps me herd the chickens back into their coop every night."

The dog dropped his piece of wood at my feet. When I picked it up, I had a feeling of dread. "Ossi, isn't this from the canoe?"

We hurried to the back yard where the canoe had leaned under the wide slanted roof of the wood shed. We stopped short. My heart sank. The canoe had a gaping crack in it. An axe lay nearby. The canoe that had brought me to Ossi and both of us to Huldor was in ruin. The canoe into which I was born and that I'd paddled through snow to my mother's portal, now had a splintered fracture.

I exploded. "Selene! Why would she do that?" I seethed and trembled as I cried. Ossi put his arms around me, held me, and calmed me by saying, "We'll fix the hole, and more. We'll re-build the bow. Piece by piece. We can make your canoe like new again."

Still seething to think I'd ever wanted to travel with Selene, I helped Ossie lay the pieces on the ground puzzling them together. We were kneeling on the ground and sorting pieces when Huldor said, "Ye finish that later. We be havin' guests all regular like from now on. Luna, I need ye to change the bedding where Magda and Selene slept."

After opening all the windows for fresh air, I flapped pillows and blankets Magda and Selene had slept in pretending to shake them out of my life. I wished I had a smudging pot of herbs. I didn't so I did the next best thing. I twirled with the blankets and pretended to be Lady Magda saying, "Arise good spirits. Let no harm come to us. Let evil have no power here. Let only goodness enter and purify this room." I spun until I was dizzy then flopped on the bed laughing, glad to have chased away all evil spirits, real or pretend.

After washing and hanging their bed linens to dry, I helped Ossi with the animals. The dog followed us from chicken coop to rabbit warrens to goat shed and then to the gardens. I said, "He follows us everywhere, like a shadow. Shadow! Let's name him Shadow."

Ossi chuckled and said to the dog, "Shadow, what do you think of your new name? Better than Dog, that's for sure." Shadow licked Ossi's hand.

When Huldor called us in for the evening meal, we were tired, but glad to be done with our chores so we could go into her warm kitchen with all its inviting aromas. "Come and see what I 'ave fer ye."

The dining table was spread, not with food, but with a beautiful blue cloth. "I'm cuttin' ye a dress from this. Goin' to make it pretty as I can even though they be plain. I know not how to make fancy ruffles and collars with scallops."

I ran my fingers over the soft cloth. It was the color of Kawishami on a bright summer day. I hugged Huldor. "Thank you. This is so beautiful, and I've never had a dress made just for me."

"That's not all," she said. Then she lay a length of emerald-colored cloth on top of the blue. "This be for a dress, too. Ossi picked the color by hisself. Ye be needing nice clothes to meet the guests that be comin' all summer."

By now I was speechless with happiness. I didn't need ruffles or scalloped collars or skirts that twirled. Huldor's thoughtfulness was plenty. Ossi fingered the cloths, too. When he looked at me, his eyes shone, and he said, "You'll be the prettiest in all the world. I know that because you already are."

Never had I heard such words of praise and felt so enveloped with tenderness. I held my chin high and smiled.

"Now we heap our plates and go outside. No eatin' on top of Luna's dresses to be!" said Huldor.

We ate sitting on the stumps around the fire pit. Ossi said that when the lads came the next day, they'd be able to finish the bath house so it'd be ready for guests. Then we could work on putting the canoe back together.

"The lads are clever," Ossi said. "They'll find ways to weave new pieces with the old to patch the hole and to make a new bow. I'll teach them how to make birch bark glue to hold it all together and water proof it. With your help, that canoe will be water ready in no time."

The thought of working with the lads and Ossi on the canoe made me very happy. As Huldor talked about the guests that would be coming, I realized that I'd be busy and happy working with her, too. She described people from faraway who told stories of traveling up and down and around mountains and sweltering deserts.

The sky darkened and little by little filled with pin pricks of light. It was like the nights Father and I had sat around a fire while he told stories.

"Tell us one of your father's stories," Huldor said.

I told about the night when he'd gotten the skunk fur for my back pack. I tried to imitate his voice as I started.

"It was a dark—well not so dark—night because there was a bulging and gib-bous moon. It was one of those spooky nights when the fairy beings that live in the sphagnum world light tiny torches called fireflies. . . .

Ossi and Huldor laughed and held their sides as I ended, still imitating my father's voice.

And then the great monster did the unthinkable.
He let loose a putrid, disgusting, awful, terrible, toxic spray that covered me
like a fetid shroud. Now my dander was up.
I reached out and grabbed him by the throat and squeezed. All the while I
coughed, choked, gagged and tried to spew the foul stuff from my mouth, but

finally the fiend lay still. I had conquered the great beast with my superior strength and intelligence!"

We all laughed until we couldn't laugh any more. Our laughter was like magic; it took away all my worries about Selene and the canoe.

Shadow lay by my feet. I heard the hens clucking softly as their chicks snuggled under their wings for the night. The raven preened his feathers on a branch above us.

The words came out before I'd even planned them. "We don't need to fix the canoe. I won't be needing it. I'm staying here. It's taken me everywhere I wanted to go and there are no more portals I want to find. Everything I want is right here."

Ossie and Huldor smiled. Ossie said, "We'll fix the canoe anyway. We'll use it, not for searching for anyone or anything, but for fishing or just floating on a lake enjoying being together."

I liked Ossi's ideas. He'd said *we*. I liked being part of *we*—with him and Huldor. I looked to the skies. Overhead the stars of the Great Bear and the Little Bear shone. "And there," I said pointing, "is Polaris. And over there are the Pleiades the home of Alcyone and her sisters."

The stars were far away twinkling in the dark sky. Untouchable and magical. I thought of Selene traveling with Lady Magda, chasing a dream of riches. She was like Father who was chasing his impossible and unreachable dream, too.

I looked at Ossi and Huldor beside me. They filled me with the magic of *we* that only a family can give. Touchable and real.

I picked up a stick and wrote in the earth.

I am Luna. I was born in a red canoe.
The canoe is broken now,
Ready to be mended like I was
When it brought me to Ossi and Huldor
To be mended.

ACKNOWLEDGEMENTS

I am so lucky I had parents who encouraged me to be a reader and lover of stories. They also raised me in Minnesota's Northwoods. It is there, surrounded by the gentle ways of nature that I drew upon for the world of *Born in A Red Canoe*.

Some of the characters in the book came to me from real life. An aunt whose love for birds and puppies and welcomed all into her house inspired Bird Woman. My mother whose kindness, and ever-ready pot of coffee for visitors found her way into all the characters who fed and cared for Purslane on her journey. The delightful (and scary) Lamb-i-kins was inspired by a tough little robber girl I once saw in a play.

Thanks to my writers' group, all of whom were patient and helpful every time I brought pieces of this story for their critiques. I am thankful for Loon Song Writers' Retreat of 2019. I especially appreciate Mari Talkin for digging into my story and for her developmental suggestions. More thanks go to Betsy and Tom Peacock for encouragement, and to Paul Nylander for his designs and expert help in helping this all become a reality. Most of all, I am grateful for my husband's patience, encouragement, and willingness to wash dishes so I can hunker down at my computer.

It's been said many times, but it bears repeating. It takes a village. . . . I am so thankful for being invited into a village of very kind people.

READING GROUP DISCUSSION QUESTIONS

1. Before Purslane sets off on her journey, two settings are important to her life: home at the hut and at the festivals. What does each signify and what does Purslane learn or experience at each?

2. Compare Father's interaction with the mayor's daughter and Purslane's with the potato-cake woman. What does each girl need and what does she receive?

3. Narcissism can be roughly defined as self-involvement such that a person disregards the needs of others because they are preoccupied with fantasies of superiority and grandiose confidence in their own successes and talents.

   Two of Father's stories illustrate his narcissism: His heroic struggle and victory over the skunk and Alcyone coming to him from the Pleiades to be his wife. In what other ways does he exhibit this character flaw?

4. What does the title of Father's book say about him? (The Complete Physiognomy of Plants and Their Spiritual and Mystical Relationship with Humans and Other Mammals.)

5. To whom and what does Purslane/Luna look when wondering what having a mother would be like? (At home and at the festivals)

6. What is the role of Alcyone's Dictionary?

7. Motifs and Symbols: How does each support important aspects of the story?

   a. Purslane/Luna writing about herself in the sand/earth. (Opening and end-ing images)
   b. The puppeteer's foreshadowing
   c. The red canoe (Consider where it takes her.)
   d. The auspicious Comet
   e. Alcyone's dress
   f. The cocoon and the Luna moth

8. What does Purslane/Luna gain or learn with the following encounters?

   a. Lily and Willem
   b. Potato-cake Woman
   c. Bird Woman
   d. Her Mother

9. Self-agency can be described in simple terms as having the ability to make one's own free choices, having a sense of control and/or taking responsibility for one's own life.

   At the beginning of the story, Purslane does not have self-agency, but as the story goes on, she shows her strong will and growth of agency. What are several incidents that illustrate this.

10. How does the breaking of Father's elixir bottles become a turning point for Purslane/Luna?

11. How do Lady Magda and Luna's twin Selene complicate Luna's life and how do Luna's previous experiences help her make her final decision?

12. Purslane's father hoped for Purslane's mystical gifts to solve his problems. If her gift to enter portals of dead had emerged earlier, would it have made them rich, as he hoped? Would it have solved his grieving for Alcyone?

ABOUT THE AUTHOR

Katharine Johnson lives in Northern Minnesota with her husband and a flock of wild turkeys. The woodlands with all the critters that come to their yard provide inspiration and setting for most of her stories.

Her two published books have brought her on journeys of self-discovery. *The Mukluk Ball* is a fun picture book. *The Wind and the Drum*, a historical fiction novel, was selected as the 2018 One Book Northland.

She has also published several short stories, biographies, and poetry in anthologies. One children's story "Company's Here" was published in the *Ladybug* children's magazine. Her short story "Ada" won the Jonis Agee Fiction Award.

She is a member of SCBWI, Lake Superior Writers, and a local writers' group.

Much of her "shelter in place" time was spent reading scads of MG and YA books to deeply explore those exciting fields of literature.